LAMAR GILES

URNED

SCHOLASTIC PRESS

NEW YORK

Library of Congress Cataloging-in-Publication Data

Names: Giles, L. R. (Lamar R.), author.
Title: Overturned / Lamar Giles.
Description: First edition. | New York : Scholastic Press, 2017. | Summary: Nikki
Tate's father has been on death row for killing his best friend in a gambling dispute,
but he has always maintained his innocence, and now his conviction has been overturned and
he is back at the casino, where high school junior Nikki has been operating illegal
poker games in the hopes of saving enough money to get out of Vegas after
graduation—and now he is determined to find the real killer, and Nikki is
inevitably drawn into his dangerous search for the truth.
Identifiers: LCCN 2016035488 | ISBN 9780545812504
Subjects: LCSH: Murder—Investigation—Nevada—Las Vegas—Juvenile fiction. | Fathers and
daughters—Juvenile fiction. | Poker—Juvenile fiction. | Gambling—Juvenile fiction. |
Casinos—Juvenile fiction. | Las Vegas (Nev.)—Juvenile fiction. | CYAC: Murder—Fiction. |
Fathers and daughters—Fiction. | Poker—Fiction. | Gambling—Fiction. | Casinos—Fiction. |
Las Vegas (Nev.)—Fiction. | African Americans—Fiction.
Classification: LCC PZ7.G39235 Ov 2017 | DDC 813.6 [Fic]—dc23

10 9 8 7 6 5 4 3 2 1   17 18 19 20 21

Printed in the U.S.A.   23
First edition, April 2017

Book design by Phil Falco and Mary Claire Cruz

For Jamie,
my partner in crime (writing)

Dan Harris was not an Uber driver. He was my dad's latest and greatest attorney from the law firm of Cheap Suit, Bald Spot & Smoker's Cough. Since we left Vegas, he'd chattered endless nothings straight from the small-talk handbook as if angling for five stars and a tip. Stuff like "It sure is hot today, huh, Nikki."

Dude, we live in the desert.

Or "UNLV's looking good this year."

Were they? He probably meant football, which wasn't my thing. Not that kind of football. The University of Nevada, Las Vegas, Lady Rebels soccer team had gotten off to a mediocre start this season with a 4–5 record. I didn't say that because if Harris knew anything about soccer, we might end up in a real conversation. I was a little too anxious for that.

My mom, sitting next to me in the backseat, was more accommodating, nodding and uh-huhing at the right moments. But her eyes and hands gave her away. She never stopped staring at the browns and grays outside her window, scrolling north from the city perimeter to barren sands, and her fingers tapped an endless nervous rhythm on the leather next to my thigh.

It was a strange thing, picking up your dad from death row.

When Harris started talking politics, I knew I couldn't deal with all our nerves tangled in one big vibrating bundle for the entire four-hour drive to Ely State.

Uncoiling the wires in my bag, I screwed buds into my ears and dialed up a long and hearty playlist usually reserved for the game I cared about more than soccer. Eyes closed, my forehead resting on the cool window, careful not to mush my big poofy hair, I zoned, then dozed. Constellations filled my dreams, all the pinpricks in the sky Dad showed me when I was little, before "Uncle" John's murder interrupted us.

A firm squeeze above my knee pulled me from the cosmos. I said, "Wha—" Or maybe I just vampire-hissed.

Mom plucked a bud from my ear. "Wake up. We're close."

Groggy, I smacked my lips, my tongue sour with the notes of afternoon breath. My Altoids tin rattled when I fished it from my bag. I chewed a handful of chalky mints into paste.

Harris got us off Route 6, drove the all-too-familiar streets lined with pool halls, trailer parks, and ice-cream stands that also sold beer. In the distance, snowcapped mountains made the horizon ragged. Dad once told me in a letter that he could see those mountains from his cell. For years I hoped it wasn't just a lie to make me feel better.

When we turned onto the final street before the prison, the change from our last trip was clear. What was usually a desolate strip of faded asphalt bordered by a set of odd businesses was crowded with vehicles. Rental cars and news vans with satellite dishes on extendable arms.

The last tenth of a mile to the prison's entrance was a slow crawl through reporters and protesters and fans (every death row inmate had them). There was a dull buzz in the parting crowd, like driving through a swarm of bees.

"I suspected we'd get some attention," Harris said, moving beyond small talk, "but I certainly didn't expect this much."

Why not? I did. The news had been going crazy over Dad ever since his release went from lofty goal to undeniable certainty. Not the big national morning shows where they mix terrorism with celebrity guests and recipes. Locally, though, it's been kind of a big deal. Black man wrongly convicted on shady circumstantial evidence, officialdom's long, hard stance on admitting no wrongdoing whatsoever because, hey, reasons. People picking sides based on as little real information as possible. Vegas loved its homegrown horror stories.

"You two okay?" Harris asked.

Mom glanced at me before answering. I nodded, and she said, "We're fine."

Neither of us were strangers to noisy packed crowds, nothing different from an average weekend at the casino. I was even dressed for it in my black Saturday night hostess dress. I'd considered buying something new, but a stylish black dress was a stylish black dress, even if a longer swath of brown thigh extending from the hem indicated a much different fit from when fourteen-year-old me bought it two years ago. There'd be time for better clothes and a generally better life than that of a hostess leading drunken oglers to dinner tables if I had my way. For the time being, I was on a budget.

Not like anyone was going to pay me much attention anyway. This was Dad's day. If I didn't already get that, the potbellied poker fan holding a "Welcome Home, Nathan" sign clued me. That poster board greeting, done up in fat Sharpie letters and punctuated with a bad drawing of a royal flush, was pleasant. Though it couldn't match the painstaking detail of a sign on the opposite sidewalk. "Whoever sheds the blood of man," the sign read, "by man shall his blood be shed," followed by the Bible chapter and verse. The wicking fire and white-hot brimstone coals on that one was a nice touch.

Fifty yards from the prison entrance, sawhorses formed a perimeter that the groupies and haters couldn't cross. Guards waited behind the line. One stone-faced, refrigerator-sized correctional officer stepped to Harris's window. Harris explained who he was, who Mom and I were, and why we dared approach the border the prison so thoughtfully erected between his world and ours. Harris's lawyer thing satisfied the CO enough to swing one sawhorse aside and let us through.

We pulled into an empty parking space, and the guard appeared in his window again. "Is everything ready?" Harris asked.

Checking his watch, the guard said, "It's time."

I'd stowed my music but heard a drum. In my chest. My hand found the door handle, and I waited for seconds that felt as long as the last five years.

A Klaxon sounded and a yellow light spun in a bubble over a massive steel-and-concrete door. I expected the huge entrance to trudge open and unleash some giant tank or humanoid battle-armor suit thingy from the sci-fi video games my Bestie #2 Gavin sometimes forced me to play, while Bestie #1 Molly reminded him we weren't that kind of girl. The big doors didn't part. All that drama for a smaller door set in the larger one. It was from there that Ely State Prison spit my father out.

He wore the gray suit Mom and I bought him, guessing at the measurements. It almost fit.

Erupting from the backseat of Harris's Cadillac, I sprinted despite my heels and flung myself at him like the earth was falling away beneath my feet and it was either his arms or oblivion. He caught me, and I buried my head in his chest, ugly-crying and soaking a patch of his suit coat to a darker gray. Mom was there a minute later sliming my bare shoulder with her tears. Dad squeezed us so tight.

Faintly, a dozen camera shutters clicked and whined. Ready to confirm to the world, to all our friends and enemies, that three-time *High Roller* magazine player of the year, two-time World Series of Poker finalist, and one-time wrongly convicted murderer Nathan "The Broker" Tate was back.

♦

Mom and I stayed in the backseat. After five years in a cage, no reason Dad shouldn't get shotgun.

On the highway, a safe distance from the news crews and crazies, Mom passed a box to the front. A lady at a Downtown Summerlin kiosk had wrapped it for us, taking extra care to puff the silver ribbon so it looked more like fireworks than tinsel. Mom offered it to Dad the way I might've offered a crayon drawing back in the day—*Please like it!*

He squinted and flexed his jaw. A blatant tell. After a second's hesitation, he manufactured a smile and took his gift. It fooled Mom, so it was a good enough recovery. I recognized his suspicion, though.

What was it like when people offered you things in prison? Was there always a hidden cost?

"What is it?" Dad asked, turning it over in his hand like someone working a Rubik's Cube.

I touched his shoulder. "It's cool. Open it."

Conceding, he undid the wrapping with care, peeling away the tape instead of just ripping the paper, revealing the white box underneath.

"It's an iPhone," I said.

"Oh. I remember those." He sat the box between his legs, never touching the actual device.

"Maybe later, then," Mom said, so chilly I was tempted to crack a window and let in some desert air.

Never one to let an awkward moment fade quietly, Harris said, "Look, Nathan, I know your head's spinning right now and I don't want to rush anything, but we probably need to make some sort of public statement soon. Capitalize."

Dad checked the rearview as if the prison was in pursuit.

"I'm thinking we should do it at Andromeda's," Harris continued. "Let the world see you back where you belong."

Andromeda's Palace. Niche casino and hotel "in the heart of Downtown Las Vegas!" Aka home.

Harris kept going, despite my dad's curled lip and narrowed eyes.

"It's not every day a capital case gets overturned," Harris said. "There could be a lot of opportunity here beyond our lawsuit against the district attorney's office and the police department. You know how things are around the country now. The brutality cases. The shootings. I mean, that's not what happened to you— and we're grateful for that—but people are fed up and won't stand for another black man getting the shaft from the system."

I watched my father closely, a habit he'd taught me when he was still around to teach me things. The annoyed head tilt, the way he clutched the silk at his knee like it was either grab fabric or Harris's neck.

"Mr. Harris," I said, an attempted intervention launched too late, "maybe we should let him relax."

"For both of us, right?" Dad said.

The car went quiet. None of us sure how to respond.

"Opportunities," Dad said, "for both us. The wronged black man and his white knight attorney."

Harris's pasty complexion went scarlet. "For all of us." His voice trembled when he waved a hand toward me and Mom, trying hard for nonchalance.

Say something, Mom!

She only pursed her lips, maintaining her habit of leaving hard stuff to me.

"Can we listen to some music?" I leaned between the seats like I had permission and tapped the satellite radio button, letting some oldies R&B singer croon about love and happiness we couldn't quite manage on our own.

CHAPTER  2

So, how did we get here?

Ask one of the corny discount comedians we sometimes booked as part of the Saturday night lounge act and you'd get "Southbound on 93!" *Ba-da-BAH!*

Ask me and you'd get a murky, confusing story told by someone who didn't understand it fully herself. Because there's no normal route to a dad on death row.

John Reedy was my dad's best friend, or something. When we opened our casino and I wore myself out daily racing around the place like I had wheels, he'd told me to call him "Uncle" John. Insisted on it. I don't have actual uncles, but I still didn't take to the charity of that artificial title. John Reedy was not very uncle-like.

He was a scruffy redhead, with eyes that often matched his hair. I only ever saw him at the casino bar. Or bothering dealers on the gaming floor. Or having heated, deep-voiced conversations in Dad's office with other adults on speakerphone before Mom caught me spying and ushered my nosy butt away.

The last time I saw John Reedy—alive, anyway—he'd been sitting down for a poker game with Dad and others. That was also the last time I had a conversation with my dad that didn't involve a reinforced glass partition or a recorded phone line.

The arrest I didn't see, and Mom didn't take me for visits right away. It was as if she thought the whole thing would blow over so there was no need to tarnish my childhood unnecessarily. In all her efforts to protect me from the reporters and the TV and the

Internet, she did the thing a lot of people did. She forgot about the newspaper.

The *Las Vegas Review-Journal* was delivered to our home daily, in several huge bundles, and it was my job to drop those papers in front of every occupied hotel room door. Of the hundreds of times I performed the task, there was only one headline I'd never forget.

"Local Man Bludgeoned to Death; Casino Owner Charged"

Every single one of those papers were damp with tears as I laid them at our guests' doors.

I'd learn more things. Foggy things during the trial. Exaggerated and wrong things from my classmates. None of it meant much beyond the certainty that my dad didn't kill anyone. I held on to that. Thankfully, it was true.

Now, the business of next.

♠

It was full night by the time we got back to Vegas, but the city's electric gleam made 8:00 p.m. seem as bright as 8:00 a.m. Harris steered us downtown and onto Stewart Avenue, where cab lines formed and weekend foot traffic thickened, bringing us home.

Andromeda was a curvy, fifty-foot silhouette rimmed by several hundred cerulean LCD bulbs. She greeted us with a thrust hip and a dainty beckoning arm that made it seem like she threw the red neon dice on top of the Binion's parking deck two blocks down.

On our sign, it appeared she was floating, her nonexistent feet lost behind the golden block letters that read Andromeda's Palace.

Each character flared a buttery gold until the entire sign was a fully lit beacon. It flashed three times before going dark, then repeated the sequence.

Dad was stiff and grumbly the whole ride. Until he saw her. He sagged in his seat at the sight.

"Home, sweet home, right?" I touched his shoulder.

He gripped my fingers lightly in his callused hand. "That it is, babygirl."

That name. He hadn't called me babygirl in years. Not even in letters. What glowed inside me felt bright enough to blind the lady in lights above our door.

So, of course, Mom ruined it.

"There's a lot to catch you up on, Nathan. A lot you missed," she said.

Her first words in a hundred miles. Dad stiffened again, leaned forward so he was just out of my reach. The slicing look I swung Mom's way was as sharp as a Fruit Ninja sword.

"Sure," Dad said. "Of course."

"New processes, procedures. Half the staff may not really know you. We should set a meeting for early next week."

Really, Mom? This on his first night back? How romantic.

"Absolutely," Dad replied. "I imagine it's been tough for you handling all this by yourself."

"She hasn't been by herself," I chimed in, my irritation fighting its leash. Half of those new processes and procedures, I wrote. While maintaining my three-point-seven GPA, extracurriculars, and a secret side hustle.

"Nikalosa," she warned.

Dan Harris may not have been an Uber driver, but he

was smart enough to know when he should act like one then. "We're here!"

He drove under the canopy beneath Andromeda, into the hotel's arching drop-off lane I called Andromeda's Loop.

We got sandwiched between a cab dropping off an elderly couple and a Hummer limo picking up some already wobbly Woo Girls. You know, packs of girls a little older than me, known for randomly throwing up their hands—especially when holding frothy drinks—and squealing, "Woooo!" They roamed Vegas like feral cats.

"Nathan! My friend! Welcome back!" The jubilant voice belonged to Mr. Héctor, Andromeda's head valet and most senior employee, who spotted us and left the ushering of guests to his underlings.

When Dad recognized his old friend, he just about dive-rolled from the car. "Héctor!"

The two of them collided in a hug, and Mom didn't push our budding argument. I sensed we'd reached the end of family night. Just in time for everyone's sake. She exited the backseat, tossing Harris a quick thanks. I did the same and thumbed a text to my crew.

Me: it's on.

Dad held Héctor at arm's length, patting his shoulders. "I'm surprised you don't own this place by now, old man."

"I'm saving, Nathaniel. My mattress is stuffed."

Harris leaned into the passenger seat, tried siphoning some of Dad's attention from Mr. Héctor. "Nathan. We're going to talk about our plans, right? Soon?"

"Okay." Dad's tone wasn't convincing, and the accompanying nod felt dismissive.

"Okay," Harris repeated, snatching the handle on Dad's still-open door and slamming it shut before gunning the engine back into city traffic.

Dad watched the car go, practically sneering. The whole vibe between those two was so weird. I didn't dwell on it—I had my own stuff happening and was running short on time. "It's good to have you back, Dad."

His head tilted. "You're going somewhere?"

"A school thing." Poker-face test right here.

"Good," he said, buying it. "Stay on top of your studies. It's the only way to get ahead in this world."

We both knew that wasn't true. "You'll be okay for the rest of the night?"

He nodded. "I will. Your mom and I need some time."

Mom stood away from us, arms crossed, missing Dad's comment because her attention was elsewhere. On the casino doors.

Beyond the tinted glass partition stood our head of security, Tomás Garcia, black suited, posted up in a way that wouldn't seem suspicious to most people. I hoped Dad fell into that oblivious group. Wouldn't do us any good if, on his first night back, Dad discovered a guy on the payroll was in love with his wife.

"Mom," I said, snatching her attention to us, her family. "I hope you and Dad have a great time tonight."

"Yes," she said, "absolutely."

Seemed in that instance, she had a heck of a poker face, too.

Good. Dad was home, I wanted my parents to be my parents again. There for each other. They'd need to be, once I was gone.

A fire-engine alarm sounded from inside, a slot machine jack-pot making someone's night. My cue to leave.

"I love you, Dad. I'm so glad you're home."

He exchanged Mr. Héctor's embrace for mine, kissed my cheek. "Love you, too, babygirl. Breakfast tomorrow? You and me?"

"Absolutely." And how many energy drinks would I need to keep me conscious for those early eats? If all went well, I was in for a long night.

♣

I sailed through Andromeda's sliding glass doors into the foyer, intending to get upstairs fast, then back downstairs faster. I thought better. Tomás and I needed a word.

Because I had way too much responsibility in our casino, I knew as much about our staff as I did about the gossip stars at school. The thing about Tomás that really bugged me . . . he was great at his job.

A one-time officer for the Las Vegas Metropolitan Police Department and a former corporate security chief for a billion-dollar tech company in San Diego, he had taken a position that was, frankly, beneath him, for the close proximity to his sick mother, a Las Vegas native.

She died last year, and he got even better at his job. Showing up earlier, staying later, never demanding a raise for his extra time. That should've made me happy; not like we could afford the pay he deserved. What made me unhappy, his looks. Tomás was hot.

I don't have a crush on him or anything. He's old and that's gross. In a way, it would be better if I *was* the enamored one.

Mr. Héctor once joked that Tomás was too pretty to escort cranky gamblers and rowdy stewbums to the cab line. "He looks too much like Alejandro Fernández."

I didn't know who that was and it showed. Mr. Héctor attempted clarification, "El Potrillo?"

I frowned and shook my head.

Sighing his disappointment, he said, "Let's just say he's got a face for the stage."

Anyhow, I'm only saying, objectively, Tomás was fine. That was a problem.

"Everything all right inside?" I asked him, motioning toward the lobby check-in and casino floor beyond that.

"Yeah, Nikki. Typical Friday." He didn't turn his head, remained fixated on my mom.

Sidestepping, blocking his view, I said, "Are you sure? There's nothing security-related we can talk about? At all?"

He blinked slowly, shaking off all those feels. "The Gaming Board alerted us to a crew cheating tables around town."

"And what are we doing about that?"

He stiffened, like a lot of the staff when they got interrogated by the boss's daughter. He shot me a look but said, "My team, floor managers, pit bosses, and the dealers know. We're switching decks every two hours. No one's seen anything unusual."

"When's the last time you checked?"

He didn't say anything. I didn't stop pushing. "Maybe you should check now."

Finally, he took the hint. "Yes. Of course."

He left, sleeve to his mouth, speaking to the rest of Andromeda's security team through Secret Service–style walkies. He slumped, seemed smaller. The posture of heartbreak.

Once, after I'd noticed Mom and Tomás having a few too many business dinners in the hotel restaurant during one of his long days, after seeing her smile with her whole face at some joke he made, I asked Mom what was up. She didn't hesitate or deflect. "We're just friends," she said. I believed her.

Don't know if Tomás would agree he had a permanent address in the Friend Zone, though. My stomach churned, sensing the potential crapstorm on the horizon.

Nope. Not tonight. No fixing all of Andromeda's problems like I've done for I don't know how long.

I moved through the lobby and onto the casino floor with forced focus.

Technically, according to the Nevada Gaming Control Board, I wasn't supposed to *be* on the casino floor, being under eighteen and all, but this was my home. Good luck making someone's living room off-limits.

Cosmos carpet stretched before me. A custom job of stars, quarter moons, ringed planets, and streaking comets over midnight blue. It gave the sensation of strolling through the heavens, and I imagined I was a celestial being blessing the compulsive gamblers on all manner of games from common to obscure. Craps and blackjack. Plinko and War and the money wheel. Of course, occasional Texas Hold'em and Omaha games in the Goddess Room, Andromeda's sparsely populated poker room. Really, we should've sealed the room off with glass and called it an aquarium for all the fish—aka sucky players—it attracted. Maybe that would change now that Dad was back in the building. A name like his might draw some whales—big-money players, high skill level optional. I hoped so.

Pushing through a Staff Only door, I navigated corridors to

a service elevator, my preferred mode of transport for avoiding liquor-soaked tourists and overeager college boys. On our floor, I let myself into my side of Mom and my—and Dad's now—family suite. It's what passed for an apartment when you lived at a budget hotel.

After shimmying out of my dress, I replaced my prison-pickup outfit with jeans, sneakers, and a red Wonder Woman tee. Then I dug through my top dresser drawer, but not for more clothes.

I pried up the drawer's false bottom, revealing the fat roll of green United States legal tender. I peeled off five hundred dollars, reconsidered, peeled off five hundred more. With my hiding place sealed and buried under stockings and super-comfy fleece socks, I stuffed the folded twenties and fifties into my hip pocket, creating a bulge.

A different elevator took me to the kitchen, where I greeted cooks and dishwashers on my way to the pantry and the door beyond. There were stairs, dark and partially blocked by long-forgotten casino junk. I took them to a not-so-secret basement room. My room.

Flinging a heavy latch, I unbolted a metal door that swung on groaning, protesting hinges. Once inside, I closed the door, putting myself in inky darkness that was pierced only by my phone's glowing screen.

I crossed the room while typing a one-handed text.

Me: you here yet?

A near-instant reply.

Gavin: you know it. let me in.

Not before setting the stage. A breaker box was mounted to the wall. I opened it without looking and flipped the lever inside. The room lit up. Small and cozy, but big enough for the only thing that mattered.

At the center, under the biggest, brightest ceiling light, was a green octagon covered in felt. A card table.

My table.

CHAPTER 3

Cards.

Before Dad's stay at Ely State Prison, that's what he was famous for. Poker, specifically. It's what he passed on to me, same as my eyes, my nose, and my stubbornness (if you let Mom tell it).

No-limit Texas Hold'em. Or stud. Or draw. It didn't matter. Anything involving diamonds, hearts, clubs, spades, a pile of chips, and someone willing to ante up was all good.

Another set of stairs led to another door that opened to the alley behind the Palace. I undid the lock and struggled against groaning hinges, until Gavin slipped in a giant hand and tugged the door open with no effort. In the unblocked doorway, it still seemed like too little room for Gavin to enter. He was six foot six and double my weight. Some of the kids at school called him The Rock (because he looked like The Rock; sometimes it's that simple). NFL scouts already had him on their radar despite him being a junior like me. Until those pro checks rolled in, he hustled to help his dad make rent and feed his three rapidly growing younger brothers. Brothers now big enough to steal his clothes, forcing him to write his name on tags of his favorite shirts. I extended to tiptoes and tucked one of those tags beneath his collar.

"Thanks, Nikki," he said.

"I'm going to be packing you a lunch and reminding you to zip up your jacket next."

"Best. Mom. Ever."

Playfully, I punched him in the arm and almost sprained my wrist; it was like hitting a tree.

He closed the door behind him and grabbed a nearby stool for his usual bouncer perch. He stripped off his hoodie and settled in. I pressed a fifty-dollar bill into his palm. He'd get another at lights-out (and maybe a little bonus if the night went as well as I anticipated). He pocketed the advance and went to work, waiting for the first of our arrivals.

We had four confirmed RSVPs and thinking of each one made my stomach feel like a butterfly reserve. So much so, a dainty knock at Gavin's door made me yelp.

Game face on, Gavin slid the eye hatch aside. "Password."

"I so want to fondle your pecs," said a voice from the other side.

Gavin's toasty complexion reddened around his cheeks. "Hey, Molly."

Yanking the bolt, he granted entrance to the marvelous Molly Martel.

Molly stood at the threshold like a model taking the runway. With her blond hair swooped over one shoulder, combined with a desert tan, she looked ready for a magazine cover shoot. Her leather skirt and patterned black stockings showed off killer legs from all our years of soccer, suggesting that magazine should be *Sports Illustrated*. From the waist up, she was all business, a tuxedo top and bow tie. When Molly played dealer, she looked the part and would've been at home slinging cards behind a table at the Palms.

She and Gavin were eye to eye, even though he was sitting. With hand on hip, she activated flirt mode. "Shouldn't you be working over at Caesar's? As one of the statues?"

"Molly, I get objectified enough by the scouts at my games."

"And I don't?"

A soccer superstar, Molly took pride in being an athlete and never let herself, her sport, or her team be counted less than any other at the school.

Gavin backed down. "Alls I'm saying is if you want a date, just say so."

Molly leaned in close enough for kissing. "Who said anything about dating?"

She sashayed down the stairs and shot me a wink. She loved all games.

"Stop accosting my security team," I said while texting players for their ETAs.

Drawing near, I expected some kind of snappy comeback. Molly only bear-hugged me. "How'd it go today?"

"Great. We're a big happy family again." I gave her a quick squeeze and pulled away. "I'm expecting a little bit of a different crowd tonight. Don't be alarmed."

Molly frowned, but rolled with the change of subject. "Alarmed? How different are we talking? Like, seniors?"

Very senior. "I'm tired of taking allowance money."

Before Molly could ask more questions, there was another knock at the door. Slow, heavy sledgehammer thumps.

"Password," Gavin said.

"Margets."

Gavin opened the door. A man nearly as tall and much wider than him entered. Tattooed sleeves ran the length of each arm. His kinky beard was an untrained pet reaching for his sterling silver belt buckle. Most noticeable was his leather biker vest—his "cut."

Gavin took it all in and hesitated in his duties. "Gotta frisk you, boss."

"I know the drill." The burly man raised his arms and rotated slowly as Gavin patted him down, giving us all a view of the dingy gray patch on his back.

It read "The Pack" above the logo of a feral wolf gnawing the back tire of a classic Harley. Most Nevada residents knew of the Wolfpack Motorcycle Club. And knew to avoid them.

Warily, Gavin gave me a thumbs-up and returned to his stool.

The lumbering biker took the steps, gave the room a once-over. "Where's Nick Tate?"

"Nikki." I met him with an extended hand. "And you're Goose."

"Goose?" Molly snorted.

The biker ignored her inappropriate amusement, remained focused on me. "You're joking."

"Not if you came to play cards," I replied.

He reexamined the room, the high corners and the floor around him, like looking for traps. He turned abruptly. "I'm gone."

"Wait." I shuffled around him, tried to block his way. "What's the problem?"

"The problem is you're a toddler."

"A toddler who can play. It's an illegal card game, Goose. Me being young doesn't make it *more* illegal."

His belly bounced with his laughs, making him look like Santa Claus the Road Warrior. "Ever hear of contributing to the delinquency of a minor? Please don't try to tell me you're over eighteen."

I didn't.

"That's what I thought." Goose stepped in close. "Don't make me move you."

Sidestepping, I dug in my pocket as he climbed the stairs. I threw my whole stash on the risers ahead of him. "I'm pretty sure that's over eighteen."

Goose stopped, stared at the fluttering bills. It occurred to me that this move was a huge mistake. What would stop him from scooping up my cash and leaving anyway? No way was I gonna let Gavin tangle with a Pack member, though he'd almost certainly try.

So I waited. Playing out my first bluff before Molly'd even dealt a single card.

Rob me or play me, whichever way Goose was leaning got interrupted by another knock, this one shattering a world of tension.

Gavin stuttered, "P-password."

The new arrival uttered the correct phrase. Gavin let in a slim, clean-shaven man with touches of gray at his temples and sunglasses on at night. His polarized lenses tipped toward the money on the stairs.

"My kind of place," the newcomer said. Then added, "What up, Goose."

Goose grunted. "Mahoney. You play with these kindergartners?"

Mahoney shook his head before aiming his chin at me. "First time, but the kid's got a nice little buzz to her. She's a legacy. Nathan Tate's."

He raised his arms to be frisked while Goose picked up my cash. My pulse thumped in my ear. Dad's name still meant something in Poker World; whether that currency could be exchanged in Biker World remained to be seen. I waited to see if the outlaw would lighten my hard-earned stash.

After a stretched second, Goose handed me my money—thank god—and removed his own tube of bills from his vest pocket. "Turn those into chips and let's see what you got, Legacy."

"Gladly." I made for my cashier's cage, which wasn't a cage at all but a worn blackjack table with drawers for holding chips and cash. Molly mouthed some choice words at me as I passed her.

No time to explain. A third player showed up and my phone hummed with texts from another en route. Besides, as competitive as Molly was in sports/school/life, tonight shouldn't mystify her too much. My dad, one of the best poker players this town ever saw, was back. Dan Harris told him he needed to make a statement. He wasn't the only one.

I separated Goose's bills and stacked chips in the appropriate denominations. "Don't worry, Goose. I'll leave you some gas money."

♥

After four hours (and many, many hands), I considered upgrading from my false-bottom drawer to a safe-deposit box down at Patriot Trust bank. I'd more than tripled the thousand bucks I started with.

With their cash dwindling, Goose, Mahoney, and the others bundled up the chips they managed to keep, calling it a night. Gavin helped a nervous Molly cash them out. For grown men who'd just gotten schooled by a "kindergartner," they seemed upbeat.

Mahoney took his haul—a tenth of what he showed up with—grinning. To one of his fellow losers he said, "Now I get what it was like seeing LeBron play as a kid."

A proud heat pricked my cheeks and forehead until an eclipse blocked the ceiling light. I was in Goose's dark-side-of-the-moon shadow, his imposing gut so close, I felt wedged between it and the wall.

"Can I help you?" I made sure I sounded tougher than I felt.

He leaned over me. "Your old man teach you to play like that?"

"Mostly." I was Dad's star pupil, his only pupil, from the time I learned to read and count. After he went in, I found other ways. Books by the game's legends. Online play where the currency wasn't real, but the lessons were. I even had an app on my phone so I could squeeze in games. Poker's a game of skill, not luck, despite popular belief. My skills had to be sharp if I was gonna reach my ultimate goal. Escape velocity.

"You ever get it in your head to do some hustling before your name really gets around," Goose said, "you let me know. I want in on that action."

"You're not worried anymore about contributing to the delinquency of a minor?"

"Not when said minor represents a promising return on my investment. You've got a bright career ahead of you. So think about it."

"Yeah, sure," I said, not meaning it. Inviting a Pack member to a single card game was way different from some sort of standing partnership. Even I knew better than that.

Goose was the last to cash out. When he was all set, I escorted him to the alley with Gavin and Molly at my back. There were some, not many, hours left before daybreak.

The xenon headlight on Goose's bike flared blue, and he said, "Remember my offer."

I only nodded as his bike growled and departed, leaving me alone with my friends. A moment I'd been kind of dreading.

"What was that?" Gavin said.

Molly tag-teamed in. "You know someone from the freaking Pack?" She got in my face like we were in a soccer huddle. "The kind of money on the table tonight can get people killed, Nikki. Have you lost your—"

"Enough!" I said. "Molly, we didn't die. Gavin, I'll keep your cut if you don't want it. We're fine, guys."

"Really," said my dad, stepping from the shadows with one of his John Player Special cigarettes dangling off his lips, eliciting an oaky sweet smell I recalled from childhood. "I'm not sure about that, babygirl. At all."

Molly screamed, recovered, smoothed nonexistent wrinkles in her skirt. "I mean, it's great to see you again, Mr. Tate."

He chuckled, a clunky forced sound that didn't mask his irritation. "Likewise, Molly. You were missing teeth the last time I saw you."

We were, what, ten, playing city league soccer and still thinking ourselves like all the other kids? Molly had gone down hard in a game, took a cleat to the face. She was very proud of that "war wound" and kept the teeth in a jar on her bookshelf.

She said, "I've had a full set for a while now. You've changed, too. You were less, grrrr, Incredible Hulk–ish back then."

Molly. She didn't mean it disrespectfully, I knew. That was just her thing, noticing muscles. Since she said it, it made me take note of my father's physique. I'd felt that latent strength when we'd hugged earlier, but his mis-sized suit disguised the hardness. In street clothes, lurking in a dark alley, he seemed a much different man from the one who used to lift me on his shoulders and dance while we watched the Bellagio fountain show.

"I'll take that as a compliment," my dad replied. "Though this young man's got me beat in the muscles department. Some growth spurt you got, Gavin."

"Hey, Mr. Tate." Gavin dipped his head, shy, a demeanor that seemed like a split personality when you saw him cracking skulls on the gridiron.

"The three of you," Dad said, "still thick as thieves. Nice to see some things don't change." Only, the way he said it didn't sound so nice. There was an edge.

"What are you doing out here, Dad?"

"Was gonna ask the same thing. Think I got it figured, though. Hope I'm wrong." His cigarette dropped, a smoldering red meteorite. He snuffed it beneath his boot. "Molly, Gavin, I'll see you two later."

Molly nodded. "Right. Later, Mr. Tate."

She drifted toward the side lot where she always parked for our games, motioning for Gavin to do the same. He didn't move his feet and kept his chin nuzzled in his chest.

"Nikki, I'm sorry. I just . . . I need . . . you know."

Chewing my bottom lip, I understood. Fishing a wad of money from my pocket, I gave Gavin what I owed, then decided to double it. He deserved it. Plus, the bump might be his severance pay if the next few minutes with Dad went sideways.

Gavin shuffled after Molly, and I slowly faced my dad.

He was stone-faced. Silent.

I broke first. "Dad—"

"You told me you had a school thing. What school do you go to again?"

"I know this looks bad."

"What looks bad? Your back-room card game with a bunch of men who look older than me?"

"They're cool. I vetted them beforehand, and the game went good. Like, really good."

"Oh, I guess that makes it okay that you're locking yourself in a basement with criminals and lowlifes." He closed the gap between us, and the John Player cig wasn't the only smell wafting off him. I detected the spicy sharpness of bourbon. Spend as much time around drunken gamblers as I had, you could just about name the brand and the year it was bottled. I winced away from the scent.

"You know what we called games like yours when I was young?" he said.

"No."

"ATMs. As in easy withdrawals. All you need is a mask and a shotgun. How much cash did you have down there anyway?"

Barely a whisper. "A few grand."

"Unbelievable. Gavin's a moose, I'll give you that. You gotta know all those muscles don't mean anything if someone wants to take you. You'll get yourself killed over this Romper Room nonsense." He spun and clocked the Dumpster with a hard jab, the collision sounding like a warped gong.

Some of the rage in him, well, I've learned it's genetic. It flashed in me, too. "You're a real hypocrite, you know."

"Excuse me?"

"'Cash games are how soft players become steel. Can't take a million-dollar pot if you can't take a thousand-dollar pot.' Sound familiar?"

He said nothing.

"It's you, Dad. A radio interview you did back in the day at the World Series of Poker. You started getting better in games like this. You talked about it all the time."

He looked genuinely confused. Maybe he had forgotten who he was. He said, "You see how great it all went for me."

"Poker wasn't your problem, Dad. Murder was." That heat Mom said I got from him, sometimes it burned a little too hot. He looked like I'd slapped him.

Backpedaling, I said, "I'm sorry, I shouldn't have said that. It's just, I need the money, Dad. Okay?"

"For what?" Whatever dark thoughts filled his mind radiated from him with near-physical force and pushed me back a step.

How much should I say? I'd been all salty at Mom for bombarding him with hard reality on his first day back, but was this the time to tell him how Andromeda's Palace was bleeding money? Should I say how tired I was of shouldering the responsibility of a junior executive in a failing venture because Mom didn't have the head for turning a profit? School, homework, sports, accounting, staff management, towers of paperwork, liquor orders, one parent with the business sense of a drowsy Monopoly player and the other with a state-mandated death sentence. My last few years in a nutshell.

I wasn't a pro-caliber athlete like Gavin and Molly, but poker was a different story. It could—would—get me out of Vegas as effectively as football and soccer for my friends. We even had a plan. They had multiple early scholarship offers, but only a single school overlapped. University of Virginia, way on the other side of the country—the other side of the world—wanted them both. I could go, too, with a big enough bankroll. That's what I played for. Freedom.

I didn't say all that. Only "I want to go to college. I'm doing this for school."

Dad was no longer paying attention, though. "What is that?" he asked, pointing.

Tracing his finger's trajectory, I turned, mistaking it for the old game where I had to name constellations. It's hard to see real stars in the city, and he wasn't looking that high.

"That building, with the three blue neon triangles along the front. What is it?" He mistook my slow response for a lack of understanding. I wasn't used to people not recognizing the landmark.

"It's the Nysos."

Tallest building in the city. One hundred and twenty stories jammed between the MGM Grand and the Polo Towers. Yet another casino/resort blocking a chunk of the sky so out-of-towners had another few thousand options for dropping their bags and toothbrushes while they ran around like drunken idiots. The three blue triangles made up a hundred-foot mountain range logo seen for miles. It'd been open a little over a year. Of course it seemed new to Dad.

"Go inside," he said, stepping past me. "You should be in bed."

"What?" How was this the end of our conversation? "Where are you going?"

"To walk a while. I'm finding it hard to stay inside tonight. Been inside a long time."

I looked to the Nysos again. "Dad . . ."

Maybe he sensed my concern, so he lied to comfort me. "Don't worry, your old man ain't looking for trouble. We'll finish talking tomorrow."

Before I could protest further, he was gone, walking into the light.

◆

The talk we were supposed to have the next day . . . didn't happen. That father-daughter breakfast he promised me? Nope. Neither Mom nor I saw Dad the whole weekend.

When he did show up at Andromeda's again, it was with several thousand extra dollars.

CHAPTER  5

On Monday morning, Molly picked me up for school in Andromeda's Loop. She and Gavin probably found it strange the way I paced the slowing SUV, yanked the door open with it still in motion, and leapt into the backseat, yelling, "Go, go!" Like a solider seeking extraction from enemy territory.

To her credit, Molly complied, gunning the engine as I closed the door and secured my seat belt. "Threat level's still high at Tate Manor, I take it," she said drily.

I groaned. Though I hadn't seen my friends since Dad surprised us early Saturday morning, I'd been texting Molly all weekend, and I was sure she'd shared details with a suspiciously mute Gavin. So they both knew about Dad's disappearance. His occasional short voice mails indicating he was still among the living, with no details beyond that. Mom's huffing exclamations of "same old Nathan"—with no fondness or nostalgia in the recollection. And casino work. Never-ending casino work.

Our ride west to Vista Rojo High was usually reserved for recapping classmate drama that blew up online over the weekend or dreadful anticipation of the coming week of sucky homework, tests we had to cram for, and rough sports practices. Not that morning. My friends knew when it was quiet time. We'd all had moments that required it over the years. Like when Molly's dads adopted another daughter, Bethany, and sort of forgot about her. Or when Gavin's mom lost her fight with cancer. My best friends, so kind and considerate, granted me silence. Until we hit the school parking lot.

"No way!" Gavin said, his spine suddenly erect, his attention on the school's front.

Escaping my own head, I leaned between their seats for a better view of the spray paint scrawled across the school's clay-colored walls. There was a series of barely coherent obscenities. The vandalism maintained a theme of maternal insults, suggested physical contortions, and stuff Vista Rojo kids do with innocent farm animals. All hastily done in the same shade of green that made up half of Cardinal Graham High School's colors.

"This already?" Molly said.

The Vista Rojo Fighting Lions and the Cardinal Graham Warrior Griffins shared an old and bitter rivalry. Every year we battled on and off the field. A mix of sports and increasingly bold/destructive "pranks" set off by one varsity gang or the other. Since no Vista Rojo team played a Cardinal Graham squad for at least three weeks, the kickoff for this year's ritual attack felt premature.

Gavin undid his seat belt and stepped from the creeping vehicle, joining a loose group of his football teammates. All of them vibrating with agitation and testosterone. The maintenance crew worked at one end of the graffiti, scrubbing what they could and priming the rest for repainting. They couldn't outpace all the amateur cell phone photographers who were, undoubtedly, posting images to all available feeds. The loitering spectators grew with each new arrival to the lot, and Molly grabbed the closest available parking space while there was still room to drive.

We waded into the onlookers together, absorbing the aggravated vibe of a mosh pit with no music.

"Oh, the many revenge plots that will be formed by second period," I uttered.

"Be nice if all these Lion Pride anarchists would help fill seats at our games." Molly's eternal sore spot. Everybody was up in arms and "Support Our Teams" until it came to actually supporting *our* team. The total number of attendees at Lady Lions soccer games wouldn't fill the concession stand during Friday night football. Anyway.

Once the warning bell rang, we could all look forward to the administrators giving us the Vandalism Response 101 lecture.

No payback, kids.

Leave it all on the field.

You're better than that!

Anyone caught trespassing on Cardinal Graham property will be punished to the fullest extent of the Vista Rojo disciplinary policy.

Blah, blah, blah . . . all the things adults had to say.

What everyone could definitely count on was simmering aggression, bordering on violence aimed at anyone even slightly affiliated with Cardinal Graham. Case in point . . .

Gavin found us in the crowd, his brow shadowy. "Nikki, your boy."

I had no clue what he was talking about or why he was handing me his phone. I took it, saw the picture filling the display, and had my mind blown with about fifty different thoughts/emotions/curse words at once.

First, Gavin knows enough to call him *my* boy? Second, god, Molly, I'm seriously considering sewing your big mouth shut.

Third, info. I needed it. "Where?"

"The equipment cage," Gavin said.

If we hurried, I might be able to save my crush from being murdered.

Okay, so not *murdered*. That's a bit of an exaggeration. Beaten and maimed? A stronger possibility.

Gavin's phone vibrated in my hand as another photo came through. Much the same as the previous pic. There he was, pressed against the wall by a half dozen beefy hands. The biggest change was the curled fist hovering an inch from the victim's chin. A text quickly followed.

come get in on this griffin blood, yo!

That thing about violence directed at anyone affiliated with Cardinal Graham. We'd reached the part of the program at lightning speed. Because the boy in question was a transfer from CG.

Davis Carlino. Here less than a month. Likely wishing he could go back.

Gavin led us down the main corridor, through the gym, and to a detached building dedicated to all things football, ridiculously dubbed the Lion's Den.

Weights, lockers, a trainer's room, and an equipment cage for the pads, helmets, and, apparently, assaults.

We heard the rowdy grunts and commotion before we reached the door, guarded by one of Gavin's fellow linemen.

The football player eyed us warily. "Bruh?"

"They're with me," Gavin said. "It's fine."

The doorman didn't look like it was fine, but Gavin outweighed and outclassed him.

The equipment cage was a wide rectangle of racks and pegs filled with football gear. It smelled of Pine-Sol and industrial laundry detergent like we used to wash linen at Andromeda's. In the far corner, a loose gathering of Vista Rojo's football elite crowded around Davis, shoving him. Everybody there was taller than me, so I only caught glimpses of him between hips and letter-jacket-clad shoulders.

There was a grunt and crunch as he collided with a rolling cart filled with athletic tape, gauze, and fungal sprays. Aerosol cans clattered, but Davis didn't make a sound.

"GRIF-FIN BLOOD!" one player crooned, setting off a chorus of the familiar battle chant. "GRIF-FIN BLOOD! GRIF-FIN BLOOD!"

"They're going to break him," Molly said, a bit too bemused for my liking. As if we were watching toddlers dismember action figures.

To Gavin, I said, "Stop them."

"I'm not *that* big."

There were upwards of ten football players in here now. No, he couldn't forcibly change the state of events. Neither could Molly and I. Force wasn't what was needed.

"Hey!" I yelled over the sounds of battery. "Who likes prime rib?"

Everything screeched to a halt.

The football players became big, mean meerkats, craning their necks in unison. Byron Richie, our quarterback, spoke first. "I love prime rib."

"Great." I dropped my satchel to the floor, crouched. Digging to the bottom, I excavated crumpled batches of coupons for the restaurant inside Andromeda's Palace, the Constellation Grill. "I got free prime rib for anyone willing to let the Griffin walk out of here right now."

Faces lit with grins. Boys. Free food. Of course.

Not all of them were so easily charmed.

"Hold up!" said a wide receiver. "I don't eat red meat. And I ain't about to let this dude off the hook after what he did to our school."

"I didn't do anything," Davis said, visible now between the parted players. Someone stiff-armed him in the chest.

Our gazes locked. Much like the first time, on his first day, my heart and lungs stuttered. I willed them to resume normal function, focused on the negotiation.

"The coupons also work on our awesome grilled chicken," I said.

The receiver's hard jaw softened.

"What do you say, guys? Deal?"

The team's kicker jumped in. "What's it matter to you anyway, Nikki?"

Davis's chin tilted up, just as curious about my motives.

I saw him every day in sixth-period chemistry but couldn't bring myself to say two words before. Now I was swooping in like Batgirl to the rescue. How to explain it? "I don't like when anyone gets blamed for stuff that's not their fault."

Recognition dawned on the faces of a few players. A familiar unease settled over me as one player attempted to relay the message about my dad to another, with no subtlety at all.

"Better do it," he said. "Her pops will . . ." he trailed off, sliding his index finger from one side of his neck to the other in a throat-slicing gesture.

Molly saw, squeezed my shoulder. Gavin glared at his teammates.

"Do we have a deal or what?" My patience was thinning.

Quarterback Byron gave an all-good nod, and Davis was released. He sidled past the players, irritated but seemingly unhurt, giving each and every one of them serious side-eye before clearing the crowd. I stood as he passed, my heart a quick-handed boxer doing speed drills on my sternum.

"Thank you," he said.

"You're welcome." There, two words. "Go." Three. You're on a roll, Nikki.

Once he was clear, I distributed the coupons to each of the knuckleheads, as promised. They traded high fives, the defacing of the school temporarily forgotten in the anticipation of well-seasoned meats. Deal done, me and my crew backed out of the cage, heading for the main building. Homeroom would be starting soon.

"Hey, Gavin?" I said.

"Yeah?"

"The one who was talking trash about my dad—hit him extra hard during practice today."

"Copy that."

♠

Thing was, Gavin couldn't tackle people in the halls. Or in the girls' bathrooms. Or on the other side of a teacher's desk.

That day, all day, it was short glimpses, huddled whispers, timely giggles as I passed with my eyes directed dead ahead, going for a willful ignorance I couldn't quite manage. The graffiti on the exterior walls only distracted when we were all outside. In here, my did-he-or-didn't-he (he didn't) Dad and I were the topic of the day.

The most awesome screw-with-Nikki exhibit was a drawing I discovered taped to my locker at my post-lunch book exchange. It featured a bird in a striped outfit—a jailbird, so clever—returning to his poofy-haired bird daughter, who waited in a nest made of money atop the iconic Welcome to Las Vegas sign.

Molly snatched it down and crumpled it in her fist. "I guess some art school's going to have no problem filling its douche quota next fall."

"Whatever. It'll taper off eventually." Even as I said it, I didn't believe it. Not with Dan Harris's lawsuits and every new development putting our names back on TV.

I'd do what I'd always done. Use my cardplayer's focus. Compartmentalize. Shove aside personal drama for calculus derivatives and *Hamlet* and the Louisiana Purchase. It's what I've done since Dad went in, and I crushed all of it. I had to. In this area, my non-superstar-athlete status made me the liability in the escape plan. Unless a UVA admissions officer was willing to throw my acceptance letter and a sweet financial aid package into a Hold'em pot, I'd be earning my entrance into our chosen school the old-fashioned way.

That Friday night game increased my bankroll to a little under twenty thousand. By the standards of my Vista Rojo classmates, that made me rich. In terms of University of Virginia's out-of-state tuition, it made me good for a semester. Not even a whole academic year.

That meant on top of my poker winnings, I'd probably still need scholarships and loans and divine intervention to make it work. What's another crushing challenge for a Tate?

In chemistry class, while Mr. Devindra droned at the front of the room, I checked my homework against the practice problems at the end of the alkenes and alkynes chapter. My phone shimmied against my thigh, the screen lit with a text.

Molly: you sure you're ok? been quiet today.

She was a couple of rows over, her heat vision warming my cheek. I tapped a quick response beneath my desk, below Mr. Devindra's phone-confiscating radar, to put her at ease.

Me: ☺ i'm fine.
Molly: emojis aren't masks. i can see your face.
Me: i'm fine.
Molly: you better be. you got a surprise coming.

Twisting so we were eye to eye, demonic smoke just about wisping from the corners of Molly's devilish grin, I knew I'd missed something important. She jutted her chin toward a clipboard making its way to the front of the room, where Mr. Devindra collected it and said, "Did everyone get the sign-up sheet?"

Sign up? For what?

The class grumbled a collective yes, and my phone vibrated before I could raise my hand to counter.

Molly: don't fight this. just let it happen.

I mouthed across the room: *Let* what *happen?*

Mr. Devindra said, "Excellent. You know the project due date. Feel free to switch seats so you're closer to your partner."

Project due date? Partners?

My classmates stood and began reorganizing themselves to be closer to the lab partners they'd chosen. Or had been chosen for them. Suddenly, I knew what Molly meant.

On the way to her partner, she made a point of walking past my desk, the same self-congratulatory smirk on her face flashed after scoring a goal.

"Why would you do this?"

"Wasn't me," she said, sincere. "I thought we were going to bang this project out together. Seems you're in high demand."

She moved on, leaving no time to dispute. I nearly chased her, but my partner arrived.

"Hey. You and me. I mean, if that's okay?" Davis Carlino said, dropping down next to me.

Seriously . . . what was I supposed to say to that?

CHAPTER 6

The scoop on Davis Carlino? He was an heir to Mount Nysos, second in line to his big brother.

Yeah, the gargantuan resort hotel that drew my father like a tractor beam, that tower of power poking into the skyline of the Las Vegas Strip—it belonged to Davis's family. A perch from where their supposed gangster father, Bertram "Big Bert" Carlino, loomed large over the city.

A side effect of my involvement with Andromeda's day-to-day operations was an encyclopedic knowledge of the town's power players. I doubted most of my classmates knew or cared about the real estate linked to the Carlino family, or the reputation that came with it. If they did, the football team might've thought better of roughing him up. What Vista Rojo knew about Davis could be summed up as rich and didn't belong.

Yet, there he was. Seated next to me. While my palms slimed sweat on my desktop.

"Are you okay?" he asked, his grin shrinking.

Be cool, Nikki. It's a near certainty he cannot see the moisture pouring from your flesh. It's all in your head.

I nodded.

"Because you're not speaking."

I nodded again.

"You're still not speaking."

No. No. No.

This was just like the first day I saw him in the hall. Worse. He didn't notice me acting like a freak then.

He'd just transferred. Lanky and a head taller than most of our classmates would've been enough to flag him as a newbie. Being so good-looking, like the star of a movie *about* our high school, pretty much made blending in impossible. I spotted him glancing up from his schedule, checking room numbers and trying not to flaunt his cluelessness. Something happened. An attack of some sort. Panic. Heart. Both. Those chestnut eyes of his locked with mine. I went breathless in a moment that was part déjà vu, part dropkick to the chest. He found the room he'd been searching for and dipped inside in time to save me from convulsing on the floor.

I was no stranger to attention from flirty boys and girls. I'd been on display in Andromeda's since I was old enough to seat guests in the restaurant or man the check-in counter when workers called in sick. I've gotten hit on a lot. Like, *a lot* a lot. I'd dated guys from Vista and other schools (never Cardinal Graham, though). I'd been heartbroken and cracked a few ventricles myself. None of that prepped me for what happened that first time I saw Davis in the halls.

Or now.

He wasn't smiling anymore. Why would he, in the presence of a sweaty mime?

A balled-up sheet of loose-leaf ricocheted off my temple. The sheer accuracy of the throw clued me to the pitcher. Ticked, I spun to Molly. She gave me the stinkiest stink-eye I'd ever seen in my life, blasting me with the Best Friend Telepathy we'd developed over the years.

She popped an eyebrow up. *You're really going to mess this up?*

I huffed. *No. I'm just getting my bearings. Don't ever embarrass me like that again.*

She sucked her teeth. *You're on the clock. Move it!*

I chewed my bottom lip. *Let a sister breathe a minute.*

When I turned back to Davis, he broadcast his own telepathy. The universally recognized *What was THAT?* look.

Awkward, yes. Also, effective. I'd found my voice again. "You signed up to be my partner."

"We're going to pretend like that weird exchange between you and the super-aggressive blond girl didn't just happen?"

"Yep. So, partner. What's up with that?"

He could reconsider at this point, and that would suck. That suckage would be on my terms.

"After you helped me this morning, I thought it was the least I could do," he replied.

"Are you really good in chemistry or something?"

"Not even a little bit."

"I fail to see how this is returning the favor."

His smile was back. Funny thing, so was mine. My pulse slowed, and while others around us chattered about the assignment, we did the exact opposite of what Mr. Devindra intended. Fine by me.

"I wanted to know why you helped me this morning," he said.

"I already said."

"You don't like when people get blamed for stuff they didn't do. But *why?*"

Did he really not know? I searched his face for a tell, some tic to clue me if he was running game, trying to be polite by not flinging my dad at me with no regard for human life like everybody else, or just out of the loop.

"People haven't been talking to you at all since you got here?"

He shrugged. "A few."

A few girls. I'd heard. Even his status as a former Griffin only repelled the more assertive Vista ladies for so long. Anyone who did muster the nerve to make conversation wouldn't make that conversation about me and mine. That was a relief. I said, "I helped because I'm a superhero."

"That explains everything. Might I request you use your powers to toss your football team into the sun?"

"Hey now, my friend's on that team."

"You mean the huge guy who didn't kidnap me."

"Yes. Gavin, he's a good—" From the corner of my eye, I detected the movement of a plain white shirt and too-short necktie. "Quick," I said, "open your book."

He didn't hesitate. I did the same. Mr. Devindra loomed a second later. "You two making progress?"

Davis said, "Absolutely. Nikki's really great at this."

My cheeks and forehead burned. It might've just been for the teacher, but hearing Davis Carlino call me great was my favorite thing that day.

♣

The early evening sun sank, giving way to purple skies and dropping desert temps. Molly drove us home, our windows down so we could catch a breeze and avoid a rolling gas chamber of soccer practice sweat and exertion. My phone buzzed with two texts from Davis. Tame messages, both about our chemistry project. They still induced a flutter in my chest like sonnets.

"Is that him?" Molly asked.

"You shouldn't text and drive. Watch the road."

"I'm not texting."

"You're worrying about my texts. It's like the same thing."

"Nikki Tate logic, wildly leaping as usual. Come on, tell me all the sordid details of your love life. Please, please."

"There's hardly anything to tell." It wasn't a lie. After Mr. Devindra started hovering, we scribbled down loose ideas for our project before class change, then traded numbers. I didn't want to get into it because the epic feel of my first real convo with Davis Carlino diminished the more I thought about the mundane reality of what was actually discussed.

"You're telling me he's not your reincarnated lover from a past life," said Molly, "because we still haven't settled that déjà vu conniption fit you threw that time."

"You're seriously not going to let that go."

"I. Will. Not."

The gift and the curse of confiding in your best friend. She always had the best ammo to use against you. I'd told her when I saw him in the hall that first day, it was like I knew him. Ever since, she's been calling us Cleopatra and Mark Antony.

Telling Molly, of course, was my only way to relieve the pressure of unrequited . . . *like*? A shoulder to lean on every time that boy had me on tilt. A listening ear for objectifying him. His eyes were so . . . and his hair was really . . . and those abs made me want to . . .

Molly's assessment of Davis? A subdued "Cute, but skinny."

It was a gross underestimation in my opinion, but I was glad Davis didn't meet Molly's chiseled-marble standards. She beat me in everything except cards, and I didn't want her competition here.

Molly turned into the Loop and came to a stop by the valet stand, where Mr. Héctor greeted us with a wave.

A yellow cab minivan pulled up to our bumper, spilling some weeknight revelers screeching their joy.

"Woo Girls," Molly said, shaking her head.

They dashed into Andromeda's, squealing. If I could only muster their enthusiasm to enter.

Molly must've sensed the change in me. She let the Davis interrogation drop and said, "Bethany's a vegan now."

"Uh, okay. Yay?"

"No. Not yay! The dads bow down to her and now there's no bacon in our house."

Slowly, carefully, I asked, "Do you want some bacon? We've got a bunch at the Grill."

"I'm just warning you. You're welcome to come crash at my place tonight, but you're going to have to eat vegan lasagna, which sounds more like a myth the more I think about it. I mean, what do you do about the cheese?"

This. Girl. "I appreciate it but . . ." My fingers grazed the door handle.

"I know. I had to offer. Go upstairs and text your boo."

On that note I bid her farewell and lugged my bags inside. I was a dirty, grass-stained, high-socked oddity that no one on the casino floor noticed. Vegas.

My sore legs got me into the elevator, and I considered how I might hibernate in my jetted tub (a perk of living in a hotel suite) without drowning.

Drawing near my door, key card in hand, a bear's growl gave me pause.

No. Not a bear growl. A buzz saw?

Keying into my room, I found neither a grizzly nor an unmanned power tool, but a missing person. My dad. Zonked out on my bed. He sprawled on his back across my comforter, his legs splayed, and his arms at odd angles. Completely still. A chill sputtered through me. If not for the rhythmic groans escaping his lips, I would've been alarmed.

"Dad." I nudged his foot with my toe. "Wake up."

He tucked his leg to get away.

"Dad!" Planting a hand in the center of his chest, I rocked him. Remembering the alley, I braced myself for a drunk's reek: alcohol and BO. He roused while I allowed myself a cautious sniff. The lavender from the hotel's complimentary soap mixed with a sharp and pleasant cologne dusted the air as he rolled over. His clothes were fresh, if a little wrinkled from sleeping in them. He was clean-shaven. What was this?

"Hey, babygirl," he said without opening his eyes. "Wanna grab some dinner?"

"Ummmm . . ."

"We can go wherever you want." With eyes still closed, his hand burrowed beneath his jacket lapel and returned with a tight tube of bills secured by a rubber band.

"You've been out playing again." I reached for the latest roll of bills cautiously, in case the prison dog in him snapped at me. He stayed cool when my fingers grazed the money. Then he let it go, forcing me to catch it before it fell on the bed.

It was as heavy as the rolls of quarters I handled in the business office when counting the drawers from the Grill. The top bill on the roll was a hundred. I resisted the urge to pop the band and count it. Whatever the mix of denominations, it was a lot of money.

"So," he said, "about that meal?"

CHAPTER  7

We ended up at SW Steakhouse inside the Wynn hotel, where they had velvety hand-stitched napkins, crystal water glasses, and a steak that cost two hundred and twenty bucks because the cow was raised in Japan and got daily massages. It was not my choice.

The Wynn, like most of the hotel/resort titans on the Vegas Strip (and very unlike our one-restaurant, one-lounge-singer setup at Andromeda's), had a range of excess all on one property. Dozens of dining options and clubs and an amphitheater for hosting mega-production music and magic shows.

There were restaurants in the Wynn that didn't have crazy people prices, like my actual choice, Wazuzu. Home of the most awesome drunken noodles with shrimp that wouldn't cost us a luxury car payment, thank you. But there was a forty-five-minute wait when we arrived, and Dad heard people talking about the lake view in SW, so he vetoed Wazuzu. Hard to argue with a newly freed convict.

When the maître d' escorted us to a table on the terrace, I was uncomfortable as other patrons shot us questioning looks. Them in suits and fancy going-to-a-show clothes, us too casual. Us, maybe, too brown.

We were seated and handed our menus, and my stomach promptly sank. We were going to have to redo that same uncomfortable walk once Dad realized how much it would cost to order anything in this place. I prepared my shame-dampening shields while he glanced over the offerings.

"Anything else for you, sir?" asked the maître d'.

"We're good, thanks," Dad said.

Our escort left us to it, and I leaned forward, queasy. "We aren't good, Dad. Did you see how much carrots cost here? More than carrots should!"

"You've still got that cash I gave you, right?"

Of course. After I showered and changed, I tried to give it back to him, and he told me to hold it for now. Which was a weird way of saying it. What was happening later?

But, yes, I still had it. I nodded.

He went under his lapel again and returned with another wad of money. "And I've got mine. Like I said, we're good."

I glanced left into the restaurant, where the probably wealthy diners now paid us no mind, then right into the black-mirror water beyond the terrace railing, in case I had to defend that money from the Wynn lake monster. "How much is that?"

He shrugged. "A little under twenty."

"Thousand?" My mind whirred. "The roll you gave me?"

"A little less."

A waiter approached, dressed spiffy enough to attend a church service after his shift. The money Dad had held was gone, returned to his inner pocket.

"Good evening," the waiter said. "If I may, I'd like to tell you a bit about the night's specials and collect your drink orders."

"Actually," Dad said, "you don't have to bother with the specials. I heard you've got those great Kobe steaks here, from the Japanese cows."

You would've thought Dad told him he had a beautiful baby, the pride he showed. "Absolutely, sir. Best in town."

"Nikki, you like steak?"

"I don't think—"

"Babygirl, do you like steak?"

That name, jeez, it softened the penny-pincher in me. "Sure."

To the waiter, Dad said, "Bring us two of those. Big ones. I feel like I haven't eaten in half a decade."

He winked at me, and I was suddenly okay with the excess.

The waiter took our drink orders, talked us into appetizers (another hundred bucks I couldn't help calculating), then left as a light show started up on the lake. As I watched it, I caught Dad going into his jacket again. That drew my full attention and my heart sped, envisioning a third wad of cash appearing. Not that time, though.

He laid a deck of cards on the table. A custom pack, straight from the Andromeda's Palace supply room.

"Tell me everything," he said.

♥

For the next three hours, we talked and ate. He asked me the kinds of questions a fan asks a star. How did I manage to play soccer and help Mom and get such good grades? What's my favorite thing to do in my free time? What inspired me? What did I want to do next? At that point the cards he laid on the table found their way into my hands. While I spoke, my fingers worked the deck. Rapid intricate shuffles all while subtly peeking at the bottom of the deck, and palming an ace from the middle. Cheater moves.

Not that I cheat. That's an unforgivable sin. But it's helpful to know how it's done so you know how to spot it. That's something he taught me. I wondered if he remembered.

Dad wasn't looking at my eyes or mouth anymore. He studied my hands. "You're good."

"Good as you?"

Smirking, he extended his palm. I gave him the deck.

His card handling reminded me of street magic. He repeated all my shuffling tricks with a supernatural speed and nimbleness, at one point spreading his hands wide and shooting cards across the gap between his palms in a near-solid accordion arc. It was impressive enough to draw applause from the haughty tables we'd passed. New approval from the previously judgmental shrank Dad's smile.

"All that's just tricks," Dad said, putting the cards down. "A clumsy, fat-fingered fish can take a pot from you if you aren't on at all times. There's a game before the game. You understand what I'm saying?"

Reminiscing was over. Nothing uncomfortable between us now.

"I can play, Dad. For real."

"You feel like showing me? I told you hang on to that stack for a reason."

My breaths felt shallow from anticipation, thinking of the poker room in the Wynn, despite an inconvenient truth. "I'm not old enough to play here."

"Not here." He signaled the waiter for our check.

I glanced at the time on my phone. It was after ten. "I've got school tomorrow."

"You've got school tonight, unless you want to keep making excuses. You don't sound like someone who really wants to play."

His tone irked me. "Ready when you are."

The waiter arrived with our check in a leather portfolio. Dad glanced at it, then pulled several hundred-dollar bills from his roll. He handed the money to the waiter and said, "I won't need any change."

CHAPTER 8

When Dad hopped on the 15, I wasn't sure what to expect. I knew we were leaving the Strip, and that made sense because I wasn't legal. Maybe we'd end up closer to home, some discreet card room downtown where one of Dad's old acquaintances wouldn't mind me sitting in on some hands. Only, Dad passed our exit and a bunch more after that until we hit East Cheyenne Avenue, where he got off the highway, and used North Fifth Street to keep climbing. North Vegas transformed into the *infamous* North Town. At Donna Street, I thought about the last shooting or three I'd heard associated with this area, hoped there wouldn't be a fourth and fifth anytime soon.

Firecracker pops of handgun shots pattered in the distance. I needed to adjust my hopes for this trip. "Dad, this is looking really shady."

"We're fine."

Another couple of turns put us on a street as humble as all the others in this neighborhood, with a massive uptick in vehicle quality. A quarter-million dollars of luxury vehicles hugged the curb before a single, pale ranch-style house. A Lexus, two Jaguars, and something low and sleek that I couldn't name, made the dark cul-de-sac with the broken streetlight look like Andromeda's Loop valet parking on our best Saturday.

"If someone wants to hide their illegal, high-stakes poker game, they aren't trying too hard," I said.

"When you pay the right people," Dad said, "hiding becomes an unnecessary inconvenience."

His sudden aloofness wasn't lost on me. He wasn't just my dad anymore. This was Nathan "The Broker" Tate. Our game had already started. He pulled up to the bumper of the car I'd be googling later, and my heart pounded.

"You ready?" he asked.

I imagined the money in my bag as a white-hot coal, threatening to burn through my purse, then the car floor, then the earth's crust if I didn't do something with it soon. "Ready."

"You better be."

◆

Music and raucous laughter leaked from behind the heavy door. My dad hammered, three quick pounds. When someone asked for a phrase, he gave it. This was a familiar routine and made me feel like I'd been doing things right with my own secret games.

Inside the house, we were met by the muscle, an alternate-reality version of Gavin. This guy wasn't as tall or hard-bodied as my friend, but the holstered pistol on his hip was an equalizer. The site of deadly weapons and the rough frisk I underwent did nothing to slow my pulse, but the adrenaline pumping through me wasn't the fight-or-flight kind. This was excitement, the first kicked ball of a soccer match. The clanking of a roller coaster about to crest the first drop.

After the security check, we made our way into a room, with a table at the center, crowded with people, cards, and chips. There were four players at the table, and another six people lounging about with drinks and cell phones in hand. Except the guy guarding the cashbox—all he held was a shotgun. My dad and I made the crowd an even dozen.

The dealer palmed the deck and began flinging all players their two hole cards, what you start with. He then dealt the first three community cards, aka the flop. A couple of players compared their hole cards to what lay in the middle of the table for all to use. The idea was to combine your hole cards with whatever three community cards gave you the best five-card hand, hopefully a hand good enough to beat everybody else's five-card hand.

You bet based on how confident you were you could win; you could bluff if you weren't confident but thought you could psych the other players into taking the third option, which was fold—quitting and leaving all the money on the table for the eventual winner. Three contestants took option three, pushing their hands forward, folding, their hole cards so bad they already knew they had no chance this time around.

The remaining players made additional bets, tossed more chips into the pot. Then the dealer laid out the fourth community card, aka the turn—an eight of spades. At the sight of it, another player folded, a freakishly tall guy. My gaze hung on him, recognition dawned.

"Is that—"

Dad squeezed my hand and whispered, "Don't act starstruck. And, yes, that's him."

Him being the All-Star shooting guard for a certain top-five NBA franchise. Him being the recipient of a blockbuster shoe deal with Nike that had Gavin hustling to save the small fortune required to buy his brothers the next iteration of overpriced sneakers this Christmas. Him having enough towering chips stacked between his custom jeweled hands and wrists to make me salivate.

Another player, a Latino man in a tank top, spun in his seat. "Nathan Tate. Back for more."

"Luciano," Dad said, "don't you mean back to *take* more. From you, in particular."

"We shall see. Who's the girl?"

"A fish."

I bit my lip. Them's fighting words. Unless Dad was doing me a favor, lowering their expectations by labeling me a noob.

Luciano gave me a long once-over. "Somehow I doubt that. Strong family resemblance. Get some chips. We'll deal you and your mini-me in on the next hand."

Dad guided me over to the cashbox and whispered in my ear, "We can still leave."

That didn't deserve a response. The man behind the cashbox asked, "How much?"

I passed him the entire roll from my purse. "Whatever this buys."

That wad of cash bought a lot of chips. Three hours and a couple of dozen hands later, I'd tripled it. Thanks mostly to Mr. Shoe Deal's money-ain't-a-thing style of play, a whole year of UVA tuition sat before me.

Dad was doing slightly better than me. Most of the other players cashed out and called it a night when they saw the kind of roll we were on. The basketball player was stubborn, and I loved him for it. He'd gone bust a couple of times. When he lost all his chips, he'd buy more. No big deal.

Luciano, our host, lost on a couple of early hands and hadn't taken a risk since. Dad was my only clear competition at the table. If I were being honest, I even found his play disappointing. Sure, he'd won nearly as much as me, but he was more conservative than I'd expected. He folded early and often. Smart, but boring. I might employ some of his caution at a table with pros, but we'd been mopping the floor with these guys. Why hold back?

When the new hand started, Dad peeked at his hole cards and folded at the flop, not liking the mix of community cards: king of hearts, four of diamonds, and seven of clubs. I gave him a condescending headshake.

My hole cards were a seven of diamonds and a king of spades. Combined with the seven and king on the table, I had a solid two pair already. I pushed more chips into the pot. Too rich for Luciano's blood, he folded. The All-Star wasn't backing down, though. He called, matching my bet, as I hoped he would.

The fourth community card dealt was a nine of clubs, and magic happened.

The NBA player raised with an obscene amount of chips. Way more than what I had in my own impressive stack. I'd either have to fold or bet everything I had to stay in.

In an instant, all my years of play allowed me to calculate the possibilities based on the cards I saw. He *could* have been chasing a flush if his hole cards were clubs, or a straight if he had an eight and a jack of any suit, hands that outranked my two pair. If the last community card were a club, or a ten of any suit, I would lose.

The thing about it, though, he touched his diamond-encrusted platinum chain before he bet. The same thing he did before every sad, unsuccessful fake-out he tried to pull off all night. He had nothing. And more than two years of tuition was staring me in the face.

I called his bluff and pushed all of my chips into the pot. I wanted that Nike money.

My father's face was stone, and it irked me. He could've cheered me on, winked, something. The odds were overwhelmingly in my favor. Only a club or a ten could beat me. The room vibrated with the force of my slamming pulse. This. Was. It.

The ball player nodded, his Joker smile gleaming across the table. "That's what I'm talking about. Play to win, right!"

Always. "Hey, dude. I hear you've got a good chance at the championship this year. That's something."

"Deal it," Dad said. Something in his tone startled me. Was he upset I'd played better than him?

The last community card was dealt.

My breathing shallowed, and I fought a ragged laugh back into the pit of my stomach, though there was nothing funny. Nothing at all. Two cards could beat me. A club or a ten.

The fifth community card, the card I'd see in nightmares for the rest of my life, was a ten of clubs.

Mr. B-Ball unfolded to his near seven-foot height, flipped his cards, revealing the eight and the jack that gave him the straight I thought impossible. With a fist pump, he said, "Yes! I think you're right, shorty. My chances at the championship are looking mighty fine this year. Show 'em."

My hands wouldn't move. Once I flipped my cards, it was over. All that money, all that potential for the future I wanted and needed, would be gone.

Luciano, who I'd forgotten about entirely, touched my forearm more gently than I deserved. "You gotta show them now, *chica*."

Mechanically, I flipped my cards, confirming my loss. The ball player's arm slithered around the chips, reeled them in, taking everything I had.

How was I still alive when there was a hole where my stomach should be?

Dad clutched my hand, pulled me up and away from the table. "That's enough for one night."

♠

We rode home in silence, save the thumping rotation of the car's tires carrying us through deserted Vegas streets. At the first red light, I blurted, "I'm sorry about losing your money."

My eyes were wet coals, burning, leaking.

Dad got us going again when the light changed. "You don't owe me an apology."

"You staked me and I blew it." I was flustered and wanted

forgiveness. All that money he'd won over the weekend. All the work he'd done to build that bankroll. I'd gone on tilt and lost it all. "I'm so, so sorry."

"You need to calm down."

"But I lost your money!"

"No, you didn't."

I sniffed and made a honking sound. "I didn't?"

"That wasn't my bankroll, babygirl. It was yours."

My elbows were pistons, my hands claws, snatching clothes from my dresser and flinging them over my head, not caring if I hit my mom and dad with socks and bras. I hesitated before popping the false bottom in my drawer. Please, don't let it be real. In my open hiding place I found what I feared: dust bunnies.

"Give me back my money!" When I spun, I yanked the whole drawer from its nook, willing myself not to throw it, too. I placed it on my bed, blinked away the tears so I could see my betrayers clearly.

Mom leaned in the doorframe between our rooms, arms crossed, unable to look me in the eye. Dad's hands stuffed deep in his pockets, where his winnings bulged the denim. "There's no giveback in cards. Once it's gone, it's gone," he said.

"You stole my money."

"No. That money was in your possession from the time we left here till when you got greedy."

"I didn't get greedy."

"All in? You played well until you didn't. Don't tell me you would've played it differently if you'd known that was your stash. I saw you, babygirl. You were going for it no matter what."

That skinny brown arm reaching across the table, reeling in all of my hopes and dreams. I couldn't bear thinking or speaking of it.

Then realization hit. I looked at my mom. "You knew."

She shuffled her feet but didn't respond.

"If I'm five minutes late for curfew, you're blowing me up." I held out my phone, the one that had been suspiciously silent all night. "It's three o'clock in the morning and I don't have a single text from you. You put him up to it, didn't you?" Then, to Dad, "Was it her idea? Did she make you do this?"

"It was *our* idea," he said. "You needed to see what that world can be. How it can get cold so fast, babygirl. Better you learn it now."

"Do you know what you've done to me?"

Dad looked to Mom for assistance.

"You needed to know the truth of what that game can be, what it can take from you," she said.

It was logical. The game could be brutal like that, and obviously, Dad wanted me to learn it early, in the safest way possible—with him. It's something I understood later. Then, in that moment, all I could see, feel, and taste was an eternity in the casino. Molly and Gavin would go off across the country, fulfilling their potential. Me? I'd be trapped at Andromeda's. Chained and waiting for the monster that was Vegas to eat me.

"Did Mom tell you about the security guy she's always flirting with? Tomás?" I said, lashing out.

Mom was in my room now, her face pinched and fists clinched. "Nikalosa Tate, that is enough."

No. It wasn't. Everyone was getting a hard lesson tonight.

Dad blinked rapidly. "Tomás? That guy who turned in a letter of resignation yesterday?"

Tomás quit? It only halfway registered; my attention was on the fuse I'd lit.

"We can talk about that later," Mom said.

"No, Mom. Let's talk now. We're all about truth tonight. Like how it's true you're a crappy business owner and you need me trapped here to do everything you can't and won't."

Dad stepped between us. "Your mother's right. You need to stop this."

"Truth: You were better at being my dad when you were just a letter in the mail."

His hand clamped my bicep, tourniquet tight, his thumb dug into the muscle and guaranteed a bruise. Some primal part of me pulled away from the pain, or tried. His grip was iron.

If he'd demanded an apology for him, or Mom, or Tomás, I would've given it. But he issued no demands, no warnings. Fear trumped my rage, because the thing using my dad's hand to hold me, and his eyes to burn through me, was a silent monster. Through the pulsing pain radiating from his tightening grasp, I faintly heard Mom say, "Nathan, stop it. Nathan, let her go."

Did he hear her? I couldn't tell. Only when Mom pounded her fist in his shoulder—"Nathan, let her go now!"—did my father regain control of his body. His fingers popped wide, a reverse bear trap, and I fell onto my bed, massaging away the dents he surely left in my flesh.

Emotions crashed into Dad's previously stony face, shattering it. Fear and horror. Sadness and still some anger.

Mom stepped between him and me. Maybe to speak to him directly, maybe to protect me if he changed his mind. I clutched my comforter, made myself not shake.

"This is over. Everyone's going to go to bed, cool off. Okay?" She rotated halfway, never turning her back fully on Dad. "Okay?"

I nodded, dreading the thought of another conversation like this, cool heads or not.

Dad backed away, eyeing that hand of his. "I'm sorry, babygirl. About all of it. Better now than later. Trust me."

Wasn't that the problem, though? I didn't trust him, or Mom. Apparently, they didn't trust me, or they wouldn't have tricked me.

Dad had been home three days. How did it get so bad so fast?

Or was good ever a thing?

Mom left me, hovered in the doorway leading to her side of our suite. Only when Dad opened the main door to the outside hallway and closed it behind him did she step fully into her room and lock herself in. It wouldn't occur to me until later that they weren't sleeping in the same room, and never would again.

In the days after the Apocalyptic Poker Game, I used every trick and alternate route I knew to avoid seeing either of my parents around the hotel. Stairs instead of the elevator. Up an hour earlier for a to-go breakfast from the Constellation Grill (on Mom's tab because, hey, I'm broke now), to be eaten on the smokers' bench in Andromeda's Loop while waiting for Molly and Gavin. It wasn't that hard. Really, I got the impression they were avoiding me, too.

My friends and I don't lie to each other, so I called what I did an exclusion. I didn't tell them my bankroll was gone and, without it, UVA was as feasible as Hogwarts for me. Over the next week, when Gavin was concerned with the thugs in his neighborhood messing with his brothers, and Molly brooded over the local sports press listing Cardinal Graham over us in the city rankings, I fake-smiled and made like the plan was still on track. Most of my world was crap. Things between me and them needed to be okay.

My Davis Carlino chemistry project proceeded and he was better at it than he let on. He did the heavy lifting by deciding our topic would be Reactivity of Metals, initiating conversations about logical steps and necessary materials, and not asking Mr. Devindra for a new partner when I responded in monosyllabic grunts. At times, I'd glance up and catch Molly mean mugging me for clearly squandering this opportunity. Too bad she couldn't lead my love life the way she led our soccer team.

We played our first away game of the season and won, and I managed to fake it through the celebration. It wasn't so hard. I assisted on a Molly goal and got a faint reminder of what joy felt like. The day after, Friday, this happened . . .

"Great game last night," Davis said.

I'd been swirling a beaker of hydrochloric acid and steel wool. It almost slipped from my grasp. "Huh?"

"You and Molly play great together."

Was Molly, tired of my obvious but persistently denied funk, now controlling Davis telepathically to force my hand? No, she seemed wholly occupied with her own chemistry project.

Backed into a corner, I said, "You came to the game?"

"Yes."

"Why?" Not smooth, at all. Quick recovery: "Most people don't come to our away games. Or our home games."

"Away games are safer for me these days."

"The Cardinal Graham beef," I said.

"Your football team is still having trouble with the concept of school transfers."

Days had passed and the understaffed maintenance crew had only managed to remove half of the offensive graffiti Davis's former classmates decorated our school with. So, each morning, the jock rage reignited. With the Vista Rojo–Cardinal Graham games still two weeks away, the only immediate revenge outlet . . . had me for a chemistry partner.

He wasn't bruised, at least not that I could see, so no one probably risked a suspension or, more important, playing time to issue a beatdown. But I knew from experience, Vista could initiate psychological warfare at a moment's notice.

"Want some advice?" I offered.

He nodded, his shaggy bangs swishing over his eyes. "Sure."

"Stop thinking of them as *my* football team. They're yours, too."

"Duly noted. Anything in addition to the power of positive thinking? I'm not sure altered vibes are going to be enough here."

Fully in fixer mode, a skill set honed by solving all sorts of wild, on-the-fly problems at Andromeda's over the years, all the problems except my own, I settled on a possible solution. "Let me talk to my friend Gavin. He plays left guard and isn't jerky like the rest of them. His influence, plus some sort of peace offering, can smooth things over significantly."

"Peace offering. So I'm negotiating with terrorists."

"What did I just say? They're your team, too. I'm not saying a million dollars in small bills. You've seen what they like."

"Food."

"Exactly. Pick up a couple bags of candy bars and throw them into the locker room. They'll love you forever. Like puppies."

"Sage advice, Nikki Tate. You're everything I've heard and more."

My mouth twitched. He'd been talking to people about me? "What have you heard?"

"You're funny. You're smart. I should never sit across from you at a card table unless I don't like money."

"That's all?"

"Is there more?"

This week, unfortunately, yes. Dan Harris got his wish, and Dad made his big public statement condemning Metro, and the city attorney's office, and American justice in general. Beamed directly from one of Andromeda's conference rooms to the homes of my worst classmates. I hadn't seen it myself. I had the texts from strange numbers I had to keep blocking and the notes wedged into my locker and the nasty posts that made me delete every social media account I was stupid enough to have started and the constant, triflingly snickering whispers. It was a crappy thing to think, but I was glad Davis was still a Cardinal Graham pariah. No one was rushing to let him in on the joke.

I forced my facial tic into submission. "Depends on how far Molly unhinged her jaw. Sometimes she does that to lessen the strain on her ever-running mouth."

He shook his head. "Actually, she gave me a pamphlet."

"What did it say?"

"It was just the word *awesome* printed over and over. It wasn't a creative pamphlet. Kind of creepy, really. You should watch that Molly. She's stalking you."

I laughed. A real laugh. It was still possible. I decked him in the shoulder and was only vaguely aware that I'd forgotten to feel sorry for myself. Forgotten my anger.

Davis Carlino, the best amnesia ever.

♣

Dad tried. He did. God, he did.

He knew enough to let some days pass—maybe Mom told him to give me space—but by the weekend he was actively making attempts to repair the damage. Amateur.

He'd wised up to my early morning to-go orders at the Grill and tried to goad me into a sit-down. I walked out. When I came home in the evenings after soccer practice, he just happened to be in the lobby, looking over a check-in clerk's shoulder as if learning the computer system. I went straight to my room. He wasn't great at the quiet slights, so every time I saw him during those angry days, I decimated him.

My mom and I had spent years perfecting our silent-treatment techniques. A passing eye roll here. A complete 180-degree avoidance turn there. Our battles eventually resulted in some unspoken stalemate. But we needed each other—Andromeda's Palace slogged along on our efforts—and that need wore down our invisible shields. The thing with Dad . . . I hadn't figured how to need him yet.

From where I stood, him being home wasn't much different from him being in prison. I felt stupid for expecting more. For wanting it.

By the time Friday hit, and things were looking up with Davis, Dad tossed subtle aside. Texting me as chemistry class let out.

Dad: I want to talk and put this behind us. Let's do something fun. Bowling at Red Rock tonight? You still like bowling, right?

"You okay?" Davis gathered his books and we drifted into the hall together.

"Fine." The text made me furious; the rage translated to a spiteful boldness I wouldn't have been capable of a week ago. "You want to go bowling at Red Rock tonight?"

He was surprised, evident by his gaping mouth. His cuteness tapered my anger, made me question the crappy thing I was about to do, but only for a second.

"Sure," Davis said, agreeing to our first date. "Let's do it."

"Awesome." I thumbed a text back to Dad.

Me: sorry. got plans.

I wanted to be clever *and* hurt Dad *and* spend more time with Davis Carlino. I wanted everything, and still got more than I bargained for.

"Remind me, why am I here?" Molly said as she sipped her cherry Coke.

Thunder echoed throughout the cavern of Red Rock Lanes, the bowling alley inside the Red Rock Resort in Summerlin. It was close to the school, but a way different vibe from Downtown or the Strip. Few tourists ventured out this far, making Red Rock more a locals' hangout, a place to get away from the televised version of the city that outsiders were most familiar with.

The weekends were Cosmic Bowling nights, where the weekday fluorescents were turned down in lieu of black lights morphing the polished lanes blue, giving the balls a candied glow. I watched bowlers fling neon orbs toward pins like Jawbreakers shotgunned at unprotected teeth. Music videos played on the displays lining the wall, the corresponding songs blaring loud enough so we had to shout to hear each other.

"Because." I got Davis's "on my way" text twenty minutes ago. I scanned the door every other second, anticipating his arrival. A new text came through, and of course I thought Davis, until I read it.

Goose: Got a game for you if you're interested.

My big-bellied biker friend was true to his word. He still wanted to stake me. And I needed to be earning money again.

"You okay?" Molly asked.

I'd been staring at my phone, maybe for a while. "I'm fine."

Me: can't tonight. sorry. but thank you.

Declining Goose's offer gave me an ache in my near-empty pockets, but it wasn't as if I could—or wanted to—bail on the night. I focused on the moment.

Molly kept expressing her concerns, undeterred by the noise. "I get I'm supposed to be your wingwoman, but does he have any friends? I'm not spending the whole night with a CG boy. Just so you know."

"I specified no Griffins."

"Who, then?"

Good question. One I honestly hadn't put much thought into because Molly and Gavin's will-they/won't-they bit was the only important romantic scenario in either of their worlds. Of course they didn't want to admit it, and the thinly veiled jealousy they exuded whenever the other one dated, or even looked at, another possible suitor just exacerbated the whole thing. So, really, whoever Davis brought was of temporary consequence.

Then Davis stepped into the place, I saw who was with him and had a change of heart.

Molly noticed, too. She sat up straighter and popped a mint.

Davis spotted me immediately, and it set my skin tingling. I stood to greet him at our table, all sorts of protocol questions scrolling through my brain. Was this a hug situation? A head nod, maybe?

Davis made it a moot point when he embraced me wholly, pulling me into him. It wasn't just my skin tingling then. I responded in kind, squeezing, tracing my fingers along his spine. I couldn't hear the noise around us until Molly cleared her throat pointedly.

"Introductions?" she said.

Davis pulled away, and it was like fighting the pull of a magnet.

"Sorry," he said. "Molly, meet my brother, Cedric."

The slightly older, more heavily muscled Carlino went with the nod option. "Hey."

Cedric Carlino, he of bulging veiny biceps on display thanks to his designer tank top, those arms demanding attention for the tattooed art adorning his flesh as much as for his rippedness.

Was *rippedness* a word? For him it should be.

He had a bronze tan, the same chocolate-brown eyes as his brother, and his scalp shaved close.

He. Was. A. Specimen.

"Hey, yourself," Molly said, flirt mode on. Her twinkly eye and half smile confirmed she was pleased. Wingwoman wasn't such a bad gig after all.

We rented ugly bowling shoes and got a game going. It was fun until it wasn't.

♥

It was too loud in there for good conversation, though we tried.

"What's up with you and the Super Friends?" he just about screamed in my ear.

"Huh?" I screamed back. I heard him, didn't get the reference.

"You, her"—he pointed at Molly—"and the biggest, strongest human I've ever seen politely ask a lunch lady for an orange Jell-O cup."

His astute observation of Gavin's affinity for that nasty dessert got me giggling. "Nothing's up. They're family."

"I figured that much. Since I came to Vista, everyone's been real cliquish. You three seem different, is all."

"Now we do. There was a time when we were very cliquish. The Outcasts. Gavin was the poor kid. Molly's adopted, has two dads, and can testify that a bunch of Las Vegas residents are way less progressive than you'd think. And I—" I hadn't planned to go there. Ever.

His smile went crooked. "It's okay. You don't have to talk about it."

So he did know. I guess this was his way of being cool about it. Could I be cool about it?

"Hey," he said. "Cedric's turn. Let's laugh in unison."

Cedric hefted his ball from the rack, immediately slung it in a manner suggesting he thought the pins were in a different building. As physically impressive as he was, he bowled like he didn't have fingers. We mocked him as Davis suggested.

Cedric spun on slick bowling shoe soles, sporting a sunny grin. "Cut me some slack. I'm doing my best over here."

"Do better," Molly chided. Glum over their combined scores.

"It is what it is. Nobody plays to lose."

"Could've fooled me."

Davis leaned into me, his warm, slightly cinnamony breath tickling my ear, whispering something about how Molly should trade Cedric for a twelve-year-old a few lanes down who was throwing strikes. I felt as jittery as the day he'd announced our partnership in class, but with excitement, not embarrassment. Even knowing stuff about my history, he wanted to be here. With me. As much as I wanted to be with him. It wasn't forced. Not awkward. No one checked their phones, hoping it was time to go.

We'd gotten through one game and started a fresh one. Davis held his ball at eye level, lining up. He began his approach and . . .

"GRIF-FIN BLOOD!"

Davis threw the ball in a hard diagonal, and it zoomed directly into the gutter.

The shout came from some ignorant, jerk, can't-let-anyone-have-a-good-time Vista classmates. I'd spotted them earlier, bowling a dozen lanes over, and hadn't thought much about it. Now they'd moved from their game to freshly vacated seats in the lane next to us. Apparently they'd run out of money and needed something to soothe their boredom. Us.

Molly reacted first. Measured and strategic. She twisted in her seat, said, "You losers trying to play us next game? Four on four?"

An out for everyone. These guys weren't our friends, but an agreed-upon friendly competition might make it so all could be forgiven.

Instead, one of them said, "Nikki, I know this isn't what I think this is. You're a Lion. Shouldn't your dad be taking out this Griffin?"

Cedric was on his feet and in their faces before I felt the shame.

"You talking about my brother," Cedric said, along with additional colorful things.

Maybe the Vista jerks didn't notice him before. Or didn't notice how jacked he was. Or how much he looked like the new kid they thought my dad might "take out."

Tense glances all around. They didn't want to back down, not when it was four on one. But Cedric didn't seem concerned about the odds.

Bystanders noticed the sudden tension spike. Moms shuffled their children behind them, while other random people skittered from the immediate area, likely seeking the nearest security officer.

"Say something now." Cedric's voice was clearly audible over the ambient noise.

Davis rushed to his brother's side, the voice of reason. "Ced, let it go."

Cedric wasn't letting it go. He jabbed his index finger into the forehead of the main mouth breather, forcing the boy back by steps.

Davis hooked Cedric's elbow, tugging him away. "Stop it. Please!"

Cedric turned his attention to his brother, still angry, but for different reasons. "Do these skid marks know who our dad is?" Back to the VJs: "You better ask somebody."

Molly got my attention. "Nikki. The door."

Sure enough, security guards. Party over.

"Davis," I said, crouched by his hip, snatching off the bowling shoes. "We should go."

He saw what we saw, leaned into his brother, whispering and soothing. Cedric was steaming, but glances at the oncoming guards had the desired effect. He took his shoes off, too. Tossed them at the troublemakers who were too dumb-scared to move.

The security guards kept at a safe distance, ready to diffuse, and prepared to do more. "We're done here, right?"

Cedric said, "Screw bowling. Told you we should've gone to the batting cages."

◆

Such a good night couldn't end like that. I gave Molly a look. Our telepathy was on point, and she wasn't about to let my first date with Davis end on a sour note. Nor was she about to let me look too pressed to keep the evening going. Casually, playing the wing-woman position to perfection, she said, "Hey, this place is lame. Let's go back to Andromeda's."

Nice and simple. She said it, allowing me to maintain a cool, not-quite-aloof vibe. A proven play.

"Fine by me," Davis said, and looked to his brother. "Ced?"

Cedric's neck craned, his gaze fixed on the guards making sure we kept on to our vehicles, as suggested.

"Ced," Davis prodded, a slight quake in his voice.

"Huh," Cedric said, his brow shadowing his face but not hiding how clearly bothered he was by the altercation. I got it. It bothered me, too.

Davis said, "Can we follow them back to Nikki's?"

"Sure, bro. It's your night."

Real cool, I said, "Awesome. Molly and me are in that SUV over there. Just follow us back."

"See you there." He gave me a quick hug. Casual. He broke off with his brother, Molly and me climbed into her SUV. Once the doors were properly sealed, and we made sure the Carlinos couldn't see us . . .

WE. FREAKED.

Squeals. Stomping the floor and rocking the suspension. Bumping fists into the ceiling. I glanced at a family walking by in the rearview. They gave us a wide berth.

"He's soooo into you!" Molly said.

"You really think?" I was fishing for more of her analysis, even though I agreed.

She started the engine and put us in motion. "Oh my god. Every time you bowled, he was checking you out."

Well, that was mutual.

It went like that the whole way home. Us breaking down everything Davis said, did, and emoted with pheromones. I felt bad monopolizing the conversation, so I asked her what she thought about Cedric. She shrugged it off. "He doesn't seem much older than us, but this has gotta be like babysitting for him. It's cool, though."

We turned in, pulling up to the curb. Mr. Héctor was on shift tonight, grinning at our approach. Only when we stopped did I hear the animal purr of the engine behind us. I'd been so consumed with my romantic progress, I hadn't noticed what a beast of a car Cedric handled. A polished silver Maserati. Its grille shaped and positioned like an animal's snarling mouth.

Mr. Héctor passed us, performing his duties, intending to offer Cedric the full-service treatment. I climbed from Molly's vehicle, waiting for Davis to emerge while Mr. Héctor went through his normal pleasantries. Only, Mr. Héctor's demeanor didn't seem pleasant at all when he stared at Cedric, and his service-with-a-smile expression went flat. He uttered a robotic "Can I park this for you?"

Cedric declined, asked if it was okay for him to leave it at the curb. Mr. Héctor nodded, then shuffled in the general direction of his valet stand.

Davis climbed from his seat, but I needed to redirect my attention for a second. "Mr. Héctor."

The look he gave me, I nearly flinched.

He'd never looked at me like that. This was something else. I glanced between him and the Carlino brothers. "Is everything okay?"

He smiled then, as fake as clown makeup. "Fine, Nikki. Fine."

He kept on to the stand and scooped up the house phone.

"That sign is sweet," Davis said, his head tilted up at *Andromeda* rimmed in blue.

"Huh?" I followed his gaze. "Oh, yeah. She's great."

Cedric joined us, his eyes on the sliding glass door leading into the casino. "How are your craps tables?"

Now my mind was in a three-way split. Héctor and the phone . . . Who was he calling? Davis and the sign. Cedric inquiring about our gaming options.

My business mind overrode everything. "We have plenty. Never too crowded. Bets from five to fifty."

"Fifty bucks?" Cedric said, his disgust a rung below what he showed those d-bags at Red Rock. "Nothing bigger? No high-roller room?"

Defensiveness washed over me, the last emotion I expected. "No, we don't. We like to keep our games accessible to players of all budgets."

It was marketing spiel, but I recited it like scripture to a nonbeliever.

Cedric gave me a *meh* shrug.

"You didn't ask me about our card games," I said, suddenly curious how far he wanted to take this high-roller thing. I could use some seed money to re-up my bankroll.

At that, he sighed heavily, exchanged some insider glance with Davis. Brother telepathy.

Molly picked up on it, too. "Did I miss something?"

Cedric said, "I'll let you take this one, bro. It's your date."

All eyes on Davis. He said, "Our dad despises cards."

"Weird, considering your poker room's the biggest in town."

"As a profit generator," Davis said, "he loves it. But as a pastime for his boys . . ."

The brothers spoke in unison, an unkind bass-heavy rendition of words they'd obviously heard too many times, presumably from the Carlino patriarch. "Cardplayers are fools leaving their hopes and dreams to paper kings and queens."

That singsongy rhyme had me bristling. The psychic wave pulsing off me must've felt like I was about to go Carrie-at-the-prom, because the brothers stopped abruptly. Davis said, "That's how our dad is. It's not how I feel."

Cedric caught up. "Oh, that's right. Davis told me you're supposed to be nice at cards. My bad. No disrespect."

"All's forgiven," I said.

Molly said, "So, if you two are done dumping on my girl's favorite pastime, why don't we go for a walk. Maybe over to Fremont."

I was about to agree when I caught aggressive movement from the corner of my eye. My dad.

Mr. Héctor met him at the doors, spoke quickly, and motioned toward us, setting Dad on his course.

"Hey!" Dad yelled, drawing not only our attention but that of a few guests, who seemed skittish at the sight of the shouting, apparently angry black man. Angry about what?

"Dad?" The first I'd spoken to him all week.

"Nikki, Molly, get inside." He moved past me and got in Davis's face. "Does your father know you're here?"

Davis glanced to his brother, asking the silent question. *What the heck is this?*

Cedric wedged himself between Dad and Davis, protective. "Dude."

"I'm not your dude, Cedric. Tell me if your father sent you here."

I reached for Dad's hands and noticed his scraped knuckles, rough with raisin-colored scabs. Something I'd missed in my days of avoidance. Even as he yelled at my date and his brother, I missed details, because I thought this was about me.

I'm not your dude, Cedric.

Dad knew them.

Damage-control time.

"Davis, I'm sorry. Please go," I said.

His lips twitched like he might argue. Cedric patted his chest. "She's right. We should leave."

"Don't come back," Dad said. "If Bertram Carlino has a problem with it, tell him to come see me himself. He knows the address."

Hurt and confusion wafted off Davis, but he didn't resist. The brothers climbed into the car, and its engine purred to life. I walked to Andromeda's entrance, not watching the Carlinos leave. Molly kept pace, but Dad lagged. Probably glaring after my rejected guests.

"Nikki, are you okay?" Molly asked.

"Yeah. I'll text you later."

"What are you about to do?"

"I'll. Text. You. Later."

She was no longer beside me. Her feelings might've been hurt. As tough as she was, I knew that was a possibility. I'd apologize later.

A quick glance over my shoulder, I saw my dad tailing me.

I had other feelings to hurt.

♠

I cut through the gaming floor and took an almost hidden path to the business offices. Separate from the cashier's cage, where the money was counted and kept, and apart from the god's eyes monitors in the security office, where our watchmen ensured no one took advantage of Andromeda, the business offices consisted of small quieter spaces, with gray carpet and beige cubicle walls. All empty this late on a Friday.

"Nikki, hold up," Dad said.

My cubicle, where I occasionally did paperwork someone older and more qualified should've been doing, was in a back corner. I'd done a lot of grown-up things in that cubicle when my classmates were probably Snapping or planning formals. I'd cut the working hours of hotel and waitstaff because Andromeda's wasn't making enough to pay them for full shifts. Responded to letters from the Nevada Gaming Control Board—aka the Casino Police— when some bitter unlucky gambler accused us of rigging games. Everything adorned with Mom's signature since I mastered forging it. This was the place I did so many of the hard things I shouldn't have to.

"How do you know the Carlinos?" Dad asked.

"How do you?"

No answer. I flopped into my chair and didn't care about the manic tone to his question. "I thought I could do this, Dad. But it's not working." It was the no-nonsense voice I used when firing the line cook who kept missing shifts to play gigs with his band.

"I don't know what you're talking about," he said, "but I need to know about your connection to that family."

"This isn't prison."

His mouth snapped shut.

"That's where you've been. You haven't been here. You don't get to be my overbearing father when you haven't been here. I've done fine without you."

"Babygirl."

"No!" It wasn't me yelling, crying, and snotting over my lost money. What I felt wasn't even anger, exactly. I was tired and needed a break from him. Five years away, and having him back for seven days felt worse than his absence. "I don't need you here, Dad. Not right now. Okay?"

I spun my chair toward the computer in my cubicle, logged in. Spreadsheets and other Andromeda documents I'd been working on earlier were already open and waiting on my desktop. Concentrating on the work, I didn't notice when he left.

♣

Another weekend spent on a different planet from my parents. I caught glimpses of a passing comet named Mom, and we grudgingly acknowledged each other without crossing the expanse of space between us. If she knew about Dad hulking out on Davis and Cedric in the Loop, she didn't let on.

I didn't see Dad at all. He didn't go back to his room after our conversation. Our fight, then gone. There was no cool-down period. Not one moment when I regretted it. No time for that. There were only chores and focus.

A Saturday morning soccer practice where Molly listened to my recap and hugged me. More hotel work because of a dentists' convention in town. Between my Saturday night hostess duties and lending a hand with the Sunday breakfast crowd in Constellation Grill, Andromeda wasn't the only girl who got paid over the weekend.

My mind whirred with the possibilities of getting my poker games started again. Rebuilding my bankroll. It was more urgent than ever to get the money to leave this place with my friends. I'd see the soccer season through, but I'd bail on softball in the spring. Couldn't waste any more energy on things that didn't generate funds.

I considered other games I knew of, the penny-ante hands out in Rancho or on the UNLV campus. I could maneuver my way into all those games, but it would take forever to earn.

An unexpected text lit my phone, interrupting my Sunday evening brooding.

Davis: you up?

I'd been flat on my back, staring at the ceiling and plotting my card comeback. Seeing his name on my phone put me on the edge of my bed, anxious. Should I launch a preemptive strike and apologize for how Dad treated him?

A bit of poker strategy came to me. Play conservative, read the table. Less is more.

Me: yep.
Davis: we never did take that walk on fremont. i'm out here now,
    if you want to join.

It was past eight o'clock on a school night. My feet hurt, and Dad wanted me nowhere near a Carlino for, I don't know, reasons.

Me: see you in 15 minutes.

♥

After the fastest shower in history, I hit the lobby and left Andromeda's through the front doors, unconcerned about who'd seen me go. If Dad caught wind of my excursion, so be it. Time he learned his paranoia had no place outside of Ely State. The Nysos logo was a bright beacon way up in the sky, and I was sneaking off with the guy who lived on top of those blue neon mountains. My stomach churned with nervous possibility.

The Fremont Street Experience was a block over from Andromeda's. You could feel its electric buzz when you neared. Blocked off from cars, the canopied walkway running between several downtown casinos was lit with, literally, millions of bulbs. You could zip-line there or chat up beautiful girls in bikinis and body paint (Gavin's favorite) or buy any number of cheesy Las Vegas souvenirs. Plenty of people did all of the above, making it hard to spot my coconspirator. Shuffling away from the foot traffic by the Golden Nugget Hotel, I fired off a text.

> **Me:** where are you?
> **Davis:** behind you.

I spun around, startled. No one was there.

> **Davis:** did you turn around? please tell me you turned around.
> **Me:** i'm at the golden nugget, jerk. come find me.

I kept my back to the wall and spotted his slim frame parting the crowd as he neared. Dressed in all black and smiling for reasons I couldn't comprehend, he stopped just shy of me. Hesitated. Then closed the gap and wrapped his arms around me.

Oh my god, he smelled amazing. It was a spicy boy smell: soap, wintergreen coolness of deodorant, and a hint of cologne, maybe.

When he let go of me, I said, "That was unexpected."

"I was thinking 'overdue.'"

"I meant . . . I thought you might be mad at me."

"What did you do?"

That was sweet of him. I knew it wasn't my actions that may have—should have—inspired his anger. So we weren't talking about the incident. Super cool. A subject change seemed in order. "How did you get here?"

"Stole one of Cedric's cars."

"No, really?"

He fished a sleek plastic-and-silver fob thingy from his pocket and I knew it would start some vehicle worthy of James Bond.

"You're a car thief?"

"Among other things."

"Oh, oh!" I bounced on my toes and popped up a hand like the only kid who knew the answer to the teacher's question. "Are you Clyde?"

"Sounds like someone wants to be Bonnie."

After the week I had, it sounded way better than being Nikki. "For tonight?"

"Let the crime spree begin."

CHAPTER 14

Our rampage was legendary. In our wake were the mangled carcasses of used ketchup packets and shredded napkins. We committed caloric felonies involving double burgers and thick-cut steak fries with Cajun seasoning. Obviously, Metro avoided engaging us for fear of public safety.

We ended up on Sunset Road, the observation area by the airport. Crumbs, greasy wrappers, and sticky soda residue would've sullied the soft leather interior of Cedric's car, and Davis didn't want to incite his brother's wrath any more than necessary. We ate our meal on the hood while planes pushed away from the earth and traced vapor trails in the sky.

There's a radio station here, 101.1, that doesn't play music. It's a public access channel for transmissions between air traffic control and the pilots coming and going. The car's custom sound system was cranked to max, and talk of "bearings" and "vectors" squawked through the open windows.

Davis said, "You know about this spot how?"

Roaring engines of a landing jet filled the silence between us, giving me an excuse to hesitate. When the plane passed, I spit it out. "My dad used to bring Mom and me here."

A louder jet took off, ascending directly over us. Davis yelled to be heard above the noise. "It matches his quiet, peaceful demeanor."

That got me laughing—a deep belly laugh. And right then, my first time being truly alone with Davis, I wanted to know him better and nothing else.

We talked sports (his favorite is basketball—reminding me of that painful night I spent in the presence of an NBA star . . . I changed the subject). We talked college (I told him about UVA and discovered he wanted to go to NYU and be closer to his mom in Manhattan).

"What do you want to study?" he asked.

Truth was, I hadn't thought that far. No one ever says that, though. Right? "Maybe business. I do a lot of stuff—fix a lot of stuff—at Andromeda's now. I guess I'd be good at it."

"My dad would love you."

I stirred and hoped the next jet sound blasted the topic of dads from the atmosphere. Davis continued, "My dad is always on us about having a head for business. And the family business. And business is never personal. Cedric cares more about all that than me. Thus—" He swept his hands over the polished paint beneath us.

"What do you care about?" I said, then backpedaled, thinking it sounded too . . . intimate. "I mean, what do you want to study?"

"Computers, maybe. Or history."

"Really?" I didn't know anybody who liked history enough to pursue it voluntarily.

"Sure. Don't know it, doomed to repeat it. That's a thing."

We talked Cedric's car fetish (I still didn't know what kind of exotic automobile we were sitting on).

"He's going to be so pissed I took one from his fleet," Davis said.

I'm glad he did. I almost said it, but wasn't bold enough to admit how much I liked us getting away together.

"Why'd you transfer to VR?"

"Ahhh." His pride was evident. "You want to hear the Fatal Flatulence story."

"The what?"

He twisted so he stared directly at the side of my face, but I kept my eyes forward, away from his intense, radiating gaze. I read once that ice skaters focus on a single fixed point when they do those super-speed spins. It helps counter dizziness so they don't swoon. Same principle here. I focused on the runways.

Davis said, "You know those safety alert systems schools have that send all the students, parents, and teachers a text or email when something dangerous is happening?"

"Okay."

"I used Cardinal Graham's system to inform everyone about a dangerous gas leak discovered inside the principal's body."

I reran that sentence in my head, nearly choked on a fry. "No! Why?"

"Everyone who'd been to his office knew the chairs smelled farty and he had stomach medicine like Mylanta and Beano lined up right on his desk. Every good prank has to graze the truth. It's ineffective if it's not personal."

Still giggling, I said, "That's not what I meant. Why'd you prank him at all?"

He chewed his lip for a second. "He talked trash about my dad and me and Cedric."

Talked trash like how his dad might be a crime king, and how Davis and his brother were the princes? Talked trash like Molly, Gavin, me, and everyone else at VR probably does?

"I get it," he said, maybe sensing my hot flash of guilt and wanting to give me a pass. That's what I hoped. "Big Bert Carlino's freaking Tony Soprano. Came in and took Vegas by force. I know I can't shake the rumors, even if they're crap."

Were they, though?

"I kept cracking jokes in class and got sent to the office. The principal went on this rant about how 'hoodlum behavior' wouldn't be tolerated, like I'd been extorting money from teachers. He was all 'seems like I'm going to have to hammer this message home for each and every one of you Carlinos.' When he berated me enough to warrant my release, I decided to spend my evening finding a back door into the system and . . ." He shrugged.

"They kicked you out for that?"

"Well, actually, they pressed charges."

"What?"

Another shrug. "A healthy donation from the Nysos got them to back off formal charges, but after that, I had to go."

My mom once had a near meltdown because a teacher overheard me singing a curse word from an old Tupac song in the hall and hit me with detention. I couldn't imagine the blast radius if cops were involved. "How angry was your dad?"

"On a scale of one to ten. Six, maybe. He was most upset about the legal action, but that's because he's heard the Carlino rumors, too, and doesn't want me and Cedric living up to everyone's exaggerations." He momentarily delved into the Big Bert Carlino voice from the other night. " '*Never get arrested! Never end up in the system!*' Deep down, I think he liked the joke."

"It was sort of boss."

"So, Nikki, is that short for Nicole? Nickels? What?" he asked, changing the subject.

"It's Nikalosa."

"That's . . . that's beautiful."

He looked at me. Like, really looked at me. "Thank you."

"Does it mean something?"

"To my mom it does. When she was pregnant with me, her and Dad"—there he goes again—"took a trip to Cabo. They were at this restaurant by the water, looking at the stars. Dad said he wanted them—us—to live in a paradise like that one day. He promised her we would. Mom said they needed to make a pact. Dad joked about the steak knives being too dull for a blood oath, but Mom said that part was taken care of already. They just needed something to anchor us to that specific place and time. When the waitress brought the check, Mom gave her a big tip. Partially for the service. Partially for stealing her name."

"She was Nikalosa," Davis said. "You were the blood oath."

"Yep."

The air around us felt heavier. Neither of us needed to state the obvious. I was there in Vegas, not on some Cabo beach, oath fulfilled.

When the next jet took off, Davis craned his neck to such an extreme I thought he'd tip backward into the windshield. "I like flying away from here."

That was unexpected. As was the gut twist and hot flash it triggered, like being shoved by a bully. "So you're a Vegas hater? Can't wait to leave?"

"Weren't you just talking about college on the East Coast and a magical Mexican paradise?"

True. A little hypocritical. But talking about Vegas was like talking about my parents. I can say bad stuff about them.

"I didn't mean it like that," he said. "It's always sunny here, so when you fly, and you get over the clouds, you see all kinds of things. Like that game when you look up and call out animal shapes in the sky, only, in like, IMAX." His voice went soft. "I don't know. It's stupid."

It was the kind of admission that you didn't make easily. It left you open, exposed.

"It's not stupid," I said, meaning it. "I've noticed something similar."

"For real?"

"For real."

The other part I didn't say. The few times I've been on planes, above those clouds, I didn't see animals. I saw gods.

Giant, angry gods. The ones that inspired the name and themes and future of my casino jail. Their protruding chins, their cocked arms ready to throw punches and lightning and judgment with no regard for the humans they'd damage as their battle wreckage fell to earth, invisible in that same Vegas sun that allowed you to see their majestic indifference so clearly.

This conversation, this thing we shared, made me nervous. I'd never talked like this with anyone before.

"One more question," he said, "is it stupid that I want to kiss you right now?"

I didn't know what to say. *Yes!* was the only word that came to mind, but it wasn't the right answer to that exact question. Was it? No one ever asked about kissing me before.

There was something kind of hot about it.

Davis waited for my answer, the one I couldn't quite formulate with blood rushing through my body. It pulsed in my ears instead of my chest. Things throbbed. Breathing had become this optional act.

"Not stupid at all," I finally managed.

A smile flickered across his face, as if he was genuinely surprised by my answer. Then he leaned in and his lips found mine, his hand snaking around the back of my neck, pulling me closer.

My eyes squeezed shut on their own. I couldn't hear or smell. Touch and taste were all I had left, all I needed. It was a sensory-deprivation kiss.

The rush and need drove me into Davis, and the sudden body collision didn't play nice with the waxed hood. We started sliding, and it was either go off the front of the car or lock together to anchor us. We went for locked together.

His hands traced my spine and the back of my ribs through my jacket. My fingers threaded into his hair. It was *everything*.

Then the hood dented.

There was a groan of stressed metal, and a *TH-WOOMPF* sound as we sank into a body-shaped depression. With equal parts reluctance and panic, I flung myself off Davis, landing beside the car, gravel crunching under my feet. He remained in the pit we created, eyes wide and slight panic on his face.

"That was so worth whatever Cedric's going to do to me."

Then he laughed. Which made it okay for me to laugh, too. By mutual decision, we decided that was enough for the night. Our kiss had the equivalent force of a fender bender. Pushing it further might down one of these planes.

Also, it was close to my curfew.

We climbed into the car, where I'd left my phone. Mom was calling, a follow-up to eight missed calls. I let it go to voice mail.

Whatever she wanted could wait.

CHAPTER  15

We hit traffic close to Andromeda's. I was no longer near curfew, I'd crossed the threshold and was sinking in the sucking sands of the Tardiness Desert, indicated by Mom blowing up my phone like a stalker.

"I'm going to need you to drop me off on the back side of the hotel." I could key into the alley door, cut through the poker room, then skirt around to the business offices. Call Mom from my desk phone, say I was working late and my cell died. Perfect.

"No problem," Davis said, "if we can ever get through this traffic jam. What's going on up there?"

Cars were moving, but with thrusters set to snail. I saw the police up ahead redirecting traffic off Stewart onto East Ogden. And *that* was backed up.

Davis said, "You up for a walk? Just a couple of blocks."

"Maybe."

"You gotta hold my hand, though. It's dark and scary."

"Don't worry, I'll protect you."

He parked in the Denny's lot off of South Fourth Street, and we strolled hand in hand. Maneuvering past the congested traffic and its unseen source was simple enough on foot. There were cops ahead, keeping congregating bystanders away from the alley. My alley. That led to my poker room.

A couple of orange traffic cones were spaced in the opening of the walkway. Poles extended from the top hole in each cone, and stretched between them was the yellow crime scene tape anyone who's ever watched TV has seen a million times. It's not so entertaining in real life.

I broke free of Davis's grasp and pushed through the onlookers, unconcerned with their annoyed grunts and admonishments. A uniformed Metro officer saw me coming, stepped up to block my path. I outmaneuvered quicker girls every day in soccer practice. Past him and under the tape before he could do a double take, I was outrunning his shouting to the other officers ahead of me. No uniforms, but they were cops. The bold DayGlo POLICE across the back of their windbreakers was the first clue, the holstered guns on their hips was the second. The big brick of a camera one of them aimed was as familiar as the crime scene tape.

"Stop!" the officer I juked yelled.

I did, too. Not because he told me. Because the wind shifted, and I got slapped by the smell.

I've thought about it so much since. Too much. It's easier to think of that smell than what I saw when that camera flash threw a spotlight on him sprawled on the ground, with the back of his head a flattened, bloody mess against the concrete.

"Dad?"

I was running. Screaming. Hands pulled me back, tried to turn me away. Three or four people and they could barely hold me.

"Dad! Dad, get up! Get off the ground! Please!"

Eventually—I couldn't tell you how long it took, a minute or a month—my strength waned. The people trying to spare me from what could never be unseen—Mr. Héctor among them somehow—took me away. Once I was out of the alley, my legs were as supportive as cooked noodles, and I was dragged along with my toes scraping the ground. Davis pushed away from the bystanders, his concern bringing him close, and Mr. Héctor shouted, "You should go!" Stopping him cold. I couldn't figure which one of them was right.

Time skipped. Those strobing cruiser lights flashed over me, I blinked, I was inside the casino. People still gambled on the gaming floor. Blink. I was in the business offices, Mom's office. She hunched over her desk, one sloppy wet hand cupped her face. My legs regained muscle and bone, and I rushed to her.

She saw me coming and ejected from her chair hard enough so it crashed into the wall behind, forcing Tomás to leap backward or endure a bruised hip.

A brief *What's he doing here?* flitted through my thoughts, when Mom embraced me, whispering "Thank god" over and over. My concern about him and his infatuation faded like a dream in daylight.

I squeezed into my mother and closed my eyes against gushing tears. But when I shut them on the world around me, I saw the photographer's flash again, illuminating the most horrible thing I'd ever seen. My father's eyes open and on the stars. Forever.

◆

There were questions. Statements. Everyone talking to Mom and not to me, even though I sat right beside her with our fingers laced. One of the police I'd seen outside, a detective named Burrows, sat on the other side of Mom's desk. Old and overweight, his pale complexion made me wonder if he spent most of his time investigating caves.

His recorder was a slim digital thing with a microphone aimed at us. Mom reiterated she didn't know where Dad had been the last two days, and she didn't know if he had enemies.

That part was a lie. Dad made enemies of the city's cops and lawyers the minute he and Dan Harris made noise about his conviction. It was a lie I understood. When Detective Burrows finally asked me if I knew anyone who had it out for my father, I told it, too.

Burrows pushed for more info. Some of his questions were precise, some vague, and some he asked three times using different words. He returned to me, said, "Where were you coming from tonight?"

I didn't answer because I honestly didn't know. It took a moment to remember there was a point when this was a good night. While I collected myself, Tomás returned to the room—I hadn't noticed he'd left—announcing news vans were outside. I fought through my haze. "They're not going to show him on TV like that, are they?"

It was calmer than I thought myself capable. Something about that chilled the room, made me ashamed. It's the thing I used to think when Dad was set to die strapped to a gurney in Ely State. Would there be cameras there? Would people know? This was a fate I thought we'd avoided.

"No." Mom had steel in her voice. "They won't."

She looked past Detective Burrows to Tomás, who nodded before chirping orders into a casino walkie. Back on the job, at least for tonight.

Detective Burrows said, "Was your husband using illegal substances?"

Mom threw her hands up. Furious. "No. Never! Why are you even asking me a stupid question like that?"

"We found some paraphernalia in the alley."

"It's an alley. I'd be surprised if you didn't find junkie paraphernalia in every alley in Vegas. Are we done?"

"A few more questions if you don't mind."

"I do mind," Mom snapped.

The detective's mouth hung open, clearly not expecting that.

"How about you answer some questions. What do you know? How'd my husband get out there? Did any of those ghouls huddling around our home see anything? Since they're out there and we're in here, maybe you ought to interrogate them and let me and my daughter have some time."

Mom was on her feet, her hands planted on her desktop so she wouldn't tip when she leaned into the detective. Burrows closed his mouth and kept his expression perfectly neutral. "I assure you the investigators outside are—"

"I'm sorry, what was that?"

Burrows frowned, confused. "The investigators outside are—"

"There's that word again. Outside."

Burrows's neutral look flickered between three or four aggressive emotions before he made a show of clearing his throat, gathering his recorder and the handheld notepad he'd scribbled next to nothing in. "Metro will do all it can to bring your husband's killer to justice."

He was halfway to the door when Mom said, "Leave your card."

Burrows faced us, no longer hiding his annoyance. "Excuse me?"

"You're going to do all you can, and I'm going to hold you to it. Leave. Your. Card."

He plucked the card from his pocket and dropped it on the desk.

She made sure he was good and gone before she picked it up. "Come with me," she said.

I followed because what else was I going to do?

We moved with purpose toward the guest elevator. I glanced across the gaming floor, spotting the security team keeping rabid reporters at bay on the other side of the sliding glass. Tomás was posted by the check-in desk, dealing with a different set of investigators. They weren't police, not the kind most people were used to. The letters NGCB were stenciled across their jackets. Nevada Gaming Control Board agents.

They kept their noses in casino scandals and crimes, but for them to be here now seemed fast, even for their Big Brother routine.

Mom gave Tomás a signal, letting him know we were going up. When the elevator dinged, and the doors parted, we entered an empty cabin. We'd gone up a floor when Mom collapsed into the sidewall, sliding down in a crouch, racked with hitching sobs.

"Mom." I went to her, hugged her, and those sobs hit me like a contagion.

Even when the elevator reached our floor, we sat there together for a long time.

CHAPTER  16

I'd avoided watching the press conference when I was mad at Dad. Now it was hard to stop. On that first day, I replayed it until my phone flashed an ominous temperature warning and shut itself down. Then I lay in the dark, wishing my brain and heart would shut down, too.

It didn't seem quite true, him being dead, because him not being around was my normal for so long. When he was in jail, it might be a week or more before he called, and a couple of months between letters. The days after his death felt like those lulls. Except when they didn't.

My dad is dead.

It was an unexpected bullet from an unseen sniper, fired over and over during a week that felt both too short and infinite. In the shower where my arms felt too heavy to lift the soap, and my eyes burned from exhaustion—my dad's dead. Forcing down a room-service lunch—my dad's dead—because I'd been excused from school until after the funeral. When Molly, post-practice, sat at the foot of my bed gossiping, the make-up assignments she delivered—my dad's dead—between us.

With the thought came an uncommon rage. Throw-something, punch-something, break-something anger. I didn't do those things. Something had to give, though. I couldn't stop the uncontrollable, unpredictable reminder of my family tragedy. It even chased me into dreams.

Jerking awake on the Wednesday after, kicking away covers that felt like clutching hands, I wanted my mom the way I did when I was little and the boogeyman lurked in my closet.

"Mom?" I nudged the door linking our rooms. Her quarters were dark, empty. The clock on her nightstand read 1:37 a.m.

Remnants of my nightmare fed my unease; my missing parent triggered full-on anxiety. Back in my room I slipped on leggings, a hoodie, and sneakers. Dialing on my way to the elevator.

The connection dropped on the ride down, not uncommon, but I couldn't remember the usual annoyances of cell reception when I didn't know where my mother was. The FAILED CALL message had me freaking.

Ding! The doors parted halfway when I squeezed through, startling a couple of sleepy-eyed guests who leapt out of my way before I barreled them over. Jogging the lobby, on a path for her office—because she had to be there, she just had to—I redialed and got a solid connection.

Mom picked up. "Nikki, are you okay?"

My ragged breathing steadied almost immediately. "I'm fine. Where are you?"

"In my office, couldn't sleep."

It's exactly what I suspected. Too bad she was lying.

I had to pass the Constellation Grill to reach the offices, but there was no longer a need. I saw my mother in a booth. Not in her office like she said. She wasn't alone.

Tomás was with her.

"Are you in my room now?" Mom asked.

"Yeah," I said, concealing myself behind a lobby fern.

"Go back to sleep, sweetie. There's some Tylenol PM in my medicine cabinet if you need it."

"Will you be working long?"

Tomás reached across the table and caressed her hand. Her lips moved slightly out of sync from the voice coming through my phone. "Probably. I need the distraction right now. Unless you're not feeling well. I can come up if you want."

"Or I could come to you."

"No," she said, her voice wavering. She pulled free of Tomás's grasp. "I don't want you having to come out at this hour. I'll bring my paperwork upstairs."

Doubtful. "Don't bother. I'm going back to bed."

"Yes. We've got a long, hard week ahead. You need your rest."

"So do you."

"I love you. See you in the morning."

"Love you, too."

We disconnected. That hard week we had coming . . . guess Mom found ways to ease the transition.

Was it that simple for her? Was all this a relief? No need for her to choose the right thing over her boy toy now that her husband was gone? I stared at my phone, squeezed it, tempted to toss it as far as I could.

Sparing my phone, I continued to my original destination, the business offices, unconcerned about Mom spotting me. Seeing how she was busy making goo-goo eyes at Tomás.

I stole an unopened bundle of legal pads and a box of pens, then returned to my room. There was a way to control that rage. Keep my mind occupied, at all times. Learn new things. Study one of Davis's favorite subjects. History.

When Dad was accused of murdering John Reedy, adults never talked about it around me. It happened. It was bad. Beyond that, I was shielded from details and legal intricacies. Your father's innocent. That's all you need to know. It's for your own good.

When the trial had concluded and Dad was sentenced, I grew numb. He and Mom said the police and the lawyers and the judge were wrong. None of what they said had kept my supposedly innocent dad from going to jail, from being told he'd die there. Even when Dan Harris appeared one day with talk of new evidence, and the possibility of an overturned conviction, the details were nothing I ever investigated on my own. Prepubescent detectives were the stuff of kid books, and I was no Harriet the Spy or Nancy Drew.

When actual sleep was elusive, and the possibility of that elusive sleep was scary, I used the late hours googling stuff.

Here's what I sort of knew and confirmed in my search engine digging. John Reedy and Dad got into a fight down in Andromeda's poker room. Dad threw Reedy out of the casino, then got drunk and left. What the fight was about, I still didn't know. It wasn't in any old articles, and seemed less important than the *second* fight.

The next morning, Reedy was found behind a liquor store on the east side of town. Killed by a blow to the back of the head. Eerily similar to the way Dad died. Some intrepid web journalist got his hands on crime scene photos of both John and my dad, and I had to take a break. Those were too hard to see.

The night Reedy died, Dad was sleeping in his car a few blocks away. The store's cashier testified he'd seen Reedy arguing with my dad. That fight is what put the jury over the edge. Despite there being no murder weapon and no conclusive DNA evidence, the prosecutor painted my poker pro dad as clever enough and "connected" enough—whatever that meant—to cover his tracks. Essentially, their argument was, who else would've had reason to kill John Reedy?

As Dan Harris pointed out a few years later, plenty of people wanted John Reedy in the ground. Like the minor drug lord who'd been hanging on to the murder weapon—"a bludgeon smeared with Reedy's blood"—for all the years since that night. Patrick Finnegan, said drug dealer, was killed in a DEA raid, but the weapon was discovered in his basement, like some trophy. He'd been small-time when Reedy died. Apparently, he'd gotten stiffed by John a couple of times too many. Dad had just been in the exact right place at the exact wrong time to get blamed for it.

There were a bunch of other things I'd found. Enough to fill a whole pad with notes, and thoughts, and suspicions. The past became clearer, but the present remained murky, and the future—at least one where justice was served—was unimaginable.

I started a notebook apart from my look into John Reedy. In this one I'd logged details from the horrible news reports about what happened. I watched cold, detached talking heads tell me my dad was beaten to death. That his body may have been moved. How he'd had a supposedly rough transition upon leaving jail, and that crap about it possibly being drug related, even though Mom insisted on an autopsy, which proved the strongest thing in Dad's system was aspirin.

Every vague unhelpful detail became my frustration log. It's what I was scribbling in, pressing the pen hard enough to tear paper in places when Mom knocked on our adjoining door, startling me, letting me know it was time to get ready.

It was Friday then, and we needed to bury Dad.

CHAPTER  17

Mom met me in the hall, inspecting my outfit as I emerged. Black dress—new this time, purchased by her sometime while I was scribbling down murder notes like a crazy person—with bell sleeves and a pair of oversized shades to finish the look.

Downstairs in the Loop a black limo idled with a discreet silver emblem for Charo & Sons Mortuary Services stenciled on the bumper and nowhere else. Behind the car sat Molly and Gavin in Molly's SUV, Gavin tugging at his starched collar and necktie with a hooked finger. They'd gotten special permission to miss school today. My friends, god, my friends.

Mr. Héctor was parked behind Molly in his old LeSabre. I scanned the area, wondering if Tomás was nearby and praying he didn't have the bad taste to show up today. He was nowhere to be seen, though I spotted a familiar face.

Across the street, at the curb bordering the Main Street public parking lot, Dan Harris sat in his car apparently waiting for our caravan to get underway. His windows were up, both hands gripping the wheel. He looked like a creeper.

Mom's shades angled toward him, and she sucked her teeth. "Get in the car, Nikki."

What was up with that?

Our black-suited driver held the door open and helped Mom and me inside. Once he was back behind the wheel, our short, three-car funeral procession was on its way, leaving the Loop, with Harris falling in behind once we were on the road.

Four cars. That's all. Not that I expected much; most of Dad's friends probably received the news in their cells at Ely State.

That's okay. Dad never cared for crowds that much anyway. No more than he could fit around a card table.

Holding that thought, I steeled myself as we went to visit him one last time.

♠

Charo & Sons wasn't a church, and the officiant overseeing Dad's service was not a preacher. Mr. Charo looked more like a somber accountant. It was okay. We'd never been very religious.

Moving through the room felt like floating. I couldn't feel my feet touch the ground, though I'd clearly taken steps. Somehow I got from the back of the room, within arm's length of the coffin, then to my front-row seat with Mom next to me, squeezing my hand as if she needed to ensure I wasn't going anywhere. The rest of our little group settled in. Dan Harris, Mr. Héctor, Gavin and Molly, plus a few other employees from Andromeda's.

Other people I didn't recognize occupied random seats in otherwise empty rows. One man looked like he might be homeless, his funeral companion being a trash bag of tin cans balanced on the neighboring seat.

Mom cried softly into a handkerchief, and I felt a flash of embarrassment because I wasn't crying.

Mr. Charo stood, approached a podium next to the casket, clearing his throat as he walked. I braced for the beginning and end of this final good-bye, waiting. And waiting.

But Mr. Charo didn't start the ceremony. His eyes traced a line to the back of the room, where some disturbance brewed.

We all twisted in our seats, expectant.

A scrawny, familiar man stood in the doorway, a bouquet of sunflowers in his fist. Mahoney?

It felt like years since I last saw the shifty cardplayer in my basement on the night Dad came home.

She's a legacy. Nathan Tate's.

Of course he'd known Dad.

With all eyes on him, Mahoney said, "Am I late?"

"No," Mr. Charo said, his voice a deep baritone befitting the Grim Reaper. "Please come in."

Mahoney, loud and tactless, yelled into the hall behind him, "It ain't started yet."

He entered fully, leading a caravan. Along with him, Goose and several members of the Pack in their biker cuts, Luciano from the Apocalyptic Poker Game, and others. The procession continued, becoming increasingly bizarre. More cardplayers came, the celebrities of the poker world, instantly recognizable from all the articles and books I'd read. I'd seen several of them take home fortunes in the World Series of Poker. All of them here honoring one of their own.

Each carried elaborate bouquets, many arrangements made to look like cards, aces and kings. They dropped their offerings before the coffin while Mom squeezed my hand in pulses. Luciano, in jeans, his signature tank top beneath a gray suit coat for a quasi-formal look, dropped off his bouquet, then took a knee right in front of my seat. "My condolences, *hermana.*"

"*Gracias,*" I said, a leftover from my nearly forgotten freshman Spanish class.

"And you are?" Mom asked.

"The guy who watched me make the dumbest move in poker history," I said with absolutely no bitterness. Don't hate the player . . .

"She's tough, though," Luciano said. "It's definitely in her blood."

He spoke with pride, pride he mistakenly thought Mom would share. Talk about misreading the opposition.

When Mom simply stared, and the long line of grievers undulated behind him like a centipede, Luciano said, "Uh, right. Well, we're all late because we had a couple of games going on in your old man's honor. We've been playing all night."

He reached into his jacket and pulled out a tight roll of bills held by a rubber band. He offered it to Mom. "We all chipped in. This should help in the coming weeks."

If all the bills were the same denomination, or higher, as the top bill, it was a few hundred at least. Maybe as much as a thousand.

Mom hesitated but conceded eventually. Neither pride nor grief led her to foolishly deny the gift. If nothing else, saying no was kind of an insult. Cardplayers don't give away cash easily.

His mission complete, Luciano departed for a seat among the rapidly filling rows.

Once the procession subsided, Mr. Charo began the ceremony, reciting words from memory, phrases that might come from the Bible or the inspirational kitten posters teachers hang in classrooms—I had no clue. Nothing he said about Dad was really personal, though. How could it be? The man probably didn't know my dad's name seven days ago.

But still, the tears came in a gush, sloshing against the rims of my shades. If Dad's eulogy were left to me, could I have done a better job than this stranger? Really?

I sobbed, and Mom patted my back in a rhythm I only recognized as comforting once she stopped. Mom wasn't the only one. Mr. Charo stopped, too, leaving the parlor in spooky silence.

I sat up and removed my glasses, mopping my eyes with the back of my wrist.

A new guest made his way down the aisle, a latecomer who had everyone's attention. For good reason.

He was Las Vegas royalty, likely worth more than everyone in the room. A rumored gangster, whispered about like some evil spirit who might come if his name was spoken too loudly. My last good memories guest-starred his son.

Big Bert Carlino approached Dad's coffin with a single white rose in hand. When he laid it on the casket, I swear the only sound in the room was the thorns scraping the wood.

CHAPTER 18

Big Bert hovered at Dad's coffin. He was the bloated, time-lapsed version of his sons. Cedric more so than Davis, but seen one, seen them all.

If Bertram Carlino has a problem with it, tell him to come see me himself.

The last thing Dad said to Davis and Cedric came to mind, along with a sensation of icy fingers playing piano on my spine.

Big Bert turned his gaze from the coffin and settled on Mom and me. Don't flinch, don't show fear. It was advice for facing down a vicious dog and felt wholly appropriate here.

Mom's gentle hand squeezes weren't so gentle anymore. If Big Bert stepped closer, the bones in my hand might break.

He stood his ground, dipped his chin in a nod that was—what? Respectful? Sorrowful? Threatening? My mind spun at the unknown history between my parents and the Carlinos.

Big Bert returned down the aisle and took a seat in the back row where an intimidating, Terminator-like companion waited.

Mr. Charo cleared his throat. "Well, then . . . Let's continue."

He did. And it was so, so hard.

All things end, though. Even good-byes.

"We will move to the interment site behind the building," said Mr. Charo. "My assistants will guide you. Look for the gentlemen with the green armbands if you need directions. Now please stand and allow the family to exit first."

The room rose as if in salutation for Mom and me. We walked

the aisle together, passing all those who'd come to pay their respects. Except Big Bert and his bodyguard.

They were already gone.

♣

Men buried Dad while cameras from all the news stations shot footage from just beyond the cemetery line. The same stations and reporters juicing my family's pain for ratings. The tragic story of Nathan Tate continues, details at six.

Those punch-kick-break-something feelings bubbled inside me. Straps hooked to a hydraulic winch slowly lowered Dad into his grave, and I pressed down the anger, replacing it with a fantasy about the casket being closed because Dad wasn't in it. He was off, somewhere, doing something fantastic that required him to fake his own death for my safety, and Mom's. Recruited to an elite team of card-playing spies. Kidnapped by aliens who need an Earthling for their intergalactic gambling zoo. Kids' stuff.

"Can we go home now?" I said.

"Yes," Mom said.

We moved toward our limo, arms linked, saying cordial good-byes to all we encountered. Suddenly, Dan Harris was pacing us, uncomfortably close to my shoulder. "Meet you two back at the casino?"

"For what?" Mom said.

He fell behind, then shuffled to catch up. "It's just—I thought we might discuss next steps. Since so many things were in motion before . . . the tragic events that have led us here."

At first I'd only noted him from the corner of my eye,

feeling like a buffer between him and Mom. His voice was whiny, desperate. More than usual, I mean. When I gave him a closer look, I noticed something I'd missed before. The side of his face was yellowish, the fading remnants of a bruise. A pink crease along his bottom lip indicated a healing gash.

"What happened to you?" I said.

Instead of answering, he crossed behind me so that he was closer to my mom and I couldn't see his busted face.

"Gwen, there's still a lot we can do for . . . yours and Nikki's security. The city's no less liable for Nathan's wrongful conviction now that he's, uh—"

"Buried over there?" Mom said, loud, pointing at the open grave and drawing stares from others.

We were rooted in place, as still as the tombstones surrounding us. I knew Mom's rage well. It bubbled, near boiling over. So was mine. Harris wanted to talk business—lawsuits—here? This conversation was the creepiest thing today, which was saying something, considering we were in a graveyard.

"I'm sorry, Gwen. You should have some time. I'll come by in a couple of days."

Mom shook her head, disgusted, and dragged me to the limo. The driver waited by the open door, a hand extended to assist us. Mom nudged me ahead, positioning herself between Harris and me, like Gavin protecting Vista's quarterback on the football field.

Inside the car, I leaned closer to the open door, straining to hear Mom's hushed response to Harris's request.

"He fired you, Dan. Get it through your head. If we owe you some money, call, and we'll settle it. Not today, and not in my home. You're no longer welcome there."

Dad fired him?

"Gwen, it doesn't work like that," he said, more forceful than I'd ever heard. "You don't get rid of me that easy."

Harris kept talking as Mom climbed into the car. The slamming door cut him off.

"Mom, what—"

Holding up a halting hand, she shook her head, tugged off her sunglasses, and rubbed her tired eyes. We sat across from each other on supple leather benches and didn't speak. I switched seats, wrapped my arms around my mom. She returned the embrace. It was enough.

But not for long.

CHAPTER 19

"I think I'm going to get it," Gavin said, rubbing his right shoulder. His shirt was untucked, and the skinny end of his necktie dangled from his back pocket between slats in the smokers' bench, like a tail.

Molly, barefoot, her itchy stockings discarded, never took her eyes off her phone as she thumbed out new texts. "You already look like him. You don't need it."

"I'm not trying to look like him. I want a tattoo on my shoulder to tell my life story. Because I'm awesome. Plus, mine's going on my right shoulder. His is on the left."

With the limo gone, and the grieving masses reduced to near nil, Mom retreated upstairs an hour ago, leaving me wedged between them in Andromeda's Loop. It was late afternoon, warm, and my best friends did everything in their power to keep my mind off my dad's funeral. Their topic of choice, Gavin's desire to get a tattoo that wasn't like The Rock's while being exactly like The Rock's.

"Don't mean to crush your dream," I said, "but a tattoo like his will cost thousands."

"It's not like his! Price won't matter when I make the league, anyway."

Molly, still texting, said, "How about you focus on Cardinal Graham now and worry about Cam Newton later?"

"I could say the same about you. You've been way preoccupied ever since you and—"

The vicious look she shot him shut him down mid-sentence.

"You and who, Molly Martel?" I asked.

She was silent, sneering at Gavin, who'd obviously let something out of the bag. I wasn't used to being uninformed when it came to these two. I'd been gone for days, physically and mentally. The effects of my grief-induced absence were showing, despite their best efforts to camouflage.

"You and who?" I asked again, edging irritation.

She held up her phone. "There's a party in the Ridges tomorrow. I've been texting Cedric."

"Davis's brother?" A dumb question with a stupidly obvious answer. They were texting now?

Gavin stopped rubbing his shoulder and focused on passing traffic. He wasn't a car-crazy guy, and none of those passing were all that interesting anyway. His and Molly's weirdo bucking-against-the-walls-of-the-Friend-Zone thing again. I waffled between feeling sympathy and frustration for Gavin.

Today was a sympathy day, though.

"Cedric's old, Molly," I pointed out.

"He's, like, a college student."

"No. He's the age of a college student. But he's unlike a college student because he's not in college."

"So. What. When we were freshmen, you dated that senior."

"He was on the chess team."

"I fail to see your point. It sounds like you want to keep the Carlinos all to yourself."

Big Bert's rose hissing along the surface of Dad's coffin was like a ghost's whisper in my ear. "That's not true."

"I can't tell. You give me a hard time, you gotta do the same thing to Gavin. He's trying to steal your boyfriend."

"Whatever," Gavin said.

"He and Davis are besties now," Molly said with a smirk.

I hit Gavin with a *What's up?* shrug.

"Davis is cool. He caught me in the hall the other day and made a really awesome offer. Team dinner at his dad's hotel the night before the Cardinal Graham game. Coach cosigned and the guys went crazy. They might vote him MVP."

"So he bribed you."

"He said it was your idea."

Okay, maybe it was. Wasn't going to admit it.

"You talk to him lately?" he asked.

If Gavin really had been spending time with Davis this week, I suspected he knew the answer. Aside from the occasional text, no.

Ignoring the question, I turned to Molly. "Doesn't let you off the hook. Cedric Carlino's, like, an adult. Is what you're doing even legal?"

"Yes," Molly said calmly. "Text messages are absolutely legal. Drop it, Tate, because you're burying the lede. Party. In the Ridges. Tomorrow. We're going."

The anxiety over the proposition stabbed me in the gut, twisted the blade. "I don't think so."

"You don't have to think. I've already made the decision for you." She stared up at Andromeda's unlit silhouette. "Let us take you away from this for a while."

When she said it like that, I knew she was right. I still wanted to argue and disagree, to show some sort of resistance to forces around me. Fatigue set in, making my back stiff and arms heavy. They'd done their jobs to the best of their abilities. With the exception of Gavin's team dinner, Bert Carlino's funeral appearance didn't come up once. It was a nice break. But I'd be thinking on it most of the night.

"I'm tired, guys."

"Go. Rest up," Molly said. "No excuses tomorrow. The crew is partying." She tossed keys to Gavin. "Pull up the car, Jeeves."

"It's right there."

Her eye roll nearly tipped her head off her neck. "Can you drive? My feet hurt."

He rose, huffed, and gave me a quick hug before taking the driver's seat. When Molly stood, I did, too. Her hug was long, her hand rubbing a circle on my back. "Love you, girl."

"Back at you."

Once in the passenger seat, her and Gavin's bickering continued all the way out of the Loop, the old married couple that they were.

Trying to hang on to that thought—because it was a good one, one that made me happy—was like holding on to smoke once I crossed the casino's threshold. Nothing about home felt the same after you put a parent in the ground.

Everything inside was normal. People gaming. Folks checking into their rooms. None of them knew Nathan Tate had ever been here.

The service elevator doors closed, but I didn't select my floor. My finger hovered, then dropped, poking the button for the floor below mine.

On that hall, I forced myself forward, removing a key card from my bag. It wasn't Nikki the Resident's key, which opened my room and my room alone. It was a master key, for managers only, which was a close enough title for all I did around the place. With it, I could enter any guest room. When we were younger, Molly and I used such a key to play hide-and-seek in empty rooms. In recent years, I've grown to understand the sacred responsibility of such access and have only used it while performing necessary duties.

Not that day.

At Dad's door I didn't hesitate. A swipe of the card and electronic chirp later, I was inside.

The room had been made up. Crisp linen, new towels, open drapes. Sunlight bathed me in warmth I didn't necessarily want. A set of mirrored double doors concealed a closet. Inside, I found all new clothes dangling from hangers, most with the tags still on. I fingered the tail of a red button-up before smushing my face in the fabric. Inhaling deeply, I searched for a trace of him. Nothing. Only off-the-rack starch.

Below the garments, on the floor, was a pile of discarded items. Dirty clothes he hadn't gotten to the laundry room before . . .

Kneeling, I shuffled through the pile until I came upon a shirt I recognized. A blue cotton Hensley. He'd worn it the night he took me to North Town. I sniffed and got a blast of all that I wanted. The new cologne we got him. Those sweet-tinged cigarettes.

With both hands I pressed that shirt into my chest, hard, fighting my stubborn sternum. The battle was a draw and I took the shirt to his bed, crawled on top of the comforter, stared out at the Vegas horizon, and cried. All the things my friends protected me from were here now. They consumed me.

CHAPTER 20

Molly leaned across Gavin's lap, ogling me through the passenger window. "Dang, girl. That outfit is fire!"

It was. Black jeans, wedge Air Jordans, two layered tank tops to show off how soccer-ripped I was, and a set of mango wood bracelets rattling along my forearm. The real secret, though . . . a bath, shampoo, deep conditioner, and a blowout that had my typically poofy hair swooping downward, grazing my shoulders, completing my masquerade as the old me. It was, by far, the best effort I'd put into my appearance in a week. No one would know eight hours before my superfly return to society, I was in my dad's room, wearing his old shirt and rewatching his press conference for the hundredth time. Dan Harris had been right beside him. They'd been smiling like friends. What changed?

Molly didn't park, no space. It was Saturday night, crowded, typically an all-hands-on-deck situation. Part of me hoped it'd be enough to make Mom keep me home, working, since we'd both been MIA most of the week.

But master strategist Molly was a step ahead of me. That snitch told my mom we had plans, an insurance policy. Mom insisted I go. So committed to us returning to some sort of normalcy, she even did my makeup.

So, party time. Yay?

Gavin climbed down from the shotgun seat. Like Cinderella's hound dog footman, he held the back door and helped me into the carriage.

"Look at you," he said. "I hope Davis ain't the type to get jelly, 'cause you about to turn heads."

Davis. Yes, he'd be there. He made it clear in several texts today. I should be looking forward to seeing him. My texts back to him indicated I would. The last time we saw each other was the night of the car-destroying make-out, but that was before I'd discovered my dad's fate. Would Davis really want to see this version of me?

We'd know soon enough.

♥

The best homes in the Ridges were too sick. Mansions, not McMansions. Real deal. High end. The funny thing about the neighborhood is it's built on what used to be barren desert. Supposedly, a lot of missing person cases would be solved if anyone ever bulldozed the mini estates and dug up the foundations.

Even the legend of a Mafia graveyard wasn't enough to discourage semi-regular debauchery when absentee parents do what they do. Someone threw a *Poltergeist*-themed party last Halloween, with a prize for the best dead mobster costume and a drinking game where players took a shot every time someone said "Fugettaboutit!"

Tonight's host was Brady Bolls. His dad specialized in marketing oddball tourist attractions, big business in Vegas. Brady, like Davis, was one of Vista's wealthy elite. Unlike Davis, he wasn't a Cardinal Graham transplant but a refugee from several prestigious private schools across the country. He's known as the Expulsion King—a nickname he might've given himself. While never a Cardinal Graham Griffin, he was neighbor to plenty of them. If you partied with him—and trust me, you *wanted* to party with him—you put rivalries aside. Them's the rules.

The arching driveway fronting the house, a mini suburban version of Andromeda's Loop, was packed with double-parked cars. In the space between vehicles, people milled.

"This is a high school party," I said, recognizing the usual suspects while Molly parked on the street.

"We're in high school, so that works," she said.

"I thought you said Cedric told you about it?"

"No. I was texting Cedric, and I told him."

Not that I was looking to party with older guys, but something seemed off. I attempted replaying yesterday's exchange in my head. Gavin's whole *You've been way preoccupied ever since you and—* thing that made Molly get twitchy. Maybe I heard her wrong, or interpreted it wrong. A minor distinction that shouldn't bug me. But tiny things bugged me more and more lately.

I shelved it when we stepped from the car and found ourselves in the company of several Lady Griffin soccer players and their boyfriends. Stink-eyes popped like spring blossoms, but that was the extent of it. On the way to the party entrance, a few mouth breathers from the CG football team recognized Gavin and began grumble posturing.

Things improved inside among more familiar faces. Plenty of VR Lions were in the house, along with popular friendlies from other high schools around town. Gavin broke off for bro hugs with teammates and city All-Stars.

Molly, perhaps fearing I'd bolt, cuffed my wrist and towed me through the crowd. My stomach plummeted as though she'd pulled me off a skyscraper.

Confession: I didn't want to be the Mood Killer. What if my casual associate classmates squirmed in the presence of Dead Dad Nikki? The news would've been all over the school, particularly in my absence when no one need worry they'd be *caught* talking behind my back.

Eventually, we came across one of our teammates, Taylor, two-stepping with a boy in a Las Vegas High School Wrestling T-shirt. Molly leaned in and asked, "You seen Davis Carlino?"

Taylor pointed away. "In the kitchen with the presidents."

Molly course-corrected and plowed us through a brightly lit doorway where a loose congregation leaned on counters, chatting and laughing. A steady flow of attendees refilled drinks from a forest of bottles atop a tile island. With prime space by the Sub-Zero fridge, Davis carried on an animated conversation, all hands and shoulders, with Sarah Parsons, our class president, and her girlfriend/vice president, Morgan Monroe. They were VR's It couple, and Davis was working them.

". . . I know most people go into class politics on false promises. Better cafeteria food, less homework. What if you really could pull off all that good stuff? With the proper connections—"

He noticed the presidents noticing us, turned, his pitchman smile faded. "Nikki."

His arms were around me before I could think or move. He felt good, better than anyone should feel when their texts have been basically ignored for a week.

"Are you okay?" he said, then quickly followed with, "No. Of course not. Forget I asked."

He backed away but kept his hands on my shoulders. I glanced left to get a read on Molly, but she'd Batman vanished on me.

President Sarah tapped Davis's shoulder. "You've got a lot of good ideas. Wanna talk more later?"

"Definitely."

Sarah and Morgan, hand in hand, disappeared among

gyrating shadows. I steeled myself for normal, pleasant conversation. Ended up in immediate awkward silence.

Davis spoke first. "I've got some good news for you. Been saving it to tell you in person."

"Okay."

"We got an A on our project."

Had I misheard him? The music was very loud. "How could we get an A when I didn't do anything?"

A shrug.

"You shouldn't let me take credit for your work. If you finished it on your own, you deserve, like, extra points."

Another shrug. "Too late. I've moved on. Reactivity of metals is so yesterday. All about those ionic bonds now."

"Is that really a thing?"

"I think I saw it in a chapter."

"Well, thank you for that." Before another lull crested, I added, "You tight with the presidents now? You've come a long way from the whole school wanting to string you up."

Grinning, he said, "Yes, I have ascended into the ranks of acceptance. Thanks to your suggestion."

"The football dinner thing. Gavin told me."

"He's a cool dude. Couldn't have done it without him vouching."

"True and true."

Our conversation stalled. The DJ mixed in a new track, and I tried covering the break by singing along. Davis bobbed awkwardly offbeat and plunged both hands into his pockets.

Grasping for something to keep the conversation alive, I said, "So, did your brother bring you or did you steal another ride?"

Davis rolled his eyes. "Ced's here. Taking advantage of all the opportunity."

"Sounds creepy when you put it like that."

"Oh no. I mean, he might have some flirty thing going on with Molly, for sure. But he's not trying to pull high school girls like some perv. He's a party promoter—like, it's his hustle—and this is the Ridges. A lot of young people with money here."

"Wait. He's *networking*?" Cocktail mixers in Andromeda's conference rooms came to mind, and clashed with images of Davis's ripped and tatted brother bouncing around a high school party.

"It's the Carlino way. He thinks if he can build relationships with some of these kids when they're young, it'll carry over when it's time for graduation and birthday bash bookings."

"That's kind of smart."

"Please don't tell him that. Both his head and mine have to fit in the car tonight. You thirsty?" He grabbed a cup off the island, emptied the remains of an orange juice container into it. He did not add booze.

I passed, and he sipped, then said, "Ced's good at the business stuff. It's what our dad pushes on us. Heirs to the throne."

He stared into the cup, contemplating something, then returned to the island to tip some tequila into his juice.

Apparently, mentioning his dad made him as uncomfortable as it made me.

"Let's find Molly. Okay?" I took off without waiting to see if Davis was following me.

I picked a path and came to a carpeted staircase, followed soft flickering light up and into a rec room that set my stomach flip-flopping.

It was Man Cave Chic. Movie posters, pennants, a sign reading "In Dog Beers, I've Only Had One"—whatever that meant. Of course, the requisite tech. A 108-inch movie screen and ceiling-mounted projector. Old-school Pac-Man and Galaga game consoles that people leaned against or sat their drinks on. The centerpiece . . . a card table.

Five players occupied it. A couple of them tossed big and small blinds into the pot, while Brady shuffled and flung them two cards each. Cedric, laughing and chatting with Molly, peeled up the corners of his hole cards, grimaced, and folded immediately.

Molly waved Davis and me over. The closer we got to the cards, the harder it was to hear the music downstairs.

Cedric turned toward me. "Deal you in the next hand?"

I had cash in my pocket, a hundred bucks or so. A yes bubbled on my lips, but not beyond. The last time I played was with Dad. "No thanks."

"You sure?" Cedric said. "I still got money you can take. Better you than these guys."

A few chuckles around the table. Cedric's chip pile was relatively low compared to some of the others. Brady; another kid in my year; Justin Simms of Simms Family Car Dealerships ("Las Vegas's One Stop Vehicle Shop"); Rashawn, one of Gavin's teammates; and a player I'd never seen before.

Still, I didn't have it in me. I shook my head and sidled closer to Molly, trembling. She gave me an up-and-down look, then stretched her eyes wide. A silent *Are you okay?*

I nodded. I'm fine. No worries. The rage barely sparked that time.

"You're lucky she's allowing you all to not go home broke," Molly said with a smug grin.

"Coach me, then," Cedric said. "I could use your help getting my dough back."

"No way!" Brady said, backed up by the rest of the table. As it should be. You play your own cards.

Cedric, conceding to the rules of engagement, said, "All right, all right. Brady, remember this when it's time to book your eighteenth birthday bash. You think you can do this well in the High Roller Room at the Nysos?"

Davis leaned into me. "He's always hustling."

I couldn't tell if that tinge in his voice was admiration or jealousy.

The game continued and Molly carried the conversation with Davis wholly. My attention was split, my major focus on the happenings at the table. Cedric really could use the coaching. Any hand he didn't fold, he lost. Brady initiated these games at every party. I've played with him enough to know he's mediocre at best, occasionally stumbling into lucky wins. Justin Simms didn't protect his hole cards. I wasn't even trying and I saw everything he had for the last three hands.

The only real competition was Rashawn and the mystery guy, who'd been splitting wins. No one was paying attention to the obvious pattern. Whenever mystery guy raised after the last community card was dealt, he won.

He looked older than us, though not by much. It was his facial hair and the way he tucked his Oxford shirt. Maybe Cedric's age. Though Cedric's presence made sense as Davis's driver and an entrepreneur looking for a young, wealthy client base.

To Molly, I said, "Do you know that guy?"

She shook her head. Cedric overheard me, though. "Chuck, introduce yourself."

"I think you just did." The player tipped his head at me. "Chuck Pearl. I'll be taking this."

He threw down a full house and raked in the current pot. He had a jackal's grin, his mouth crowded with teeth that seemed too big or too numerous. I couldn't tell which.

"You sure you don't want to play?" Cedric pressed.

"I'm sure." A lie. I wasn't sure about anything other than I now felt uncomfortable around a game I'd played my whole life. The rage sparked again. Maybe Molly was ready to go.

Cards gathered and stacked, Rashawn passed the deck to Chuck for the deal. His fingers were nimble, barely moving as he spewed cards the way machine guns spew bullets. Again, Justin did a poor job guarding his hand. He had a king of hearts and a seven of diamonds. Meh.

Chuck dealt the flop. With three community cards on the table, Justin didn't have anything, but he played bold and tossed chips into the pot, forcing others to do the same.

The fourth community card was a king of clubs. Rashawn and Cedric folded. Brady stayed with it.

The last card was a king of spades. Justin went from a set of nothing hole cards to three of kind. Odds totally in his favor for the first time all night.

And he folded.

Dude!! I screamed in my head, stepping closer to the table.

That left Chuck and Brady in a showdown. Chuck raised again. Brady called, oblivious to Chuck winning every hand where he's raised this late. Over seven hundred dollars in the pot now. Should be interesting.

"Let's see 'em!" Chuck said.

Brady flipped his cards. Ace of diamonds and ten of clubs.

Combined with the queen, jack, and either of the kings on the table, he had a straight. A great hand. Not great enough.

He turned over his cards one at a time, relishing the victory. A king of diamonds and . . . *A king of hearts?*

"Four of a kind!" Chuck said.

My eyes bounced from Chuck's winning hand to the face-down cards Justin pushed toward center table when he folded. "What the—"

Justin saw me coming, attempted to mix his cards in with other cards. I was standing, with superior leverage and shoved him in the chest, tipping him and his chair. While he toppled, I flipped his cards, showing the stunned room what I knew.

"This is a single-deck game. Justin's got a king of hearts. How's Chuck got a king of hearts, too?"

All night, I'd been skirting the edges of anxiety and anger. I shouldn't have come here, shouldn't have put myself in a situation where others could see me cycle from one extreme to another. No undoing it now. I was my father's daughter, and I didn't deal well with cheaters.

I stepped over Justin, grazing his chin with one of my heels hard enough to bruise. "Grab them."

"You heard her," Brady said.

Rashawn seized Chuck's arms when he tried to push from the table and run. Davis and Cedric lifted Justin to his feet.

There was an umbrella stand filled with sports equipment—tennis racket, a putter, and others—next to the rec room doors. I rifled through and came across a field hockey stick.

Chuck Pearl wasn't smiling now.

"This will do," I said. "Outside. Let's go."

I shoved open the door, crossed the driveway, examining all the cars in view. On the lawn, Gavin and other VR football players squared off with Cardinal Graham's quarterback and his crew. The conversation seemed dangerously close to breaking Brady's truce, but our host wasn't exactly keeping score.

I stalked straight through bickering jocks, the field hockey stick propped on my shoulder. Rashawn, Brady, and the rest dragged Chuck and Justin behind me.

Gavin motioned to Molly, alarmed. "What's going on?"

"Not sure, but you should come," Molly answered.

He did. The VR Lions followed, as did the CG Griffins. After them, more of the party was in tow.

At the street, I spun on Chuck. "Tell me which car is yours."

He twisted and squirmed, still trying to wrestle away. I lowered the stick so it hovered inches from his crotch.

"You're being difficult," I said, feeling almost jubilant now that I'd let the rage roam wild. "Should I be difficult, too?"

"Over there." Resigned, he motioned left with his head. "The blue Lexus."

I went to it and the mob made sure Chuck and Justin kept pace. I pointed the stick at the grille. "There."

Chuck fell in place before me, back to the bumper. Justin next.

"This is not a town that takes kindly to cheaters," I said. "Would you like blindfolds?"

Justin's chin thunked on his chest like a dropped hammer. Chuck steeled himself. A tough guy.

Him first, then.

I swung my stick for Chuck's head, pulling back at the last second so I only tapped the car's bumper. He yelped.

"Where are you from?" I butted his shoulder with the stick.

"Arizona!"

It didn't even sound true. He said it too fast. Where he came from wasn't important. This lesson was.

I smacked the bumper again, hard that time. "Justin, you're helping him. Why?"

Justin broke immediately, looking almost relieved, "I—I lost one of the cars off my dad's lot to him, okay? It was a stupid bet and I couldn't pay up and he said if I got him into some rich kids' games, he'd . . . he'd . . ."

"When you let him put one of his dad's cars up, you really thought he could honor that?" I asked Chuck.

"A bet's a bet," he said with a shrug.

Beginning a slow circle of the Lexus, I said, "I can't imagine you came by this honestly, Chuck." The cream leather upholstery inside was pristine. The dashboard was loaded with buttons and displays. "You don't deserve something this nice when you disrespect the game. Would you agree?"

Chuck said nothing, so I threw the question to the crowd. "Would you?"

Cheers and fist pumps from most. Though Molly, Gavin, and Davis looked on with something like horror.

"See, Chuck, I think it would be in your best interest to leave. While you still have a vehicle to—"

Through the back passenger window, I saw a torn plastic bundle with an assortment of boxed card decks spilling from it. On the boxes, familiar logos. The Tropicana. Harrah's. The Rio. Official casino decks, in sealed boxes.

Casino decks differed from run-of-the-mill Bicycle cards you bought from drugstores or Toys "R" Us. They were customized with lush coatings, beveled edges for better dealer control, watermarks, and proprietary artwork. They're bought in huge quantities with delivery procedures as rigorous as an armored car moving cash from bank to bank. Because in Vegas, fraudulent playing cards could be as lucrative as fraudulent credit cards.

Selling used decks to tourists was a small piece of the souvenir trade, *after* the casino's done with them. Used cards always had the corners machined off, so they were easily recognizable should they ever make it back to an official table with an ambitious cheater. Like Chuck.

Opening the door and dipping into the backseat, I rifled through the various decks. All new and sealed. The Luxor. Flamingo. The Quad. Andromeda's Palace.

Breaking the seal on the box featuring my casino's logo exposed a fresh set of cards with corners intact.

Chuck Pearl wasn't just some lowlife out to cheat kids. He was the kind of top-tier grifter that had our security team on alert whenever the Gaming Control Board caught wind of the next great schemer. The kind like John Reedy before his untimely demise.

I backed away from the car and flung the deck at Chuck.

"You were going to come into my home? Steal from me?" My arms flailed wide. I'd forgotten I still held a field hockey stick. It still didn't quite register when that stick shattered Chuck's front passenger window.

I swung the stick again, purposely this time, and broke the headlight next to Chuck's head.

"Time to go." It was Davis, looping an arm around my waist and lifting me away.

I bicycle-kicked the air and threw the stick in Chuck Pearl's general direction. It skittered across the pavement five feet shy of him.

Davis carried me, tossed me sideways into Molly's backseat, the slamming door colliding with the bottom of my heels and sending a mild shock wave up my legs. Outside the vehicle, a small-scale argument erupted between him and his brother.

"No," Cedric said.

"I'm going with her. Just follow."

"Dude!"

"Dude, what? Come get me."

All the other doors swung open. Davis jumped in the backseat with me. Molly hopped behind the wheel and was in motion before Gavin closed his door. A well-executed escape plan. Though I couldn't figure the point at which the plan was conceived.

Sitting up, fighting not to aim my frustration at them, I managed actual words. "Why did you stop me?"

"The cops were coming," Gavin said. "You didn't hear those sirens."

"What sirens?" An unnecessary question, now that my ears weren't thrumming with my own fury, and I caught them in the distance. I pounded a fist into the seat, imagining it was Chuck Pearl's face.

"Hey," Molly said. "I didn't cheat you out of anything. Stop beating up my ride."

I opened the window and screamed into the night. My lungs burned before I stopped. Empty. I folded in on myself, elbows on knees, and head tucked the way they tell you to do on airplanes before you crash.

Spiraling, down, and down further.

Davis patted my back the whole way home, and said the right things, like "You're fine" and "Breathe."

None of it brought comfort.

At Andromeda's Loop, I pulled myself together enough so Molly and Gavin agreed I didn't need an escort to my room. Davis followed me from the SUV as Cedric's trailing car cruised to Molly's bumper.

Davis said, "Nikki—"

Please don't ask me if I'm okay.

"—what do you need?"

Surprised, I said, "Find out how your father knows my family."

I skulked inside.

"Excuse me. Nikki."

My head whipped toward the check-in desk. "What?"

Veronica, a hospitality specialist who'd been with us a couple of years, flinched. Taking it down a notch, I said, "Sorry, sorry. Yes?"

Skittish, she pushed forward. "A patrolman came by. With a box."

A patrolman? "Where is it?"

"He said it was for your mom, but she's not here, and when I saw the label, I didn't want to leave it in the offices—"

"I'll take it."

She ducked beneath the desk, returned with something similar to a shoe box but plain, no logos. Only a label adorned with Sharpie script.

N. Tate Personal Effects

The world froze. Someone hit MUTE on the sounds from the gaming floor. That winding rage in me stopped. I touched the box with shaky fingers. It was real. I snatched it off the counter.

"You did the right thing, Veronica."

She nodded, gave a pinched cautious smile.

"Don't worry about telling my mom. I'll let her know."

CHAPTER 22

N. Tate Personal Effects

It sounded like dragons or robots from movies. My computer-generated dead dad.

I sat in his room, on his bed. The box balanced on my knees. The items were from his car. The cops confiscated his ride for a cursory examination only—photos and cataloging. They indicated everything in it would likely be returned. One of their few kept promises.

There were a few loose chips—five-dollars and tens, nothing major—from casinos around town, chewing gum, an all-you-can-eat buffet coupon. Junk. Except for the iPhone.

Scooping it up, I examined the white glass smudged with dark dust. Was it fingerprint powder like I'd seen on all sorts of police shows, or dirt from the box? Flipping it over and powering it on, that white Apple with the missing chunk glowed on the scuffed display.

I blinked away tears. Everything about the night crashed down. How I'd turned into a lunatic on that cheater's car. Who does that?

Dad never set a passcode. I swiped off the lock screen and got a low-battery message; the phone's remaining power was at 7 percent.

After dismissing the warning, I swiped right to left. Dad still had the default apps, nothing extra. No surprise. When I gave it to him, he'd eyed it like a suspicious time traveler.

He had unread texts (twenty-two) and missed calls (twelve). Scrolling the menus revealed some were from Mom, but most were from unrecognizable numbers Dad hadn't bothered linking to contact names.

The phone buzzed in my hand, startling me, and I dropped it facedown. Recovering quickly, I snatched it up. The incoming call screen didn't show an unidentified number but one of the few contacts from Dad's missed calls list. Just initials. F.S.

Panicking, I answered, "Hello?"

"Izz thish Nathan's goil?" The slur in the voice was extreme, but having been exposed to more than a few Vegas drunks, I translated expertly. *Is this Nathan's girl?*

"Who is this?"

The caller spoke slow, straining to enunciate properly. "Nathan told me to . . . call if something . . . happened."

Urgency overtook me. A drunk man calling on my dead dad's phone should inspire a hang-up. It really should.

"This is Nathan's daughter. Who are you?"

Back to slurring again. "Thanksh god. I been callings for dayss."

"Okay, you got me. Say what you have to say." Silence. My pulse thumped hollow in my ears. "Hello?"

I lowered the phone, the screen was black.

The battery died.

I lunged for the box the phone came from, searched for the charger. Not there. Spinning in place, I checked each visible outlet for that distinct white cube and cable. Pulled the nightstand away from the wall in hopes of locating the power supply. Nothing.

Bolting from the room, I bypassed the elevator for the stairs. On my floor, I shouldered past guests congregating in the hall and let myself into my room, seeking my own charger.

Jamming the cable into the dead phone's port, the reboot time was purgatory. It took three minutes before the phone lit up, functioning. I redialed F.S. from the call history. It rang five times . . . ten . . . before a generic voice mail greeting informed me the user's mailbox was full and I should try again later.

"No!"

Redialed. Again and again. Same result.

Nathan told me to call if something happened . . .

What did that *mean*?

Flopping on my bed, I cradled the phone in my lap. Maybe F.S. left a message on one of his previous calls. No, there was nothing. Text messages offered no clues either.

A scream bubbled. It would've escaped—not like Mom was around to get alarmed—but I'd tapped Dad's photo icon accidentally.

His albums did not show the same neglect as other features on his phone. He'd been busy with his camera. Hundreds, maybe as many as a thousand, pics. Locations around town. Iconic signs, buildings, and landmarks.

Really, the photos were plain fare. The sort of pics a tourist with a twitchy finger and oversized memory card snapped and never looked at again. Only . . . Dad wasn't a tourist. He grew up in Vegas and often lamented how the visual aesthetic of the Strip cheapened the richness of the city, like the tacky homes in nice neighborhoods that went crazy with holiday decorations. His taking so many pictures around the city was strange. Even stranger: More than half of the photos showed the latest, greatest casino resort in the city.

The Nysos.

CHAPTER 23

I slept better that night than I had since . . . since it happened. That Sunday, energized and ready to work, I spent the morning in Andromeda's business office, reviewing the month's dismal financial reports and filing some of the minor but infinite paperwork that was a part of casino ownership.

At mid-morning, Mom walked in and seemed taken aback by the sight of me. "She rises!"

"Drama. Queen," I said.

"When I peeked in on you earlier, you were comatose."

What time was that, Mom? When I peeked in your room, after midnight, you weren't there.

"I took it the party went well," she added.

"Meh."

An awkward silence flared. In it, I became hyperaware of the shuffle-hum coming from the Xerox machine in the next room. When she craned her neck that way, I cleared my throat. "Mom, a patrolman brought a box of Dad's things by yesterday."

The box rested in the footwell beneath my desk. The contents rattled when I passed it to her.

Serious now, she upended the lid, then shook the box without touching anything in it. "There's not much here."

There really wasn't. Especially since the phone was in my pocket. "Have the police said anything? Are there any new leads?"

A heavy sigh. "They're exploring the possibilities."

"What does that mean?"

"Nikki, how much of this do you want to hear? It's not pretty, or comfortable."

"Have we ever been comfortable here?" I said it with a pointedness that might've gone over her head. Or not.

She pulled a chair from a nearby desk and sat. "Detective Burrows told me your father fought his attacker. They found skin under his nails. That may be helpful, but initial testing isn't coming up with hits in the state's database. They're going to check nationwide, because there are a lot of transient people in the city. They might get lucky."

"What if they don't get lucky? What if there are no hits?"

Her eyes flitted to the printer room again.

"Mom?"

"We'll cross that bridge when we come to it. In the meantime, I'm interviewing lawyers who may help push the police a bit, make sure they don't forget about Nathan. Us."

"Not Dan Harris?"

"Not Dan Harris."

"Why? He knows us, right?"

"Unfortunately, he does." She stood as if we were done, taking the box with her.

"Why are you keeping so many secrets from me?"

"Because I love you. Because telling you every little thing in my head and heart won't help you sleep better, or do well in school, or live the way a child should."

"Thank you." I meant it. I wasn't mad. I only needed the confirmation.

"I'm going to be in my office. Get out of here, go do something fun."

"I'm almost done."

"Good. Want to get lunch with me?"

"Can't. I've got plans."

"With Molly?"

A grin and shrug sold it without me verbalizing a lie.

"Some other time, then." She left the office, content and none the wiser.

The Xerox machine ran on.

♠

Molly sent several dozen text messages throughout the day while I worked in Dad's room. My slow response time made her desperate enough to actually call. I answered to stop the harassment and brushed her off by first claiming exhaustion, then lying about dinner with Mom. I wasn't ready to talk about what happened at the party. She'd have to deal.

On Monday morning, I still wasn't ready.

Me: mom's taking me to school early to talk with principal about days i missed. see you in class.

I had a valet drive me to school and never looked at her response.

♣

Forty-five minutes before homeroom and the halls of Vista Rojo were desolate. In the solitude, I repeatedly dialed the mysterious caller on Dad's fully charged phone. As with the fifty other times I'd called, no answer.

Knowing Molly's routine, I stuck to alternate routes and corridors as the halls filled, making it all the way through first bell without colliding with her. From there it was a steady string of teacher condolences and awkwardness as everyone tried pretending they weren't giving me side-eye either for my family tragedy or for what they'd heard about my party meltdown.

I crossed paths with Davis between third and fourth periods. A familiar, yet intensified heat rushing over me. He saw me and didn't run away, so that was something. Angling away from the flow of hall traffic, we met against a bank of lockers.

"How are you?" he said.

"I'd be better if you've got some info for me. Anything on our dads?"

"Right to it, then. No. Not yet. My dad's been in Atlantic City on business."

"You haven't talked to him at all?" Impatience tinged my words.

He frowned. "Yes. This didn't seem like a phone thing, though."

Tension crackled between us. It was my fault. "Sorry. I shouldn't be so pushy."

His head bounced a half nod, like he wanted to agree but couldn't quite get there. "He'll be back tomorrow. I'll talk to him face-to-face."

"Thank you." Warning bell rung. "See you in chem."

I didn't wait for a good-bye.

♥

I dodged Molly at lunch by striking up a conversation with my guidance counselor about the pros and cons of attending an out-of-state university. Molly passed us on the way to the cafeteria, eyebrows arched high, silently questioning. It was a short reprieve, since she was in chemistry, too. I expected her to be bolder, force my neighbor from his desk. She kept her usual seat, only sent a single text.

Molly: why are you avoiding me?
Me: i'm not. you're imagining things.

I powered my phone down, packed up my books two minutes before the class bell rang, then hustled into the hall and melted into the crowd. It was simply postponing the inevitable. There was a place where there'd be no hiding and no outrunning my best friend. A place where she was queen, and defying her was an act of treason.

The soccer field.

◆

After final bell, I hit the locker room at a sprint, dressed for practice, and was on the field thirty minutes early. Coach Riley was already there, jotting notes on a clipboard. When she spotted me, she placed her clipboard on the bench and wrapped both arms around me like her prodigal daughter. "Glad to have you back, Tate."

"Thanks," I managed, despite having the air squeezed from my lungs.

Coach Riley backed off. "Since you're the early bird, give me ten laps. You been away too long. Gotta get your motor going again."

Laps? I'd thanked her too soon.

The first few laps were rough, but I hit my stride on the fourth and it hardly felt like I'd been away at all. There was comfort in the way my cleats gnawed the turf, the way my legs and lungs burned with low heat. Another runner appeared beside me, matching my pace and erasing the comfort.

"Dude," Molly said.

I exaggerated a gasp. "Been running . . . a while. Hard to . . . talk."

"Are you mad at me for something?"

"No." That was absolutely true.

"Well, I'm starting to get real pissed at you. We need to talk about Saturday."

I sped up slightly. "Practice is about to start."

Molly pulled a Flash, sprinting way ahead in effortless strides, then stopping on a dime directly in front of me, forcing me to a skidding halt. "Fine," she replied. "Let's practice. You're on B squad today."

"What?"

B squad. Second string. Team captain could assign select starters to B squad if she felt it beneficial for certain scenarios. Traditionally, the move was less strategy, more demoralizing. A demotion ensuring everyone knew you'd fallen from grace. Since making captain at the start of this season, Molly had never exercised the symbolic smackdown. Until now.

"Just for today," Molly stressed. "Because I know you can't resist a bet."

Where was she going with this?

She said, "Anytime it's you and me one-on-one, if I can shake you, I get to ask you one question—no dodging—after practice."

"That's a crap bet! You know how good you are."

"Fine. When it's you and me, I'll only dribble with my left foot."

Okay. That was a decent handicap. "What do I get for good defense, or if I shake you?"

"I'll deal at your card games for free. Anytime you stop or juke me, it's another freebie."

"Screw that! Too easy." Also, I didn't know if there'd be more card games. They hurt.

"What, then?"

"If I get you—even once—I get a demand. A no-strings freebie. You must comply." She'd hate that. Good bets were anything that made you uncomfortable.

Molly's hubris didn't allow for hesitation. She thrust her hand forward. I shook. Deal.

Coach blew the whistle, and everyone hit the grass for burpees and stretches. Then the war began.

CHAPTER 24

My leading B squad on my first day back triggered concerned murmurs from the team (Coach included), but the whistle was god on the field, and soon we were into agility and endurance drills. *Intense* wasn't even the right word for how those went. Everyone knew what to do, but Molly barked orders at her group like they were marines on their first day of boot camp. I followed suit, and B squad feared me.

Through the sweat and burn, anticipation drove them because they *knew* what drill was coming.

Cone goals.

It's a drill meant to sharpen offensive and defensive skills. Essentially, it's one-on-one soccer. Attack and defend. Me vs. You.

Or in this case, Me vs. All-State, top college recruit, undisputed sports killer Molly.

A few B-squad members scrambled the cones in place, forming an approximate rectangle, ten yards by four yards. The four-yard gaps represented the goals Molly and I would take turns defending. The ten yards between those goals, our personal battlefield.

Molly stepped into the perimeter, softened her knees, and shifted her weight toward her toes. "Ball!"

An A-squad member passed the ball into the coned area, and Molly received it on the run, keeping her word by dribbling left-foot only. I rushed to Molly's right hip, forcing her off balance, hoping she'd cough up the ball. A mistake.

Molly countered with her own hip bump, then lifted her foot over the ball so the outside edge of her cleat controlled it. The way Molly was positioned, I couldn't even see the ball.

When A-squad cheered and Coach blew the whistle, I knew Molly had scored. One of my B-squad girls chased it down so we could go again.

"That's one," Molly said, not mean.

The chaser returned and tossed the ball into me. I dribbled to Molly's left, keeping the ball to my right. If Molly blocked, I'd stop, spin around her, and shoot from a distance. It was a great plan that I never executed because Molly was a freaking ninja. She swept in, stole the ball, and dribbled directly into my goal.

"That's two."

We went again. Molly dribbled, I dropped my shoulder and rammed into her sternum, riling up A squad and knocking the ball loose. I sprinted after it, shot a split second before Molly blocked. Score. Barely.

Molly sneered, and I took pride in rattling her.

On the next possession, she got fancy, popping the ball up with her heel and sending it through my goal with a bounce off her head.

"Three."

A squad cheered, and I knew Coach stopped this drill whenever someone scored five. On offense now, I had no plans of going down easy. As Molly took her defensive position, I sped up, channeled everything—numbness, rage, grief, isolation. Molly never saw it coming. I mowed her down full force and kept going, one of my cleats catching something meaty, not turf. Molly screamed. I didn't look back as the whistle blew.

"What are you thinking, Tate?" Coach yelled.

I kicked the ball through Molly's goal. Turned and saw my friend clutching her injured forearm, blood oozing between her fingers. Accusatory glances assaulted me.

Coach kneeled by Molly, examined her puncture wounds. "They aren't deep," she said, uncharacteristically soothing. "Get to the nurse's office, okay?"

On her feet, Coach stomped to me, pointing her whistle like a weapon. "You're running for the rest of practice. Only break to throw up. You hear me?"

I processed it but didn't react.

"Tate! Are you deaf?"

"No."

"Then run."

I repeated myself. "No."

"Excuse me?"

I should have felt something. But I didn't. The next part was easy.

"I quit."

♠

Walking the perimeter of the school with duffel and book bags, I heard the whistle and bouncing balls as practice resumed. The team would be fine without me. Better without me. My head was elsewhere.

Powering up my phone revealed a missed text.

Mom: What did you print? All the toner from the office machine is gone.

Ignoring it, I called Mr. Héctor at the valet stand. Thirty minutes later, I was in the backseat of a town car heading home. Once there, I went straight to Dad's room, got back to work on what mattered.

The room became home base. I had taken a few minutes yesterday flagging it in our booking software so no incoming guests would get it. As far as the check-in desk and housekeeping were concerned, my father's room no longer existed.

Hours sailed by, with a timer going off every fifteen minutes, for another call to F.S. Him not answering was expected but didn't change my new routine. The quick (perhaps pointless) calls gave me a chance to rest my tired hand. All that writing.

Eating was still a necessity I couldn't forsake. The absolute best perk of living in a hotel: room service.

After placing my order, I had no reason to believe that the knock at the door was anything but my Cobb salad and Coca-Cola on a rolling cart with good silverware. With a pen behind my ear and the legal pad tucked under my arm, I answered the dainty knocks, instantly regretting it.

Molly, grass-stained, gauze-wrapped, and wearing a no-nonsense expression, said, "By my count, I get three questions. I'll be asking them now."

Andromeda's Palace hotel rooms were designed with a short and narrow entryway giving a restricted view of the room. This allowed guests to open their doors a smidgen while still maintaining a degree of privacy. What happens in Vegas . . .

I didn't open the door fully, taking advantage of the design choice. While Molly couldn't see everything inside, I saw well into the hall and got queasy. She wasn't alone.

Gavin, in his VR football sweats, face damp and flushed from his own practice, stood at her side. The two of them there, then, wasn't necessarily a shock, though I had to ask. "How'd you know to find me here?"

"Your mom," Molly said. "She's worried."

Mom knew I'd been spending time in Dad's room? My paranoia cranked to an eleven. She hadn't been in here since yesterday, or we would've had a sit-down, probably with suggestions of therapy. Could I keep her out of here now? Block her access through the key card system?

"We're all worried." Davis sidestepped Gavin, having been fully obscured by my ginormous friend, then wedged his way to the forefront of this, what? Confrontation? Intervention?

"You're worried?" That familiar, unpredictable rage sizzled. "You don't have your own problems to deal with?"

Davis flinched, and Gavin's gaze shifted to the general direction of the elevator.

"I was hoping it wouldn't go this way. You leave me no choice," Molly said.

Before I could brace the door with my feet, Molly muscled her way into the room.

"No, don't—" I grabbed her arm, but it was still practice sweaty. Slippery. Molly slid by easily enough. Caught a glimpse of what I'd done to Dad's room and shuddered like someone who suddenly found herself in a lion's cage. Panic and awe.

"Nikki, what the—"

My chest rose and fell too fast, a slight hyperventilation. No one else was supposed to see this. No one else was supposed to *know*.

Gavin entered, joining Molly. His head on a swivel, taking it all in.

Davis trailed but didn't join the others. He stayed next to me, took my hand. "What's wrong? I want to help."

He hadn't seen yet. When he did, he'd know his offer of help was laughable. I was *way* beyond that.

Molly turned her back on my project. "I think you know my first question."

Davis stepped forward, dropping my hand. To his credit, his body language did not mirror the strangeness around him.

On each wall, on every available space, from the floor to the edge of my extended, tiptoe/stretched-arm reach, were photos. Each one printed on a standard sheet of paper. Hundreds of sheets. Overlapping, but neat. The last few were faded and grainy, the final products squeezed from Mom's precious toner cartridges. They were the photos Dad took in his last days, arranged chronologically with tape, patience, and a tiny bit of insanity. I could admit that.

Silence and tension. Both thick enough to make the room feel stuffy despite the air-conditioner breeze flapping the photos' loose edges.

Two hard knocks on the ajar door made everyone jump and spin.

"Room service."

Molly, with her superior reflexes, jogged over, using her body to obscure the employee's view into the room. "Thanks. Whatever this is, can you bring up three more? We're going to be here a while."

♣

"I've been retracing his steps. He started taking pictures the night he got home." I pointed to the wall closest to the entrance, swept my finger right, along the adjoining walls, nearly 360 degrees. "All the way until maybe hours before he died."

The last picture I printed was taken in the early afternoon

outside the Aria. "The police don't think these pictures are important. I don't see how they're not."

There were trays of half-eaten salads, crusty bread, and empty soda cans on various pieces of furniture throughout the room. They digested their food and my explanation of the CSI-style displays of evidence around them. All eyes bounced about, their reactions hidden. I never figured the best poker faces I'd ever seen would belong to my friends in that moment.

While Molly and Gavin jumped from wall to wall and photo to photo at random, Davis hovered around select sections. Particularly the photos from Dad's first night. And his fourth, and his ninth. Those were the Nysos photos, Davis's home. I spent a lot of time on those, too.

Molly interrupted me watching Davis. "Where are you with all this? Do you, like, know anything?"

In a split-second decision, I decided not to mention Dad's apparent obsession with the Nysos, because awkward, and instead pointed to a grouping of other properties I'd tagged with small yellow Post-it notes. "He was really taken by properties with this sign. I've counted at least nine instances of it in different locations."

The sign read: "Owned and Managed by the Poseidon Group."

The words were done in a simple white Helvetica font with a golden trident watermark behind the lettering.

"Okay. What's the Poseidon Group?" Molly asked.

I was embarrassed to answer. "I checked their website. They just seem like some development company. They specialize in small-scale properties. The pictures are taken at some liquor stores, a no-name coffee spot, a barber shop."

"Why would your dad care about those?"

It's the very question I'd been asking myself.

My phone buzzed softly on the bed, my timer going off again. The third time since they'd arrived.

"Are you going to call him?" Molly says, now aware of F.S. and my inability to reach him. She uttered the question slowly, carefully, in neutral voice. Neither encouraging nor discouraging.

I wanted to try so bad. I also wanted to show them I didn't *have* to.

"No." I deactivated the timer. "It's pointless."

Molly nodded, almost imperceptibly. I couldn't tell if it was an acknowledgment or approval.

Davis walked the room, moved on to the non-Nysos photos, but what was *he* thinking?

"What now, guys?" I asked. A question and a challenge.

"Your mom's concerned," Molly said in reply.

"So you need to file a report?" The edges of my vision pulsed. Molly and Mom were awful tight lately.

"I *can* file a report," Molly said, "but what it actually says is debatable."

"And that means what, exactly?"

"It can mean—" Molly began before the chiming, buzzing phone interrupted. "I thought you turned that thing off."

"I did!"

It wasn't my phone's timer going off again, but the phone *beside* my phone.

Dad's.

Me staying away from the phone was as likely as the unluckiest gamblers in the world staying away from the posh game rooms around town. I snatched the phone off the nightstand and tapped the ACCEPT icon.

"Hello?"

"Is this Nathan's girl?" Gravelly this time, but no alcohol-soaked slur.

"This is Nikki." All eyes on me, I lowered the phone from my ear, put it on speaker. *See, I'm not crazy.*

"I'm Freddy. Freddy Spliff."

"Okay." Should I know that name? "I tried to call you back from before."

"I got locked up. I'm out now. We should meet."

CHAPTER 25

Ummm, definitely not, Molly mouthed.

The boys had their stern, false-bravado looks going, as if Freddy Spliff might burst into the room with outstretched groping hands. I got it. Stranger danger. Hang up. Run. Hide. This was everything parents warned us about from the moment we're old enough to waddle out of sight.

Yet . . .

"For what? Say what you need to say now."

"No! No, no, no! *They* might be listening."

The man sounded sober, but also skeezy and loony-bin paranoid. What were you hoping for here, Nikki? "How did you even know my dad?" I asked.

"From Ely State."

Prison. It kept getting better. "Look, dude. If you can't say what you have to say, then we're done."

His response was quick, shocking. "The papers say Nathan was killed in a bad drug deal. That sound right to you? That's surprising, girl. Real surprising."

My blood dipped below freezing.

Molly reached across me and tapped MUTE. "This guy sounds über-creepy. You know that, don't you?"

"Of course!" But then I promptly added, "So what's a good public place to meet, guys?"

Molly slapped her forehead and paced away.

"Caesar's," Davis offered. "The Forum Shops stay crowded. You can meet him, and we can be there."

Molly spread her arms wide, her not-happening posture, and zeroed in on Gavin. "Some help here."

Gavin said simply, "It's about her dad."

From the phone, his mic still live, Freddy said, "You there? Did the call drop?"

I unmuted quickly, afraid of losing the connection and never hearing from him again. "Yes, let's meet. Midday at Cae—"

Molly grasped my shoulder, shook her head while mouthing, *Cosmo.*

No time to question the team captain, I rolled with it. "The Cosmopolitan. Tomorrow."

"Noon, then. We can still take them down. For Nathan."

Take *who* down?

The line went dead. About four billion unanswered questions lingered. I asked Molly the first one that came to mind, "Why the Cosmo?"

Everyone waited for the brilliant strategy, the likes of which Molly's concocted on the playing field many, many times over.

"Holsteins is in the Cosmo," she said.

The muscles in my face nearly cramped from my sudden hard frown. "The burger joint?"

"Yeah. If I'm going to skip school to watch your back, I want one of their crème brûlée milkshakes. They're magical."

♥

I walked them all to the Loop. When we hit the lobby, Molly sped up, her gravity pulling Gavin along, leaving me paces behind them. With Davis. He hadn't said anything since we left my dad's room.

The general cheer wafting off the gaming floor was an inappropriate soundtrack for the tension between us.

"Is there any way to make this less awkward?" I asked.

"A talking dog and a van we call the Mystery Machine."

I snort-laughed. "Oh my god, I so needed that."

"I was worried about that one. Like, is an obscure Scooby-Doo joke offensive? Should I go more modern? *iZombie*, maybe?"

Dead serious suddenly, I asked, "Do you think I'm crazy?"

His shoulders tightened. "I think you're looking at it the wrong way. You have questions about what happened to your dad. That's not crazy, that's natural. That guy Freddy, though. He might be a total psycho. You should be ready so you don't get hurt."

"That's why you guys will be there. If he tries something—"

"No. I mean, yes, we don't want him to BTK you. I was talking about a different kind of hurt. Disappointment if he tells you him and your dad were on the run from aliens or werewolves. Whatever."

What he said wasn't far from my own thoughts, but it was still hard to hear. Freddy Spliff did not sound like America's most trusted news source. Indulging him in this meeting was likely a prelude to an emotional crash-and-burn, yet I couldn't steer away.

He said the other thing on his mind. "Your dad really had a thing about my dad, huh?"

I'd been hesitant to bring it up, but it kept hitting us both over the head, didn't it? "Maybe. Your dad came to the funeral."

He stopped me in the foyer. "What? You didn't say anything before."

"I didn't know how to say it. My head's been all over the place and you always catch so much crap over who everyone thinks your dad is."

He wiped a hand over his face, smoothing all the tics there. "So what did you think? Did you see his horns? The pitchfork?"

"For someone named 'Big' Bert, he was smaller than I expected."

"That's something." He laughed, a pained sound. "This is not the second date I envisioned."

"That you envisioned a second date at all is amazing. I couldn't blame you if you felt differently about it."

"Sure you could. You *should* blame me if I wasn't here doing what you once did for me. Helping."

That left me speechless. Our night at the airport felt like it happened years ago, to a different girl. But this boy who owed me nothing was as sweet as ever. All my decisions from before hadn't been bad.

Mr. Héctor was working the valet stand and already had a sports car—another of Cedric's, I guessed—parked and ready behind Molly's SUV. With a tight-lipped expression, he handed Davis his keys.

Davis thanked him and said to me, "Before I go, can I see your dad's phone?"

I thought I'd been discreet about slipping it into my pocket. I didn't go anywhere without it now.

"Please," he said quietly.

Was Molly watching in her rearview? I passed the phone to Davis under the cover of his open car door, like a spy.

"You've got pictures," he said, "but if you want to know where he was most often, there's a better way. Watch."

He thumbed the SETTINGS icon and walked me through a series of subsequent menus I'd never seen, eventually ending up on a screen labeled Frequent Locations. "There's a History option that gives a rough approximation of places he went often."

"You're kidding me." I retrieved the phone, looking at maps. Dates and times. "How did you . . . ?"

"It's a standard feature built into the phone's GPS. Most people don't even know they're walking around like tagged animals."

Having my friends see what I'd been up to in my dad's room felt horrible at first, like being forced to walk the Strip naked. How wrong was I? They're watching my back. Counting on them felt like something old me would do.

I glanced up from the phone and before I knew it, I'd stepped in, closing the space between us. "Thanks," I said softly.

"You're welcome," he replied just as softly.

I felt a ghost of a smile on my face before leaning up to kiss him. It was meant to be a peck, but as soon as my lips hit his, I felt my hand fisting his sweatshirt and pulling him even closer. A delicious shiver bolted up my spine as he kissed me back. When we finally broke apart, he looked me in the eye and said, "Thanks."

I burst out laughing before replying, "You're welcome."

Then he slipped into his ride and roared off. I stood there a beat, Dad's phone and Location History cupped in my hand.

Molly leaned from her window. "Boy toy's gone. Get over here."

Pocketing the phone, I complied, approaching Molly's window cautiously. "You shouldn't have come here. But I'm glad you did."

"I got you, Tate. No matter how hard you try being a jerk. We will get to those final two questions."

"Fair enough. And I'll get to make my demand."

"A deal's a deal," she sneered, "even though you maimed me."

I gave a half shrug. "I'll try my best never to do that again. No promises."

◆

The gift shop had souvenir maps of Las Vegas. I grabbed one, then stopped in the offices for a box of pushpins. When I returned to Dad's room, I took the generic framed painting of a ship listing at sea from the wall over the bed, and tacked the map to it. My feet sank into the spongy mattress while I used the locations in the phone to mark Dad's travels with more pins. An hour into the task a call came through on the room line. Mom.

"Are your friends still here?" she asked.

"No, they left a while ago."

"Can I come down and talk?"

I tamped down the swelling panic. "I'm actually on my way up."

A few minutes later I stood in her side of our suite. Mom had abandoned her casino-floor pantsuit for loose pajama pants and a T-shirt. She wrapped her hair for bed.

"Is it helping, you spending time in your dad's room?" she asked.

"It is." Short, ambiguous answers felt safest.

"Good. I'm willing to give you whatever time and space you need for now. I think we can both use that."

I bet. Time and space with Tomás was a little more than what I needed. If he was enough of a distraction so she left me alone, cool. "Sure, Mom."

Her back was to me, eyes on her mirror. "If you want to talk, though, just know . . ."

Her hesitation was discomforting. We weren't the best at heart-to-hearts, and never had been. "I get it. Is there something *you* want to talk about?"

"A lot of things. I don't know how to say them." She still wouldn't look at me.

"Are you happy he's gone?".

She spun on me, her face hard. She waited before speaking, let calm back in. "Not in the slightest."

"Because it's weird to me that he had his own room. What was going on with you two before he . . . ?" I shrugged. Didn't need to say it.

"Adjustments. Figuring what it meant with him back. For everybody."

"Were you going to divorce him? Now that you didn't have to feel guilty about him being in jail?"

No outrage, and no straight answer. Both telling. She did say, "We discussed a lot of possibilities."

"Is that what's on your mind?"

"No. I wanted to ask you to leave tomorrow night free. Don't make plans with your friends or anything. We should have dinner and really talk. About what happened, and what's going to happen."

All the cryptic crap got to me. "Can't we do that now?"

"I think our conversation will be a long one. I have a couple of meetings early tomorrow."

"What kind of meetings?" I'd gotten a glimpse of her calendar when I was in the office yesterday, saw nothing.

"Important ones."

That's how you want to play, Mom. You're not the only one with important stuff to do tomorrow. "Fine." I was no longer in the sharing mood. "I'll see you tomorrow night, right after soccer practice."

CHAPTER  26

I kissed Mom on the cheek the next morning. It was important that she see me leave with my schoolbag and my soccer duffel, which no longer held sports gear I wouldn't need.

"You look nice today," she said. I knew she saw it as a sign of me progressing. Moving on.

My outfit wasn't far from my usual school attire. Jeans. Tee. Blocky platforms instead of sneakers. I didn't feel like hiding those in my duffel with the change of clothes and makeup I'd already stuffed in there.

"Felt like switching it up," I said. Not a total lie. Molly, Gavin, Davis, and I discussed the benefits of looking older today. "See you tonight for dinner."

Mom nodded as I headed out the door.

In the Loop, Molly waited alone, tapping a drum solo on her steering wheel.

"Where's Gavin?" I asked.

"Coach Peoples called early morning practice. There was another incident and he's punishing them for it."

"Oh god," I said, climbing in beside her. "What now?"

She took us into traffic, the opposite direction from school. "Grammar's been beheaded. Finally."

"Shut. Up." Grammar, the Cardinal Graham's eagle-headed mascot. For as long as I'd been at Vista Rojo, there'd been healthy debates on how someone might grab the head off the rival mascot's costume. Teams dared each other; some of the genius types in the school drew up Mission: Impossible–like plans to accomplish the feat. No one ever went through with it. Until now.

"Coach Peoples thinks his team pulled it off?"

"They did. Gavin sent me a pic last night." She motioned to her phone resting in the cupholder. I tapped in her security code and navigated to her texts. I glanced at a couple from Cedric Carlino—winky emojis and LOLs—that we'd deal with later and found the incriminating photo from Gavin. A shot of the Griffin's detached head propped on top of the Vista Rojo High School marquee.

"How'd they do this?"

"Intel from your Davis."

"My Davis?" I kept my voice high and light.

"*We* should've been the ones stealing that head. But you had to go and quit on me."

"We never planned to steal it. We always said that was stupid."

"True. Still. Quitter. You're not really done with soccer, are you?"

"Um, yeah. If for no other reason, the Hades-style torment Coach Riley would put me through if I tried to come back now."

Molly held her freshly bandaged arm in front of my face. "Not just Coach. I'd have some B-squad beatdowns lined up for you, too."

I turned away, shamefaced. "I'm sorry about that. My head's been weird lately."

"Save it. I've had teeth kicked out before. This was a bug bite."

Glancing at the picture again, I said, "It's kind of awesome that they got it. CG's going to come back at us hard."

"Us? See, you're still on the team. If only in spirit."

Okay, I had all the school pride feels. I was still capable of enjoying moments like this.

Morning rush traffic on the Strip was a real and horrid thing. Bumper to impatient, maniacally honking bumper on the way to the Nysos. The steel-and-glass behemoth was a looming waypoint ahead, reflecting morning sun and blocking our view of anything beyond. A divisive landmark despite its youth, it became part of Las Vegas's navigational landscape. You were north of the Nysos or south of it. East or west. Davis's home was the new center of the universe.

We continued down Las Vegas Boulevard, the looming hotel growing closer, closer. Some of the landmarks we passed were in Dad's photo log. The boxy towers of the SLS and the mirrored glass of the Riviera. Thanks to Davis's tip about navigation history, I knew they weren't the important properties. They're one-time visits, maybe even real sightseeing on Dad's part. It was the Nysos, and a few other properties around town, that drew him again and again.

What were you looking for, Dad?

Molly steered us into the cavernous underworld of the Nysos's parking deck, putting us in a slow-moving line of cabs and tourists. I fired off a text.

Me: we're about to hit the valet stand. get down here.
Davis: as you wish.

"He's coming," I said.

"Awesome! So is he, like, your boyfriend now or what? That's my second question, by the way. You're obligated here."

I'd been expecting that one. "We haven't talked about it."

"You've thought about it, though?"

"Is that your third question?"

She considered it a moment. "No. I'm going to keep that one for a while."

Traffic sped up and split, the taxis veered far left, and paying drivers seeking assistance angled toward the tip-hungry valets.

Ahead of us a polished black party bus spilled spent people into the offloading area. I've seen a bunch of these rent-and-roll vans—with their tiled floor and optional stripper poles—all year. Bachelor's playing dress-up, suits and ties. Birthday parties where the ladies all do short sequined skirts, and the eternally twenty-five birthday girl got a sash and tiara like Miss America. Occasionally, there were nuns.

The groups on these buses were, typically, pretty much the same. As my mom said, dogs with the dogs, and foxes with the foxes. The group evacuating this bus were like the animals from the Madagascar movies, an unlikely group bonded by . . . what?

One guy looked like an aging CEO. Another was college age, in cargo shorts and a tank top. There was a woman with knitting needles and yarn protruding from her purse. An old man with a cane.

A final passenger exited, tatted arms visible up to the short sleeves of his polo tee. He didn't quite fit the group either, but he'd never seem out of place at this hotel since, technically, he owned it. Cedric Carlino belly-laughed and patted the CEO-looking dude on the shoulder.

Glancing our way, his eyes were sharp despite their pinkish, sleep-deprived tint. Nodding his recognition, he jogged over, yelled toward the valet, "You taking care of my friends?"

The valet's relaxed swagger vanished, clearly uncomfortable. "Mr. Carlino," he said, "can I pull up something from the fleet?"

"Naw, naw. I just got in. Was gonna go sleep for, like, twelve hours, then I saw the lovely ladies." The valet took it as a dismissal and moved on to the next car.

"Hey there, Molly," Cedric said.

"Hey, yourself? So you were out being bad last night."

His grin curled up to his ears. "You know it. Another promoting gig. Had to take care of my people."

"What kind of gig was it?" I asked, perhaps overstepping my boundaries. But the crew on that bus was so not like what I was used to in this town.

"Corporate thing. Fast-food franchise—Monte Fishto, ever heard of it?"

Before I could answer, he said, "They got a bunch of the owners at a convention here. Wanted a bus to see the town. Me, being a full-service kind of guy, was happy to oblige. What are you two doing here?"

"Picking Davis up for school."

Cedric leaned on Molly's door, his body jutting into the incoming traffic lane, forcing other cars to veer around him. "Little brother finally got tired of the Richie Rich routine, huh?"

"I . . . guess." What else could I say?

"Good." His tone shifted suddenly from jovial to something more serious. "I'm glad he's getting to have fun and be normal. I'm glad he's got friends like you."

Molly's eyes flicked to me, and I returned the gesture. *What's that about?*

A couple of awkward beats, then Cedric looked past Molly, to me. "So you know about our poker room?"

Okay, that was a turn. "I know it exists. That it's huge."

"Forty-five tables. Crystal card shoes. Ergonomic memory-foam chairs, I swear you could play for days without so much as a back spasm." He looked more than a little proud.

"So you're trying to convince me to book my eighteenth birthday party here?" I was way more comfortable with hustler Cedric than with the weird introspective version from a moment ago.

"ABC. Always be closing. My dad's saying. I think he stole it from a movie. But no. Not that. I like the way you handled that cheater Saturday."

I was uncomfortable again. He might be the only one who liked it.

"I see you got mad respect for the game, is all. You can come through, play some hands here anytime."

This felt eerily reminiscent of a conversation with my father. "I'm not old enough."

"If you're a Carlino guest, no one's gonna sweat you about ID."

"What's this about sweat?" Davis said, joining his brother.

"I just gave Nikki the golden ticket to some Hold'em here at the Nysos."

Davis shook his head. "What's in it for you?"

"Good players attract good players. If what you say about her is true . . ."

"Could you please stop trying to use my friends for your own personal gain?" he said as he climbed into the car.

Cedric raised his hands in surrender. "Fine, fine. Invitation stands, Nikki. You all have a good day. By the way, don't know if you noticed, but you're half an hour late for school." He winked and backed into the revolving doors until they swallowed him whole.

CHAPTER 27

"Anybody up for some window-shopping?" Davis asked, leading the way through the Caesar's Palace gaming floor into the corridors of the Forum Shops, a relatively short walk from the Cosmopolitan. We were plenty late for school, but plenty early for the meet. With three hours to kill, we blended in with tourists and tried to appear older than we were, lest we attract security guards seeking IDs and explanations.

In the presence of such retail, Molly lost her mind, abandoning us for dressing rooms of things she couldn't afford. While she frolicked, Davis and I retreated to the shadows of the Atlantis animatronic show at the hub of the Forum Shops. It was a storytelling contraption made of fountains, stage lighting, and scary Muppet-like statues that recounted the sinking of Atlantis, or something. Mostly it made babies cry.

"I spoke to my dad," he said.

"And?"

Davis shrugged. "He said he knew of your dad from the early days of Andromeda's Palace. '*Casino owners are part of an exclusive club. I went to the funeral to pay respects.*' His words, not mine."

"My dad didn't respect *him* very much."

"I got the same impression."

"What he told you can't be all there is to it."

"I know. I never said my father was very forthcoming. At least not with me and Ced."

His mood shifted, same as Brady's party when the subject of his dad came up. I didn't want to push him, but we couldn't keep skating around it, either. Our parents were keeping secrets.

"Can I ask you a question that's kind of personal, and might make you a little mad?"

"You want to know if any of it's true. The gangster stuff."

"How did you know?"

"When I went to Cardinal Graham, anyone who knew me long enough eventually asked. It's all right."

It wasn't all right. Forget that I'd done *anything* like someone from Cardinal Graham, I could tell the topic exhausted him. I was sorry for going there, for doing to him what so many mean kids had done to me. I was sorry, but I didn't stop. "Is it?"

"I have no idea. Think about it, you know you were named after a waitress in Mexico because they told you. What if your parents and the waitress knocked over a bank that same weekend? They don't say it, it didn't happen. Right?"

Except, if other people said it, I'd sure be curious.

"My dad is a lot of things. Things I hate. He's obsessed with his business. His kingdom. That doesn't make him a killer. A not-so-nice guy at times, yes."

"Does Cedric share your opinion?"

"What makes you ask that?"

"Something he said." *I'm glad he's getting to have fun and be normal. I'm glad he's got friends like you.*

"Ced's had it rougher than me, for longer than me. Dad wants heirs. Ced's the oldest. When our parents split up, Dad brought him out here immediately, while I spent seven or eight years in New York with Mom. Trust me, I got the better deal."

"How so?"

"Dad's intense now. And he's made it. Back then, when he was trying to get to the top, he was obsessed with more, more, more. It's why him and Mom split up. She thought he loved the business more than her. She was probably right. When he came here, he didn't bring Ced to be his son, he brought him to be a junior executive. Or something. For a long time, Cedric told Mom he wanted to come back to New York. Back home."

Fake thunder and lightning crashed around us and the Atlantis statues yawned to life. Tourists crowded with phone cameras on. Functional families on display.

I said, "He seems like he's handling the pressure well. All those cars. His promotion business."

"What choice did he have? Dad shuts down all frivolous activity as soon as he thinks it's a distraction. Ced wanted to be a baseball player. He was good, too. Dad pulled him out of sports at his peak, said it was a waste of time."

"That sucks."

Davis shrugged. "Like you said, he's handling it well. He's the son with potential."

"Not the way I see it." I grabbed his hand and pulled him along. "Let's walk."

"You want to come to the football dinner with me?"

An abrupt change, which got me stammering. "You think that's a good idea?"

"Until yesterday you played soccer. Most sports fans around the world consider that football. Feels appropriate."

"No, goof. I mean our family drama."

"I know what you meant. I'm still asking."

I squeezed his hand. "It might be a bad idea. Not the worst I've heard this week. Yeah, I'll go."

♠

Ten minutes before noon, we took our positions in the Cosmopolitan. Like the Wynn, the hotel resort mixed gaming, shopping, clubbing, and dining in a beehive. China Poblano was open for lunch, so I nabbed a table in the patio section, ordering water and a couple of pricey tacos to keep the waitress happy. Molly and Davis set up in Holsteins, thirty yards away. I saw them through the window, where Molly's head bobbed joyfully over her crème brûlée milkshake.

This close to midday, hundreds of people bustled along with their bags and their plans. The low murmur of commerce echoed throughout the cavernous floor. My duck-tongue tacos cooled on my plate while I searched the crowd for Freddy-ish faces. I had no clue what he looked like. Only imagined a grizzled, aged man, based on his voice alone. Lines deep-cut in his face, a mix of thick facial hair and silver neck stubble, yellow eyes that weren't the windows to his soul but portholes to his damaged liver.

No one fit my description. From Holsteins, Davis stared unblinking. Intense. Molly slurped her empty calories.

He mouthed, *You okay?*

Before I gave my thumbs-up, a woman screamed.

"El Potrillo! *Dios mío!*"

Twisting toward the main floor and crouching from my seat, prepared to hide fully if necessary, I spotted the woman. Latina and elderly in a Cirque du Soleil T-shirt, she was in a full freak-out, with two younger women—a daughter and granddaughter by the resemblance—attempting to calm her. Unsuccessfully.

"El Potrillo! El Potrillo!"

The singer Mr. Héctor once told me about? Here?

The younger women restrained her from chasing the object of her desire. A dark-haired, denim-jacketed man fleeing the crowd. I didn't see his face, though I'm certain it was not the singer. It's a man who looked like him.

Tomás?

A voice behind me said, "You're Nathan's kid."

It was not a question. I turned my attention. The man I came to meet stood at my table. Hello, Freddy Spliff.

CHAPTER 28

He looked nothing like I'd imagined. He was old, like my dad's age, but neater than I expected. He wore pleated khakis—too big in the waist, a belt cinched to the last buckle hole kept them on— and a pressed sky-blue shirt. The outfit had a borrowed feel, like when Molly and I wore each other's clothes.

His tanned cheeks were clean-shaven, blowing my stewbum image away. His hair oiled and combed. The eyes, though . . . they were the eyes of a drunk—yellow, crackling with red lightning. His breath was flammable, so much so, I checked his pockets for the telltale impression of a flask.

I flicked a glance toward Holsteins. Davis signaled Molly, who turned in her seat so fast, she disconnected from her straw, drib-bling milkshake down the front of her shirt.

"You drop something?" Freddy asked, shuffling his feet, surveying our immediate area.

My knees remained bent in the defensive crouch I'd taken when that woman screamed for El Potrillo. Or Tomás. Or I didn't know. Too much was happening, and Freddy Spliff was the priority. I could easily find Tomás later.

"Just my napkin." I reclaimed my seat, grasping for my former composure.

Freddy Spliff's eyes seemed loosely moored in his head, bounc-ing around the vast retail floor, never settling on any one person or thing.

"You are?" he said, his certainty softening. "Nathan's kid?"

"I'm Nikki. Sit down." I nudged the seat across from me askew with my foot.

The way wobbly Freddy collapsed into the chair, I felt I'd offered it just in time. He gave one more sweep of the area with his omnivision, lowered his head onto the table before curling his arm over his eyes, a shield from the light.

Awesome. My potential source was a second grader in need of a nap.

"Is he okay?" The suddenly-there waitress startled me.

Freddy sprang up from the hip, wavering, an on-guard cobra. "Coffee. If you got espresso, I need a shot in there."

"No food, sir?"

He glanced at the exotic uneaten tacos on my plate, winced. "Just coffee."

"Sure thing." The waitress disappeared, her aloof chilliness wafting.

"What information do you have about my dad?"

Freddy's rolling marble eyes settled on me finally. I preferred his unfocused mode. His gaze penetrated so deeply I craved one of those lead blankets the dentist gave you before X-rays. "Nathan really didn't tell you anything about *them*?"

"Them who?"

He waved his arm in a wide arc over his head. "The watchers *every*where! Unseen by us."

"Like ghosts?" This drunken nonsense was the reason I skipped school?

Freddy Spliff's eyes narrowed. "No, girl. Like cameras!"

When he swept his arm again, I keyed on the globes mounted in the ceiling. Typical surveillance. Obvious and overdone. Vegas casinos rivaled airports in paranoia. So what?

The waitress returned with Freddy Spliff's coffee in a porcelain mug and a chrome basket of sugars and creams. Unsubtly, she pressed her hand to her nose, like she couldn't stand the reek emanating from our table. "Will you be needing the check soon?"

I snapped, "You can bring it, but we may be here a while. Thank you." She skulked off, and I said, "What about the cameras?"

"Nathan was watching, too. He told me that the night before he was killed."

"Freddy, you might think you're making sense, but you're not. Please tell me exactly what my dad said to you."

"He said it was the same scam, the way it happened. He said it was like history repeating."

History repeating. What history? Dad's death was like John Reedy's. Eerily so. I knew that already. That couldn't be what Freddy's talking about. Unless Dad *knew* he was going to die the way he did . . .

Which. Was. Insane.

"What about the cameras? Is there a surveillance video from the night my dad died?"

Freddy Spliff sighed and smacked his forehead. Like I was the one talking nonsense. When he sprang to his feet, I gripped my armrest, defeating my flight-or-fight response. Beyond Freddy, Davis and Molly mirrored my tight posture.

Freddy Spliff rooted in his shirt pocket. When his skeletal fingers emerged, a flash drive on a lanyard dangled from them. "Nathan didn't know a thing about modern computers, but I learned some things in lockup. I helped him put it all together."

I wouldn't have been more rapt if he'd flashed a ten-thousand-dollar casino chip just for me. Shifting to the edge of my chair, I reached for it.

Freddy Spliff snatched the drive away. "You were supposed to come alone."

"I—I didn't—" At first I feared my own violations of our terms would keep me from the apparent gold mine of information. But Freddy Spliff hadn't discovered Molly and Davis; he never even looked in their direction. He gazed past me. I twisted, spotted a couple of men in dark denim pants and solid black polo shirts, staring.

"Them? I don't know those guys."

"You're working with them, too. Aren't you?"

"Freddy, please, I promise, I—"

Freddy Spliff ran before I could convince him.

CHAPTER 29

For a lumbering drunk, the man was sneaky quick. He escaped the China Poblano dining area before I left my seat, nearly fading into the lunchtime crowd. He couldn't get away, not with that flash drive. Grabbing the two phones on the table, I chased. Only barely registered the chilly waitress shouting, "Hey, your check!"

Past Holsteins. Davis was up, yelling something at Molly. I couldn't wait for them.

A set of escalators led to the ground floor, and to fancier restaurants on higher levels. Freddy angled toward them while I weaved around human roadblocks, trying to anticipate if he'd go up or down. Neither. He dipped into a side corridor.

Making that corridor a second too late, elevator doors closed on Freddy Spliff, the down arrow winking red. The placard next to the elevator indicated two levels of parking deck beneath us. Kicking off my platforms for speed, I shoved a phone into each of my back pockets and descended into the stairwell. At the next level, I leaned from the door, saw the elevator moving down, and I kept going, too.

At the ground-floor landing, I caught a glimpse of Freddy Spliff's shirt fluttering around him like loose skin. He ducked between bumpers and fenders like a maze runner, sparing an occasional glance over his shoulder.

"Hey!" I yelled, still following.

He had a significant lead, but no longer hindered by clunky shoes, I put on soccer speed. Gained. The secret to my speed—my bare feet—was also my downfall.

I planted one foot solidly in a patch of shattered glass. It hurt like a mother, even if not all the tiny pebbles pierced the skin.

Whimpering, slowing, I did not stop, but each step was a hot needle drilling into my sole.

Freddy Spliff made for the far end of the lot, not going for a vehicle but an emergency exit. He bounced the door open, stepped through a blazing-white rectangle into the populated desert. My orientation was completely off. Were we facing the front or back of the Cosmopolitan? If that door put Freddy Spliff close to the clogged and crowded Strip, I'd never find him again. I willed myself along faster, despite the pain.

Moving through that same door, wincing at the sunlight, I emerged not on the Strip. This was the back side of the hotel. A loading dock ran adjacent to giant rolling doors meant to accept crates and pallets. No trucks were offloading, so the empty loading bay felt like an abandoned part of the city. No crowds, no sounds of joy. Only the hum of unseen machinery. A single engine.

Suddenly interrupted by Freddy Spliff's screams.

At the far end of the loading dock a black van idled, it's back door spread wide like wings. Two men in dark denim and polos, the same pair from upstairs, held a kicking and screaming Freddy Spliff by the arms, forced him into the vehicle.

I nearly yelled out. But if I called to them, if I let them know I was a witness to this bold daylight kidnapping . . . would they take me, too?

They got Freddy inside the van, the doors closed. I ducked behind a recycle bin while the kidnappers returned to the van's cabin. When the driver closed his door, I spotted an emblem stenciled below the window. Too far away to make it out clearly and lacking the courage to get closer, I went for Dad's phone, the camera app. I steadied my hands and zoomed in as much as I could, then tapped the shutter icon, taking multiple pics in a rapid burst.

The van pulled away, and I returned Dad's phone to my pocket and removed my own. My thumb hovered over Molly's number when someone yelled, "Don't move!"

Fearing a fleet of clandestine vans and an army of black-golf-shirted cultists, I turned slowly toward the voice. These weren't the same guys. This pair wore khakis and shirts identifying them as Cosmopolitan security team members.

Relief sagged my muscles, siphoned my adrenaline. I became more sensitive to the pain in my foot, but it was okay. Help was here.

"Thank god you're here," I said. "They took him. I thought he was crazy paranoid, but he wasn't. They really took—"

"Miss," Security Team Member One said, clutching his radio tightly, "did you run out on a check at China Poblano?"

"That?" I reached for the loose twenties in my back pocket.

"We said *don't move*!" Security Team Member Two fingered the extendable baton fixed to his belt.

Those bulky men were, essentially, three of me. Yet they felt threatened enough to ready their weapons? I made up my mind, not another move. Every brown person in America knew how quickly this could go wrong. How quickly it *has* gone wrong.

"I was going to pay. I have the money in my pocket. If you could walk me back to the restaurant, I'll take care of the bill. Then I want to tell you about the man I was chasing. How he was taken." My enunciation improved with terror. Each word was loud enough and clear enough to impress a speech therapist. But I still spoke another language they couldn't bother translating.

Security Team Member One said, "Can we see some ID, miss?"

Sure, plenty. My driver's license. My school ID. Each exposing me as an underage truant in a restricted area of an established Strip resort.

I really should've paid for those tacos.

CHAPTER 30

The skipped China Poblano check was easily reconciled.

The Cosmopolitan security team had the ability to take cash, debit, or credit. And they provided a receipt. Yay! No petty larceny charge. I reminded Mom of those fortunate and timely conveniences on the drive back to Andromeda's.

"I don't care one little bit about those tacos, Nikalosa! Don't say the word *taco* to me again."

We spoke of tacos no further.

"How did you get there?" Mom said as we emerged from the Cosmopolitan parking deck in one of the Andromeda's town cars. "Did Molly bring you? You left with her this morning, didn't you?"

"No," I said quickly and convincingly, summoning every bit of my poker table deceitfulness so as not to implicate my friend. Or Davis. "I got an Uber after first bell."

Getting caught by security was never part of the plan. Molly and Davis didn't sign up for this kind of trouble. When Cosmo security granted me a phone call to summon a parent, I also texted Molly a warning.

Me: DISAVOW.

Though Molly, to her credit, didn't blindly follow the order.

Molly: where are you?
Me: with security. mom on the way. don't get caught, too, and
      don't respond. deleting these texts now.

Aside from deleting incriminating evidence, I forwarded all the calls from my phone to Dad's. The best preemptive strike of my life.

Mom had arrived at the security office in record time, and she'd taken my phone the moment she saw my face.

Driving too fast and aggressive for Strip traffic, Mom said, "What were you doing in a restricted area?"

Telling her about Freddy Spliff was never an option. "I was spying."

Her response was a perplexed scowl.

"Our business isn't doing so hot, Mom. The Cosmopolitan's been doing great, booking conferences and conventions. I wanted to scope the grounds on a day when it wouldn't be very crowded. Get a feel for what a successful establishment is *doing right*." I emphasized the last words with the intent to burn.

"You skipped school to play corporate espionage at this hotel?"

"Not just the Cosmopolitan. I checked the Bellagio and Caesar's, too."

"For what? What did you learn? Please, tell! I hope it's worth me grounding you for two months."

I feigned hurt. "Does that mean dinner's off? I was so looking forward to that."

"Keep it up, young lady. Three months isn't a stretch."

Three months. Six months. A year. Whatever. Nothing short of bars and shackles was stopping me. Not after what I'd seen today.

"What happened to your foot?"

An Ace bandage coiled around my ankle and heel . . . another gift from the Cosmopolitan's full-service security team since I'd tossed my shoes.

"A gold-and-diamond chandelier fell and shattered. I stepped on the pieces so I could smuggle them out. When we get home, you can pick them from my flesh and pay the mortgage."

"Three months it is. School and soccer practice. That's it for you."

"Sounds fair."

♣

Ordered to my room, I stayed put into the evening. A struggle. Dad's room, my notes and photos within, called like a siren's song. Couldn't give into it. Things went terribly wrong and I needed to project what Mom considered normal behavior as much as possible. So I sat, considered dropping an anonymous tip to the cops about Freddy Spliff's kidnapping. It was a distinct possibility for a hot five seconds, but three things—which might be summed up as one thing, fear, if I thought about it too hard—kept me from doing what would be sensible in someone else's city.

One, what proof did I have? I should've gone for video instead of a photo. That 20/20 hindsight.

Two, if I called the cops, and my anonymous tip—they always seemed suspect to me—wasn't as anonymous as I thought, it circled back to my mom, and we got nuclear fallout I didn't want to think about.

Three, the cops weren't being helpful in Dad's death. The van that took Freddy felt like the law . . . though that logo didn't look like Metro. Bottom line: No cops.

With no good options, I resorted to my old hopeless mode. Dialing Freddy's phone. Like old times, there was no answer.

♥

Late that evening, I got a group text going from Dad's phone. Molly informed me she and Davis made it back to school without incident on the strength of forged doctors' notes. In a lengthy exchange, I told them all I remembered about the strange, incoherent Freddy Spliff conversation. How I wrote it off as cuckoo speak until he got snatched by the men in black (golf shirts). I sent the fuzzy kidnap van photo to both of them for opinions. They couldn't make out the emblem either.

The afternoon went so wrong/weird, I'd almost forgotten about what happened right before Freddy Spliff showed. I hesitated bringing it up, but who else was I going to run this by?

Me: you remember that lady screaming right before FS showed?

Molly: yes

Davis: ✓

Me: i think she was yelling for tomas.

Molly: the guy who likes your mom?

Davis: ?

Molly: @D—N's mom is smoking. a dude who works for them
knows it. details later. @N—you sure?

Me: no

Me: but . . .

That lady could've been screaming for the real El Potrillo, for all I knew.

Me: idk.

Davis: that's real coincidental, right? if it was him?

That's just it. The part I was unwilling to say, even in a text. If it was him, it felt like the opposite of coincidental.

But . . . what did that mean?

◆

Our texting continued sporadically. Gavin joining late, taking us on a much-needed tangent about—what else?—that Griffin head.

Gavin: word is CG's pissed.

Davis: wait until we launch phase 2. total psychological warfare.

Me: phase 2?

Molly: phase 2?

Davis: @N—remember that safe alert story i told you?

Gavin: dude! no evidence!

Davis: no worries. all i'm sayin is i gave G a tutorial. ☺

Me: oh god!

The boys continued their thinly veiled discussion of torturing Cardinal Graham, while Molly started a separate private exchange with me.

Molly: what now? that freddy dude made it sound like your dad
was onto something. and i know you.

It wasn't a lie. She knew me, knew I wasn't going to let it rest. I had no clue what to do next. Bring up Tomás to Mom? Couldn't see that going well.

Freddy Spliff mentioned a scam. Might be worth hitting up Luciano, a cardplayer like him might know more about that.

Though, if his number was in Dad's phone, it wasn't tagged with a name, and I couldn't see going by that house, with its armed security and sketchy surroundings, unannounced.

I scrolled through the contacts, trying to guess which random phone number might be the right one, and paused on a name I definitely knew.

Dan Harris had been fighting for our family nearly three years. More than willing to go out of his way for us when there was talk of lawsuits and bestsellers and movies. Something went south between him and my parents. Having a little chat with him about it might be worth my time while I figure my next move.

Me: i'm thinking about seeing a lawyer.

CHAPTER 31

Mom didn't trust me getting to school with Molly but couldn't break away from an early morning hotel emergency (something about a guitar and a toilet) to personally ensure my safe arrival. She left chauffeur duties to Mr. Hectór. In his sweet-as-can-be grandpa way, he gave me the business over my disobedience, and it was worse than getting grounded. If he had kids of his own, his disappointed look would've crushed their will in infancy.

"Your mother, she worries about you a great deal, Nika," he said. Not Nikki. Mr. Héctor did things his own way. "You should be behaving better."

"You're right. I know. Is it okay if I turn on the radio?"

When I reached for the dial, he popped my hand, a sound like a whipcrack. "No radio. We haven't talked in a while. We should now."

"Ow!" I massaged my stung flesh, flexed fingers, wondered about nerve damage. "Okay. No radio."

Peppermint and Old Spice was his signature scent. I was used to it being attached to smiles, welcome-home gestures, even a polite curtsy in the days before his bad hip. Not now. His lips were tight, and I knew whatever talk was coming wouldn't be one I'd enjoy. I rolled down the window.

"You and your mama seem to be butting heads lately."

"That's us, a couple of rams."

"I know things are hard for you, with all that's happened. It's hard for her, too. You know that, don't you, Nika?"

"Of course, but—" I stopped short of saying it wasn't so hard that Dad should be forgotten, his last days of life dropped in a shoe box and tucked in a closet. This was the first time since the night of the party that a rage wave crashed into me. It felt good, but it needed direction. Not at Mr. Héctor, never him. He might share it with me, given how much he loved Dad.

"She's got Tomás to help her work through the pain, I guess."

Even through the jowls that had grown floppy in the last few years, I could tell he'd clenched his jaw. Moments passed before he spoke again, and I thought we might spend the rest of the ride trashing Tomás for line-crossing. Possibly Mom, too, for letting him.

"You lost your father. She lost her husband. Measuring one against the other is a mistake, Nikalosa. A shameful one." The words came through a grumble at the back of his throat, like a dog's growl.

"That's not what I'm doing."

"What are you doing?"

What no one else would. "You're okay with it? Dad was your friend, and she's all in that dude's face like—"

"Someone who's shown your father nothing but respect in a difficult situation."

"Respect?"

This was not going the way I expected. I willed the school closer.

"Your mother's made plenty of sacrifices for the love of your father, his dreams. You don't think a strong black woman like her longed for a life of servitude inside a Greek myth, do you?"

"It's the family business. What else was she going to do?"

"Maybe you should ask her sometime."

Mom never complained about running Andromeda's. She complained about stress, and missed quarterly projections, and unreliable staffers. Never the whole. That was my thing. I wanted out. Mr. Héctor probably sensed it—saw me walking in with college brochures or something—and tried playing it like that was something Mom and me had in common. Peacemaking.

"Andromeda's and Tomás aren't the same thing," I said stubbornly.

"What good does it do you hating him? From what I can tell, he's done nothing wrong other than having misplaced affection and poor timing."

Taking Mom's side was one thing, but he was not making me the bad guy over Tomás. "What if he fixed his mistakes?"

Mr. Héctor shook his head. "I don't understand."

"My dad's gone. Forever. That worked real good for Tomas's affection, didn't it?"

"Nika! Stop! What you're suggesting is cruel. The man is guilty of nothing but having feelings for a woman you don't give enough credit to."

He'd never yelled at me before. Never. Guess we're all trying new things.

He turned the radio on.

Great talk, then.

♠

Mr. Héctor dropped me off at the main entrance, breaking his vow of silence. "Be good, learn plenty. And think."

Only one of his directives interested me. I nodded, weak-smiled, waved him away.

What did I know about Tomás? Ex-cop. Security guy. Where was he the night Dad died?

I texted the besties.

Me: meet at my locker.

Gavin was slouched against the wall when I arrived, and Molly met me halfway with open arms. "I'm sorry we let you down yesterday," she said.

"You didn't. I'm glad you and Davis escaped. Everybody doesn't need to take a fall."

She breathed heavy. "Those fake notes we put together worked. The dads never even got a phone call about the classes I missed."

"Told you we were golden as long as we showed up by end of day," Davis chimed in.

Nobody heard him approach, and Gavin actually goose-jumped.

"You're a mastermind," I said. "Think it'll work again?"

Molly's face went slack. "No, sweetie. I don't. Please tell me that's enough to keep you attending your regularly scheduled classes today? I mean, we're already here."

Davis scanned up and down the hall. "Who's paying attention?"

Some of Molly's swagger dissipated. Gavin offered no backup despite her pleading glances.

"I'm not letting you take my car." In other words, she wasn't going. That was a problem.

Before I protested further, Davis said, "I drove today."

Blank stares from us all.

"Cedric got the idea I was 'riding to school like a real boy,' told my driver he didn't have to come in today," he explained. "I paid him back for being so helpful by stealing one of his cars."

"Makes perfect sense," said Molly.

"I'll help you. Any way you need," Davis said to me.

My heart climbed into my throat. His offer, with no hesitation whatsoever. Not only that, another Bonnie and Clyde outing. Swoon.

"If that's okay," he said, doing a full-on hot and awkward thing.

Molly gave him the team captain stare; she had no power here. When he didn't back down, she turned on me. "Nikki. No. It's not going to go your way."

Sure, I was already in trouble. For doing the right thing, though. If I found good intel, and finally told Mom what I was doing, she'd see how wrong she'd been. How . . . passive. We could go to the cops, or the news, or something together.

"Molly, take good notes today. Okay?"

CHAPTER 32

Davis maneuvered a yellow drop-top McLaren Sport onto the 15 with deft coordination of his hands, feet, steering wheel, and gear-shift. I luxuriated in the ride, my schoolbag on the floor because there was no other room for it in the tiny car.

His aviator glasses reflected the oncoming road, and with the morning sun hitting his face just right, I got an eerie premonition of the next decade, what Davis would look like at age twenty-six.

Would we still know each other years from now? Would we have Davis and Nikki stories worth telling?

Implications of such thoughts startled me. I shifted closer to my door, reclined my seat as far as the cramped sports car allowed. Then I propped one foot on the dash. Enjoying now, despite our grim mission.

"Where we going?" Davis asked.

Such. A. Loaded. Question.

"To see a lawyer."

"Are we getting divorced?"

Laughter, couldn't help it. "This guy worked for my dad. He might know something about, well, all of it."

"You know Molly was right. We probably won't be able to sneak back into the school like yesterday. Your mom's going to know."

"So will your dad. You don't seem worried."

"I haven't broken the Carlino Prime Directives, so it will only be so bad."

"Good for you." I wasn't sure I could count on such a casual reaction from Mom. But we were too far gone now. I pointed at the sign over our exit. "Get off here."

By my directions, Davis put us on East Bonanza Road. Ahead, there was a peach stucco strip mall across from the clustered garages of a U-Store franchise. I checked the address in my phone, assumed Dan Harris's office was in the strip mall. Though, judging by his clothes, a rent-by-the-month storage unit might be just as likely.

Davis turned into the lot and plucked the sunglasses from the bridge of his nose. "Is this the spot?"

Reading the signs above the businesses, I still wasn't sure. There was a dentist office, a dance studio, a hair salon, and a soaped-up window with a "Coming Soon! Count of Monte Fishto's" sign taped to the glass. Nothing indicated a law office existed within ten miles of this place.

Then, "Oh, wait."

There was a single door with a rusty, wrought iron grate over it. No adjacent windows. It occupied a space directly between a dry cleaner and a discount electronics repair, like something from the fantasy novels I read in the summers when I was little. A portal to Narnia.

There was a small placard next to that strange door. It said: "Attorney."

I tugged the handle, and the door swung open on oiled hinges. Davis bowed. *After you.*

The door opened on a corridor lit well with overhead fluorescent bars. Inside we came upon another door, frosted glass obscuring any view beyond. "Harris & Harris Law Firm" was stenciled across the pane. Beneath that, "Free Consultations."

Inside the office, I found the man I came for. Asleep at his desk, rank take-out containers emitting noxious fumes from the wastebasket.

"Mr. Harris." I covered my nose after saying it.

He sat up, palmed drool off his chin. With red, squinty eyes he stared as if he'd never seen me before. The bruise around his eye was almost completely gone, and his split lip looked more chapped than injured. His gaze shifted beyond me to Davis. He tensed. Looked beyond Davis as if expecting my entire class to mill in, too. "What is this?"

A roach skittered up the wall behind him and disappeared beneath his framed law degree. *This* is the legal genius who finally got Dad exonerated?

"It's me, Nikki Tate."

He pulled his gaze from Davis to me. Still looked confused.

"Nathan Tate's daughter."

"Stop talking to me like that. I know who you are."

Okay. Fine. "Your sign says Harris and Harris? There's more than one of you?"

"I work like I'm two lawyers. What do you want?"

"I've gotta ask you some questions about my dad."

He yawned and finally said, "Your mother was pretty clear about me keeping away from her and hers."

"Is she here?"

"Touché." He shuffled the papers on his desk in a pantomime of busyness. More than a few sheets were betting slips from local sport books. I recognized the logos. Dan Harris suffered from the most popular addiction in town.

Gambling debts might explain such low-level digs. Plenty of Rock Bottom Bettors came through Andromeda's. Their dazed, maniacal energy screaming stubborn loser. Never got that vibe from Harris, though. He'd won a big bet by getting Dad off.

This all smelled funny, and not because of the rotten garbage.

Davis spoke up. "On your door it says free consultations. She at least gets that, right?"

Harris flinched, staring Davis down for uncomfortable seconds before addressing me again. "Fine. What do you want to know? I'm an open book."

Well, that's a pleasant surprise. "You and Dad talked a lot, before he . . ."

His eyes softened, saved me from saying it. "We spent nearly three years talking. Exoneration's a slow process. No prosecutor wants to be the one who put an innocent black man away, not these days. They fought hard to maintain that he wasn't innocent. So they could stay right."

Brushing crumbs off the chair across from Harris, I took a seat and dropped my bag at my feet. "I get that. So how'd you win?"

"New DNA evidence."

That phrase was in the papers and on the news when word of a possible overturned conviction broke. Since I started poking, I found it played a factor in a lot of overturned cases. Nobody elaborated much on it, though. "New" might mean a new process, or new forensics people working the case, thus new results. I would've thought the same if I hadn't rewatched Dad's press conference again last night, anticipating today's visit, and paying close attention to Dan Harris's remarks.

I placed Dad's phone on the desk, next to a potato chip, and played the cued-up video.

Dan Harris frowned at the sound of his own voice, tinny through the iPhone speakers. "—*it's always an uphill battle to reverse legal decisions of this magnitude. However, when my office was tipped about new DNA evidence, triggering the raid on the real killer's drug compound, we had undeniable proof of*

Nathan Tate's innocence. That the Clark County DA's Office still
fought for eighteen months—"

I paused the clip. "You said the new DNA evidence triggered
the raid."

"Correct. I got the tip and was able to point the authorities in
the right direction."

"Why *you*, though?"

"Who else would get the tip?" He laughed. "I *was* Nathan's
lawyer."

"Except you weren't." I leaned over, unzipped my bag. Inside
were the folded, yellowing sheets of cheap loose-leaf paper I'd
pulled from a box in Mom's closet, the box where she kept all of
Dad's jail letters.

"When you contacted my dad because you were willing to take
on his case, he wrote us about it." I read the obsessively neat cur-
sive: *"This guy says he can help. Says he can do it pro bono with an
understanding that any future lawsuits or residuals that come
from him getting me off, we'll share. It sounds almost too good to
be true, but what else do we have now? His name's Dan Harris.
I'm going to meet him later today."*

"Okay?" Harris said.

"The letter's dated the same day that drug raid happened. I
checked against all the news articles referencing it. If Dad wrote
this letter that day, that means you got the tip and pointed the
authorities in the right direction *before* he'd accepted you as his
lawyer."

Harris pushed back into his chair, pressed his fingers into a
steeple beneath his chin. A shadow drifted across the letter, Davis
leaning in for a better look.

"That's got to be a mistake," Harris said.

"No, the prison reviews all incoming and outgoing mail, makes sure it's not like an escape plan. They time-stamped it." I turned the page so he could see the red ink verifying what I'd already explained. "How did you get a tip that helped a client you didn't have yet?"

"I don't recall."

"Wow. What happened to being an open book?"

"You know, Nikki, when you have as much knowledge as me, it's hard to remember every little detail quickly. You'll see one day when you're older."

"Fine." I'd hoped this would go a little smoother. "Why did my dad beat you up?"

He lunged forward. "He didn't beat me up. I chose not to harm my client when he was clearly unhinged."

"Unhinged about what? Why was he mad at you?"

"As I said, everything I know doesn't always rise to the surface of my mind quickly. Time and a little extra assistance can help."

"What the heck are you talking about, Dan?"

"Money," said Davis. "That's what you want, right?"

"Your words, young man. Not mine. All I'm saying is there's no telling what'll help dredge up those details I may or may not have."

"I only want to know what happened to my father. I can't pay you," I said.

"I know, Nikki. Unfortunately, pro bono only goes so far. Consultation's over." Harris stood, motioned to the door. "Now get out of this office."

CHAPTER  33

"That didn't seem helpful," Davis said. We were back in the car, en route to nowhere. I punched the dashboard.

Dan Harris was hiding something. A lot of somethings. In times like this I longed for the Vegas I'd heard about in old-timer stories and in the movies. The town where mob enforcers motivated anyone to talk, given enough time. That's where I was. Considering torture as an option.

"I'm not crazy," I reminded myself.

"No one said you were."

"The stuff with Freddy Spliff, Dan Harris lying. It's all connected. You get that, right?"

Davis answered slowly, "I get we met with a guy who probably needs to hit a Gamblers Anonymous meeting. He basically told you to come back with cash. Who does that?"

My stomach dragged on the asphalt behind us. "I saw the betting slips on his desk, but—"

"What about those pink Past Due letters in his trash under that nasty food? Or that eviction notice?"

I didn't see those things, too busy reading Harris instead of reading the room. Davis had been free to roam.

"Your mom doesn't want that guy around," Davis said. "Probably for good reason."

"Stop sounding so sensible!"

"Look, all of this is horrible, and strange. I think—"

"What? What do you think?"

Say I'm being desperate. Say this is the grief. Say it so I can get out and Uber . . . wherever. Say all of it. I dare you.

"I think we need to look more closely at what happened to Freddy yesterday. Or that dude that's crushing on your mom. That lawyer feels like a dead end."

"Oh." His extremely helpful offer calmed me down. "That is pretty sensible."

Unsheathing Dad's phone, intending to revisit the photo evidence I'd been working off for the last few days, I had several missed calls and a single text.

Mom: You've had your dad's phone this whole time? And you're not in school? Get your butt home now, Nikalosa!

Crap. I face-palmed.

"What's up?" Davis asked.

The end of life as I know it. "Nothing at all," I said, with a headshake.

There was also a voice mail, but not from Mom's number. I pressed PLAY, bringing the phone to my ear.

"This is Goose. Got one for you. Whenever you're free, we're here all day. You interested? If not, I can take a hint."

The call was forwarded from my confiscated phone. Another offer to be a biker's pet cardplayer. That's where I was. My options: Convince Davis to drive us aimlessly, go home and let Mom drop the hammer on me, or . . .

I called Goose back. He picked up on the first ring. I said, "I'm in."

♣

Goose provided the address. Beyond the borders of Las Vegas, into neighboring Henderson. The whole ride over, what I'd hastily assessed as my only good option eroded, melted into a lead ball that sat heavy in my gut. Playing for Goose hadn't seemed like a great idea when my world wasn't upside down. Except, I hadn't played since the night I lost all my money. With Dad. I'd been avoiding it.

The thing I excelled at more than any other, the last great gift my father gave me. I was afraid in a place where I was once fearless.

You interested? If not, I can take a hint.

I'd passed on the kiddie game at Brady's party. The closer we got to the rendezvous, the more I felt like ordering Davis to reverse course. I could back out. Easiest thing in the world. It would only get easier to refuse on the next game, and the next. Heck, if Mom buried me in a hole beneath the hotel, I wouldn't have a next game to worry about.

Everything around me was so wrong these days. I needed to know if I could still do this right.

We arrived. Not a casino, a bar. Four muscular chrome Harleys canted side by side next to a few random vehicles, and one not so random.

"Unbelievable," I said.

A blue Lexus with a broken headlight and a cardboard pane duct-taped over the broken window sat in the otherwise deserted lot. A certain cheater was in the house.

"Is that . . . ?" Davis said, recognizing Chuck Pearl's car, too.

"It is."

He swung a wide arc in the lot, parked with the McLaren's nose pointed at the street. Like a getaway driver.

"This is a biker bar," he said.

I didn't answer, my mind on the Lexus. If Chuck was here doing what he does, a broken window might be the least of his worries. I shouldn't care, but that piece of cardboard wasn't just patching shattered glass. It was an ugly reminder of when I'd lost control. I regretted people seeing me like that, regretted being that.

"Nikki, what are we doing here?" Davis finally asked.

Chuck, Chuck, Chuck. "First, I'm going to save a fool's life. After that, we'll see."

♥

Inside, laughs and groans. We passed from bright midday glare into dim yeasty surroundings. Old cigarette smoke flavored the air, and partially filled liquor bottles four shelves high obscured the mirror behind the varnished bar. The place was empty except for a woman, who might be a rough twenty-five or a great fifty, keeping the bar and a couple of construction workers sipping brew and clacking balls at the billiards table. We were five steps in before a lax doorman hopped off his stool.

"Think y'all got the wrong establishment." Shorter and slimmer than the patron saint who invited me, he was also a Pack member, adorned in their trademark leather vest and wielding a ball-peen hammer with a stained head I didn't want to think too hard about.

"Goose here?" I asked.

"Who's asking?"

"A potential business partner."

He seemed skeptical but didn't waste time puzzling it out on his own. He drifted to a hallway next to the bar, were the raucous noise emanated. "Goose! You got people."

The mammoth biker emerged and waved us over, a big grin splitting his scraggly beard. "She's with me." He led us to the back room. Looking past Goose, I spotted Chuck, whose face paled at the sight of me.

Other players at the table included a variety of types. All adults. All in good spirits. I only knew one thing about them, true of all cardplayers. Those good spirits got dark if they discovered a cheater.

Goose embraced me like his long-lost niece, nearly smothering me in his girth, bike leather, and cologne. In the hug, he spoke low. "I'm staking you a thousand. Can you work with that?"

He let me go, his blue eyes like spotlights. I nodded. A thousand dollars to start? No problem.

Goose noticed Davis, and I prepared to soothe any frazzled nerves my wealthy friend might be exhibiting. But Davis was not frazzled. His hand darted forward, comfortable and assertive.

"Davis."

The biker shook the extended hand. "Goose, kid. You play?"

"Nah. Never learned."

Goose shrugged and walked us to the table. Introductions were made, Goose taking me around the table, no deception. I was Nikki Tate, daughter of the late great Nathan, and Goose's potential protégé.

It wasn't cheating, not a hustle. Whatever I won with Goose's money, I got a (hopefully) fair cut. What I lost, I wasn't responsible for paying back. It's how I *thought* I was playing that night I lost my own bankroll.

I needed the game today. More than the money, I needed reassurance that I was still me.

Goose made the last introduction. "This here is Perry Sapphire."

"Have we met before?" I said to Chuck—Perry, whatever.

"I don't believe so."

Chuck's pile of chips was a bit healthier than everyone else's, though not by much. Perhaps he hadn't done too much damage yet.

"Is that your Lexus outside?"

"Yeah, that's mine." He folded, pushed away from the game. "I actually lost track of time and need to get going. Early day tomorrow."

Chuck raked his chips off the table with his forearm, and they clink-clink-clinked into a knapsack that he walked over to the banker.

"Come on," a cigar chomper in shades and a sports coat over a Def Leppard T-shirt yelled after him. "You're not going to give me a chance to win my money back?"

Chuck spoke over his shoulder. "Another time."

"Perry," I said, forcing Chuck to face me. Fresh sweat dotted his forehead. "Would you mind me taking a look at your Lexus before you leave? I've always wanted one."

"Sh-sure."

To Goose, I asked, "You all have been going a while, right?"

"About time for a smoke break."

"Good. Be right back."

I followed Chuck and his cash to the exit. Davis tailed, but gave me space.

Outside, at the Lexus, with no one in earshot, Chuck said, "Look, you crazy—"

A flash of party anger welled in me. I held up a single finger. "Uh-uh. All I gotta do is yell to my biker buddies in there, and maybe your kneecaps get a new range of motion. If you're lucky."

"It's not your money on that table."

"Not yours, either, not if you got it by cheating. Are you insane?"

"I should've stayed in Atlantic City."

"Maybe. In any case, I'm not going to rat you out."

"Gee, thanks for small favors. You only cost me a grand in car damage."

"Is your life worth a grand? That's what I just saved. Those aren't rich kids in the Ridges."

He sighed, backed off. "Tell me about it. An old buddy got me into that game, told me they were lightweights. It didn't take me long to figure they weren't that light, or that me and my buddy ain't as friendly as I thought. Not if he put me in a pool with sharks instead of whales."

"They're probably okay if you play them fair."

"Keep telling yourself that," Chuck said bitterly. "It was cool of you to let me just go. I halfway want to thank you. But I won't."

He attempted to climb into his car, but I grabbed him by the arm. He flinched.

"You don't have to thank me. Just give me your number."

"What?"

"Phone. Number. Someday, and that day may never come, I will call upon you to do me a service in return." I handed over Dad's phone.

Sneering, he punched in a number. "Didn't know chicks liked *The Godfather*."

"I love *The Godfather.*" I snatched back Dad's phone. "Answer if I call."

An eye roll and engine rev later, he was gone. I returned to the bar's entrance, where Davis waited.

"What was that about?" he asked.

"Nothing. Just the way this town works. Let's play."

CHAPTER 34

Fresh, stacked chips—courtesy of Goose—sat before me as the cigar-chomping Def Leppard fan dealt my first hand. Davis took a chair in the corner, patient, fulfilling his promise to help in any way I needed. This was it.

Three hours later and I'd turned Goose's one thousand into five. Chomper took the largest hit, calling bets on pots he had no hope of taking. Not strategic, personal. He didn't like losing to a girl, the Achilles' heel of misogynists everywhere.

Davis hung in the whole time. Really, I forgot about him for long stretches. More concerned with Dad's constantly vibrating phone. More messages from Mom, no doubt.

We hit early afternoon, and the other players called for another smoke break. I glanced to my driver and saw him in an animated conversation with Goose. Curious, I headed over and said, "Hello? I thought I was having my performance evaluated."

"I stopped watching you after the first few hands. Me and your friend here had a little chat about motor vehicles," Goose said.

Davis blushed mildly, but he had a sleepy look about him. He'd been patient, but pushing it further bordered on rude.

"Goose, I should probably go."

"Feel free. You did good today, Little Nate."

I flinched, stung. "What did you call me?"

"Little *Tate*. That's your name, ain't it?"

"Yes. You're right."

While he cashed me out, I turned to Davis. "You look like you're in need of caffeine. I'm sorry you had to sit through that."

"Been through worse." He checked the time on his phone. "School's almost over. Where to now?"

Good question. I still wasn't ready for the wrath of Mom. "Is there anyone at your place?"

Davis's cheeks flared. "*My* place?"

"Not like that," I hurried to say, heat prickling my entire body. Although I kind of wished it was like that. "I just mean . . . can we hang there? Without anyone bothering us?"

My babbling clarification didn't really make it any better. Too late to turn back.

"No one should bother us there," Davis answered with a small shake of his head.

Goose returned, handing over a roll of cash. "Fifteen hundred here. Good haul, wouldn't you say?"

"Absolutely."

"I'll be in touch if some other opportunities arise. You do the same?"

Nodding, my eyes never left the cash in my hand. Seeds to a money tree, the start of a newer, bigger bankroll to put me back on track.

"Let's go." I took Davis's hand, trying not to lose my cool (again) as electricity bolted up my arm, and led him back to the lot. Halfway to his car an angry dog started barking. At least that's what Chomper sounded like.

"Hey, girlie! Hold up a sec. We need to talk."

Girlie? I spun, defensive. Chomper, rage-faced, drew close.

Davis stepped in front of me. Chivalrous but unnecessary.

"Yeah?" I said.

"You're real good. You're going to be a monster in this game."

I'm already a monster, tool. "If you say so."

"Now hand over my coaching fee, I'll let you be on your way."

"Your coaching *what*?"

"Goose gave you something like two grand. That's about what you took off me while you were getting in some of that good practice. I'll take it back now and we won't have any problems."

The street, so far from the bustle of Downtown and the Strip, was quiet this time of day. Suddenly, coming here felt like a mistake. A trap.

Cigar Chomper extended his hand, palm up, the calluses giving a visual history of hard manual labor.

"I won this money." I felt the futility in the words. He already knew that and didn't care.

"Little girls can't win here. This is a man's game. Give me my money."

"Dude," Davis said, reinserting himself between me and the lowlife. "Walk away."

Chomper sidestepped Davis, not sparing his scrawny junior a second glance. Until Davis said, "You know Big Bert Carlino?"

Chomper paused. Whatever intimidation tactic he'd been planning in the quest for my money was preempted. "Who doesn't?"

Davis waved a hand near his own face. "Notice the resemblance?"

The next seconds ticked by long and slow, time stretching like taffy. Chomper leaned into Davis, removed his sunglasses, squinted. His eyes popped wide, recognizing bad news. "Wait. You're not—"

"Look," Davis said, clapping a hand on the stocky brute's shoulder, "what if you came to the Nysos one weekend and played some hands? Give me your name, and I'll tell my dad what a good coach you've been to my friend. Have him put you on our VIP list."

A friendly invite that didn't sound friendly at all. That charming side Davis showed with me, and at Brady's party, and with Goose wasn't on display now. This was something else.

Chomper's eyes flicked to me, uncertain.

"Seriously," Davis said, his voice so cold I expected a puff of condensation from his lips. "What's your name?"

Chomper backed away, breaking Davis's grip. "You know what, kids, I'm good. It's been a pleasure."

He shuffled toward the bar as Goose stepped out, lighting a smoke. He assessed Chomper's shifty demeanor, then cast his gaze toward us. "Everything okay here, Little Tate?"

Davis never took his eyes off the startled goon. I said, "Everything's fine. Thanks."

Chomper ducked around Goose, disappearing into the shadowy watering hole. Davis turned to me, grim, forcing a smile. "You ready?"

CHAPTER  35

"What *was* that?"

Davis shifted gears, maneuvering us back toward the Nysos. Engine noise and heat. Always the heat. I waited for his response.

He said, "You shouldn't read too much into what happened back there."

"You mean the totally not subtle way you threatened that sore loser?"

"He was going to rob you. So I just—I used a trick."

"A trick. That was total dark side of the Force, Davis. I thought that stuff about your family wasn't true."

"He doesn't know that. Are you mad at me?"

"Of course not. I just . . ."

"What?"

"I get you were trying to scare him. You scared me, too."

A good minute of silent riding passed. Sixty seconds for me to regret the way I'd said that, or that I'd said anything at all.

Davis, speaking softly, no trace of annoyance in the question, asked, "Would you rather I took you home?"

No! Absolutely not. I'd have to go eventually. Visions of my basement card room converted to a medieval dungeon inspired me to stretch this time together. "I was scared for him. Not for me. I'm fine. We're fine."

For the moment.

At the Nysos parking deck, Davis asked the valet to detail Cedric's car and keep quiet about seeing us. The man seemed hesitant until Davis punctuated the request with folded bills. With our cover bought and paid for, he took us through the Valets Only entrance, which led to a spartan cinder-block-lined corridor resembling the back passages of Andromeda's Palace. The similarities ended when we reached the elevator. No buttons, only a digital keypad. Davis punched in a code, and the doors hissed open. The cabin wasn't the boxy cars I was used to, but a glass cylinder loaded into a vertical tube like a bullet. We stepped in and were fired upward.

We cleared the first few floors in a breath, and once we passed the tenth story, views of the inner elevator shaft transitioned to more glass, the exterior panes of the hotel. Each story we rocketed past gave us a higher, more expansive few of Las Vegas. Traffic became ants milling along sanctioned routes, and people shrank, organisms under a microscope. Davis's great glass elevator began slowing around the sixtieth floor and crested to a complete stop on the seventy-seventh. We stepped into a short corridor of bleached wood floors that led to huge mahogany doors with long steel handles like you'd see on refrigerators. Davis retrieved a key card from his back pocket and touched it to a sensor in the doorjamb. The lock clacked, and one of the doors nudged outward as if by a breeze.

"Welcome to Casa Carlino."

A penthouse I expected. Without any real experience in this kind of luxury, I thought that meant a single floor. I still don't know if I was underestimating, or if this family was overachieving. The Carlino residence, with floor-to-ceiling windows as big as Jumbotron screens in football stadiums, was three stories high. Easy.

The huge living room rivaled the gaming floor at Andromeda's. Pale bamboo flooring stretched before me, decorated only by slim beige couches and welded-steel coffee tables.

Beyond the lounge area, chrome appliances in a kitchen worthy of world-class chefs. To my right, a daunting view of North Vegas and the ridges beyond. Left, a staircase leading to a partitioned-off second level. I assumed that's where the bedrooms were. Davis's bed would be up there.

He went that way, beckoning me. I climbed stairs into the lavish living quarters of one of Vegas's wealthiest families, my bag bouncing on my shoulder. In the corridor at the top of the stairs, photos were arranged in neat grids along the wall. Casual smiling pics of a round-bellied Big Bert when he was a size more fitting his name. Cheesy matching sweater family photos featuring super-young Carlino brothers, Big Bert, and a pretty brunette woman.

I lingered on those. "Your mom?"

"Yes. And those are all our horrible haircuts."

"Please. Your haircut's way worse in this one." I pointed to a grade-school photo of snaggletoothed Davis rocking shaggy, foppish locks. He didn't disagree.

A whole section of wall was dedicated to Davis and his brother. Davis receiving a blue ribbon at a science fair. Cedric in peewee football pads. Davis dressed as a cowboy at some Wild West–looking amusement park. Several snaps of Cedric in his baseball glory days, sliding into base, or looking every bit an all-star in pinstripes with his bat cocked.

Of all the dark stuff I'd heard about Big Bert Carlino, this elaborate display presented undisputed truth. He loved his sons.

"You little turd!"

I spun at the shout. Cedric shot past me and decked Davis in the jaw, sent him sprawling.

"Take my car? Again? You know how much it cost to fix that dent in my Bugatti?"

Davis shifted onto his butt, massaging his jaw. "More than my orthodontia, I'm guessing."

Cedric huffed, his eyes flicked to me. "Nikki, you might need a new boyfriend after today. This one's gonna get broken."

My mind whirred with the sudden ferocity, and the question of whether Davis was my boyfriend. Also how calmly Davis took the sneak attack. Did this happen a lot?

With clenched fists and jaw, Cedric rushed Davis. Before I could stop myself, I had jumped on his back, trying to redirect him. "Cedric, no!"

"Get off me," Cedric said, whipping back and forth, trying to throw me as gently as he could, though I hung tight.

Davis was on his feet then. "Stop before you hurt her."

Too late. One hip twist and lost grip later, I collided with the wall, sending about a dozen photos clattering to the floor with me in a rain of sharp, poking frame edges. "Ow!"

At that, calm and self-deprecating Davis disappeared. He caught a distracted Cedric—who was trying to help me up—off guard with a swift hook that rocked his brother. Cedric stumbled, rebounded off the opposite wall, regained his footing in a bouncy boxer's stance.

But a referee ended it before it began. "Enough, you two!"

Big Bert stood at the top of the stairs, taking it all in, none too pleased.

Cedric said, "Dad, he—"

"Shut it!" He was speaking to his son, but looking at me. "Nikki, come with me."

The casual use of my name shook me more than if he'd sprouted fangs and pinned me with glowing red eyes. "Wh-where?" I stammered.

Davis interrupted. "Dad."

"Quiet." Barely a whisper, it shut Davis down. To me, Big Bert said, "Come on, young lady."

He offered a hand to help me up. I was scared not to take it. When his fleshy fingers grasped me, I felt the potential power in them. The palm was sandpaper rough, and the knuckles were bolts beneath his skin. Tugged back on my feet, I accidently stepped on one of the downed frames and cracked it. "I'm sorry, really sorry."

I attempted kneeling to collect the things I'd knocked over and destroyed, but Big Bert still had my hand, and his grip tightened. "No need. Delano!"

Was Delano an Italian curse word? Did he just recite an incantation like Harry freaking Potter?

Footsteps reverberated, the sound growing louder and closer. Big Bert's funeral escort and Davis's sometimes driver rose from the stairwell. "Yes, sir?"

"Could you collect these pictures and make sure my sons don't kill each other while I attend to Nikki."

There it was again. My name rolling off his tongue with such ease.

He finally released my hand and I knew I should follow. Davis and I locked eyes, his concern for me obvious. For the first time, our own telepathy kicked in. Each of us silently assuring the other we'd be okay.

I left the brothers, followed Big Bert downstairs.

He walked to the nearest couch, motioned for me to sit. I did.

"Does your mother know where you are?" he asked.

I almost lied. This felt like a lying situation. I had my own questions, though, and gambled on some honesty quid pro quo. "No. Why were you at my dad's funeral?"

He heavy-sighed. Focused on the city well beyond his glass walls. "We knew each other before his incarceration," he said plainly, unexpected. "Vegas isn't as big as you think."

"Knew each other how?"

A cordless phone sat on a table next to me. He passed me the handset. "You should call your mother."

Him, a few feet from me, concentrating on the view, was different from the cool and scary demeanor he'd perfected in news photos, and when he'd come to offer condolences. He seemed sad. Torn.

Something hit me. A remote possibility that never crossed my mind during these trying days since Dad died. "Mr. Carlino, were you and my father friends?"

His back straightened, raising his height to something more appropriate for his nickname. "Call. Your. Mother. Right—" He erupted into a coughing fit, doubling over and clapping a hand to his mouth. The sound like an old car engine fighting to start.

"Mr. Carlino." I was on my feet, unsure how I could help.

"I'm fine," he managed between moist, harsh hacks. He took the seat I'd abandoned.

"I'll get Davis and Ced—"

"No. It's passing." His breathing steadied. He planted the hand he'd used to stifle the cough on the couch cushion by his thigh. "I'm going to have to insist you call your mother now."

I might've resisted more, pushed to know if him and Dad were indeed friends. But he lifted his hand, the one that caught those horrible coughs, from the couch and didn't realize what he'd left behind.

"Yes, sir." I dialed Mom's phone, putting one hundred percent of my attention on the numbers I punched. Anything so I didn't look at that cushion. The one smeared with Big Bert's blood.

CHAPTER 36

My call with Mom was scary brief. She ripped into me immediately. What did I think I was doing? Where did I get off running wild all day? Where was I?

That last question was the only one I answered. "I'm at the Nysos."

Silence.

"Mom?"

"Bert's there, isn't he? Put him on the phone."

I passed the handset.

"Gwen," he said.

Notes and inflections flitted from the handset. Nothing I could make out. Big Bert nodded and pinched the bridge of his nose as if staving off a headache.

"She's fine," he said. "I'll have security escort you up when you arrive."

Mom's volume increased sharply. Big Bert twisted away from me. "Yes, I like all my parts exactly where they are. No need for threats, Gwen. She'll be waiting for—" He held the phone at arm's length, perplexed. The universal look of getting hung up on.

"That went about as well as expected," he said.

"How'd you know my dad, Mr. Carlino?"

"It'll take your mom a while to get here in traffic," he said, totally glossing over my question.

"Mr. Carlino—"

"I have Davis to deal with. Your mother has you. That's all you're getting." That came with an edge. I didn't push further.

"Wait here." He said it like I had options.

He ascended the stairs, letting out a few light coughs, but nothing like before. I sat there for the eternity it took Mom to reach the Nysos. For every single second of it, Big Bert berated his youngest son in thumping bass tones that reverberated throughout the residence. I couldn't discern words from where I sat, but I took it as a preview of what I'd be getting soon enough. In the midst of it, Cedric descended to my level, smirking. He flopped onto the far end of the couch, kicked his feet up on the coffee table, and bobbed his head like his father's yelling was his favorite song.

I said, "You didn't have to hit him, you know."

"Oh, yes I did! Little thief."

"So you're enjoying this?"

"A little. He'll probably hear about it for the rest of the night. Maybe lose his phone and Internet privileges for a while. It'll blow over."

"Lucky him."

His smile retracted. "How bad will it be for you? I have a hard time thinking your mom's going to take this well."

He was right, but I didn't feel like agreeing with him, so I said nothing.

"Your family doesn't seem to like us much," Cedric continued.

That, I couldn't resist. "But why? Your dad said he knew my father back in the day. Then he shut down. Do you know anything at all?"

He shook his head. "Above my pay grade. Everybody in town knows us, and half of them hate us."

"Is that something you get used to?"

"Yeah. You learn to live with it, then use it. There's a certain satisfaction in being better than the people who don't like you. You know that, Little Miss Card Shark."

Truth. On the field, at the card table. There's nothing like beating an enemy.

"Speaking of"—Cedric leaned toward me, his words slicker than before, the always hustling pitchman—"I got a proposition for you. Poker. I want in on those famous skills of yours."

"In how?" I asked suspiciously.

"Teach me. Teach some of my friends. You know I can pay whatever."

That was unexpected. Flattering. One problem. "I'm really close to being sentenced to solitary confinement. It's going to hit the fan when my mom gets here."

He shook his head. "You won't be locked down forever. I want to know how you think when you play, how you spot cheaters, all of it."

"Why me? You're a Carlino. You could hire Phil Ivey if you wanted."

"Who?"

He really did need lessons. "Don't worry about it. I thought Big Bert didn't want his boys in card games."

Quietly, with eyes on the stairs, he said, "Big Bert's stubborn and short-sighted. Texas Hold'em is the most popular card game in any casino with a poker room. It's the game to know."

Gongs sounded. Big Bert thundered down the stairs. Fee-fi-fo-fum. Cedric leaned away, whispered, "Think it over."

At the door, Big Bert smoothed imaginary wrinkles from his pants and suit coat before letting my mom in. A Nysos security guard followed her, clutching a walkie. "Anything else, Mr. Carlino?"

"Not now. Thank you."

The guard stepped out, and Mom stood rooted in place, her neck craning; she seemed to forget she'd come with war in mind.

On the staircase, Davis appeared, sulking. He came only half-way down before stopping. Maybe he knew what I knew, that we shouldn't get near each other in this moment. The other Carlino-Tate meeting taking place in the room was going to be volatile enough.

"Hi there, Gwen," Big Bert said.

"Bertram."

We knew each other before his incarceration. Vegas isn't as big as you think.

Moms eyes settled on me. Hardness resumed. "Get up!"

I sprang from the couch. She crossed the room in quick strides, her hand clamping on to my arm, yanking like a violent dog owner snatching a scared pup's leash.

"Mom!"

"Walk, Nikki."

I shuffled, my pace controlled by the maternal vise squeezing my soft underarm.

"Ma'am," the manservant Delano said, suddenly appearing. He held my bag. "Don't forget this."

It must have fallen during the commotion from before. Mom allowed me a slight reprieve to reclaim my belongings.

Safely across the threshold, Mom faced Big Bert. "I don't know what's going on here—"

"It's okay." He was as gracious as the day of the funeral. "I'm sure Davis is just as responsible for all of this as Nikki."

"Oh, I wasn't apologizing," Mom said. "I'm telling you and your boy to keep away from my daughter. I don't care what you've done or how much money you have or what you're capable of, come near her again and I will *kill* you. Nikki, let's go."

Another glimpse of Davis was all I wanted, because I believed my mother, believed she'd do anything to keep us apart, even murder. One last glimpse, just in case she succeeded.

Big Bert closed the door, robbing me of even that.

♠

"Is that where you were all day? Lounging in the penthouse with that boy like some—" She stopped herself, kneaded three fingers into her temple while keeping her other hand on the steering wheel. "Just tell me where you were today. If you lie to me, I swear . . ."

"I went to see Dan Harris." All the James Bond spy stuff was wearing on me. Plus, admitting a little like that, I wouldn't have to tell about Goose's card game. Or the new bankroll in my pocket. A blaring horn to my right gave me an excuse to look away from her without seeming like I was *trying* to look away.

"You . . . what?"

Something in her voice. I sensed a misstep but couldn't change direction quick enough. "I talked to him about Dad's murder."

"You're a detective now? Are you crazy? God, I let you watch too much TV."

We're doing this? Fine. "The cops are useless. You don't care. Somebody has to."

"Did he tell you anything helpful so you can solve your mystery?"

"You don't have to patronize me."

"Dan Harris is a parasite. I told you he doesn't have our best interests at heart. Did you learn anything that contradicts that?"

No. I didn't. But I'd never admit it. "Do you care?"

She clucked her tongue. Her breaths gained weight until they were the heavy exhales of a bull. "You don't know what you think you know."

"Obviously! How did you and Dad know Mr. Carlino? Let's start there."

"Let's start with you skipping school, disobeying me—*disrespecting* me—over and over again. We'll start there, and stay there for, say, the next six months. All this running around, doing any and everything you want . . . over. School and home. That's all. Don't even think about playing the soccer card—I know you quit."

"But—"

"Accept it. That's your best move right now."

"Like the way you accepted Dad was going to die in jail, and when he didn't, it messed up your plans to move on."

"Don't get *slapped*, Nikalosa."

"You want it to be easy and neat. Nothing for you and Tomás to be guilty about. Right."

"Nothing about Tomás and me concerns you today. You're the one in trouble. Sneaking around with a boy you've got no business being with."

What a hypocrite. "Learned it by watching you."

Traffic kept us still, trapped together. Her upper lip curled and her brow furrowed as if attempting to switch places. She squeezed her eyes shut. The expression was familiar, burned in my memory from the time I smeared the carpet with chocolate pudding or got caught smoking cigarettes under the middle school bleachers. The peak frustration look. Good.

She said, "Nikki, I will always love your father. Always. He's gone, though."

"For like a"—my voice cracked—"a week."

"No. For five years. He's been gone a very long time."

Hadn't I considered how normal it seemed with Dad no longer around, too? Didn't I treat him like an overbearing nuisance when he was still here? But my gut said keep fighting. Our bickering felt as natural as corner kicks and raising bets.

"I'm right here, Mom. Say what you have to say."

"When they locked him in a cell, they put us in one, too. A bigger one. You're making yourself not understand because, I don't know, you're grieving and that's what you need. I need things, too. If you don't want to be coddled, then you'll hear this straight. I wanted to do this differently, but I can't see this getting easier between us anytime soon. I'm selling Andromeda's Palace."

The shock flung me forward like a collision, with so much force my safety belt bit into my neck and collarbone. I wrestled the harness for some slack, then twisted in my seat, facing her. "Did Tomás talk you into it?"

"No."

"You're like the worst business person ever. Now you're wheeling and dealing prime Vegas real estate? All on your own. Hardly."

"What I've done to inspire such a lack of faith from you, I'll never know. Rest assured, this decision is all me. If I hadn't been concerned with being the loyal wife who supported her husband's dreams no matter what, I'd have put Andromeda's on the auction block years ago."

"Without talking to me first, of course."

"About what? You're leaving. That's your plan. Play in those god-awful card games, win four years of tuition, and leave Vegas in the dust because you feel all alone in the big bad world."

Stunned, I stared.

"I used to think my mother didn't know what I was up to, either," Mom said. "Surprise. Here's something that'll really shake your bratty woe-is-me routine: The right price and buyer means your tuition's covered for any school you want on the planet. It means *I* can go to school and learn something other than how to clean vomit off craps tables, if I want. That sale means all the things you ever complained about are—*poof!*—gone. We both get to have the life we want. So who you mad at now, little girl?"

The words rattled around my head like the dice at those tables she hated so much. Who, indeed?

CHAPTER 37

We didn't speak again in the car, or in the elevator. Mom selected the floor while I stared at her shoes. The doors opened on Dad's floor, not ours.

"Come on." Mom let us into Dad's room with her manager's key. It was clean. The pristine arrangement of a housekeeping visit. Bed made. Bathroom scrubbed. Dad's closet empty. His—my—photos gone.

I rushed ahead of Mom, ran my fingers over the wallpaper . . . not even remnants of tape.

"What did you do?" I said, my voice rising. "Where is it all?"

"Those photos have been shredded. Your father's clothes are on their way to the Goodwill."

"No." I stepped fully into his closest. Was there clothing the housekeepers missed? "You should've asked me."

The tears came. I shouldn't have been so weak over clothes and photos. They weren't him.

"The next guest that checks in is getting this room," Mom said.

I blinked through a wet prism. "You're so glad he's gone!"

"You didn't get enough of this in the car?"

"You don't cry for him. You throw his stuff away." I ripped the comforter off the bed, just because. "You said things were better when he wasn't here."

A head tilt, the posture of a curious cat. "I never said that to him. Nikki"—panic usurped the frustration in her tone—"I did not. Who told you that?"

No one told me she said those things. I wasn't talking about her at all.

I skirted past her, up the stairs to my room, sealed myself inside. Or tried to. My locks were gone.

Adjoining hotel suites have two interior doors that face each other like the bread in a sandwich. Each room can close and lock their respective door to prevent the neighbor from crossing into the other suite. Usually. Where there used to be a knob and a dead bolt on my side, there were now empty holes. I poked my fingers through and wiggled them.

All this running around, doing any and everything you want . . . over.

No. It wasn't. Because as bad as that fight was, Mom forgot to take Dad's phone.

With my door permanently ajar, I sat in the floor, my back pressed against my bed, and texted Davis. No response at all. Big Bert might still be yelling at him.

On a whim, I dialed Freddy Spliff. A desperate, futile act.

He answered.

"Hello?"

I rocked forward on my knees, whispering in case Mom had made her way upstairs. "Freddy?"

"Hi, Nikki."

I checked the display, ensuring I'd dialed the right contact. It *was* Freddy Spliff's number, but the coherent gentleman on the line sounded like an impostor.

"I'm glad you called," he said. "I may not have been brave enough to call you myself."

"Are you all right? I saw men take you. Who were they?"

"The Helpers."

"Like elves?"

He laughed, a kind sound. Better than any sound he made

drunk. "They work at Help House. It's a halfway house. Where I live right now."

A halfway house? I knew what they were, vaguely. Housing for people fresh from jail who didn't have a permanent residence. I always understood them as way stations for ex-cons trying to get back on their feet. Not employers of goon squads to snatch people into dark vans.

"Why would people from a halfway house grab you like that?"

Stuttering, flustered, he answered, "Because I asked them to. I know my weaknesses, and I made it clear to them what those were, and how they might help me."

"Weaknesses?"

"Drinking," he said. "Lying."

My throat constricted. "You weren't lying to me. Not about my dad."

"I was so drunk, I barely remember what I told you."

"It was about scams my dad was looking into and the people who were onto him. You said—"

"When I'm like that, Nikki, not much of what I say can be relied upon. That's some of what Nathan and I did talk about. The way I messed up with my family, how my drinking and ending up in jail made it so I can't go talk to my own daughter. When I heard about your dad's death, I fell off the wagon. Hard."

"But—"

In the background, a muffled voice spoke and the line went mute. Someone's in the room with Freddy. Who? Why?

Background sound broke the silence as Freddy unmuted the line. "I have to go. I'm sorry if I upset you. Remember Nathan was a good man. That's what he would've wanted you to know."

"He would've wanted his killer brought to justice. He would've wanted to not be beaten to death in an alley. He would've wanted to be home for five years instead of rotting in a cell for something he didn't do. Don't tell me what my dad wanted. He's dead, and he doesn't want anything anymore."

My words weren't spoken. They were shouted. The kind no one really listened to. Freddy was no different. He'd hung up.

♣

Along with Dad's phone were all those photos. When Mom was in the deepest part of her sleep, I snuck downstairs to the offices. Printed select pictures, stole a tape dispenser. I spent the rest of the night redecorating.

CHAPTER 38

"Get up. Time for school." Mom didn't bother knocking as she unlatched her still-functioning lock and granted herself entrance into my space. "What have you done?"

Pushing up from my sprawled state, the position I'd collapsed in sometime around 3:00 a.m., tape strips stuck to my fingers, I joined her in admiring the collage I'd pieced together over my windows. A sampling of Dad's pictures. Nowhere near as numerous as those she'd disposed of. Equally obsessive, though.

I waited.

"Get dressed," she said, and left.

My tiny protest was a victory.

♥

Radio and road noise were the only sounds between us until we hit the crowded Vista Rojo lot. My agitated classmates milled about in familiar droves. Cardinal Graham had struck back.

"Is this a fire drill?" Mom asked, inching the car forward. Chants of "GRIF-FIN BLOOD! GRIF-FIN BLOOD!" ringing, Mom's face clouded. This was supposed to be my return to order.

"Don't worry," I said. "This is just your public-education dollars at work. See you this afternoon."

I waded into the crowd, wedging between shoulders. A maintenance man balanced precariously at the top of an extension ladder, unmooring something like a charred corpse from above the main entrance.

"It's the mascot," Molly announced, appearing by my shoulder like my good angel. "The costume, anyway."

Gavin was at my other side. "Minus the head."

He held his phone for me. There was a picture of the VR Lions mascot Leonard's head on a pike, *Game of Thrones*–style.

"You okay? Did you get what you needed yesterday?" Molly asked.

"Not exactly."

She didn't push for details. I didn't offer them. I just wanted a normal school day.

We made our locker rounds. When I spun the combination on mine, a flurry of loose projectiles fell to the floor.

Playing cards. Five of them. Two were faceup with a word scribbled on each in silver Sharpie ink. The ace of clubs scrawled with the word *OR*, and the eight of spades featuring the word *OFF*. The other three showed their customized backs, deep dark space and misty cosmos. Cards from Andromeda's Palace.

"Nikki?" Molly said.

Kneeling, I flipped over the facedown cards. All except one. I turned it three times before realizing it wasn't a playing card but a cut card. No suit, face, or number. Just the starry background design repeated on both sides, meant to cover the card on the bottom of the deck so no one got a glimpse when the dealer unloaded. The remaining two cards were playing cards, each scrawled with a single word: the eight of clubs (*BACK*) and the ace of spades (*ELSE*).

Gavin leaned over me, eclipsing the overhead light. "What's it mean?"

I arranged the five cards in the only order that made sense.

BACK OFF OR ELSE.

The phrase was clear. There was an additional message, though. The cards—their suits and denominations—were not random. The hand was specific. Some cardplayers would call it mythic. Legend.

It was the same five-card draw hand held by the lawman/gunfighter Wild Bill Hickok when he was murdered way back in the day. A single shot to the back of his head. It's most common name . . .

The dead man's hand.

CHAPTER 39

"Is this the way you run your school?" Mom fanned the cards across Principal Flagstaff's desk in their proper order, then tapped her index finger on the cut card, hard.

"Mrs. Tate, as I've explained—"

"You had an incident. Misguided football pranks. But football players didn't do this." Another poke at the cards for emphasis.

I didn't call Mom. Molly did. Big bad team captain said this had gone too far. Gavin backed her up. Traitors.

Principal Flagstaff made another attempt to rationalize. "Typically, our campus is a model of safety and discipline. The week of the Cardinal Graham game is one of heightened emotion."

"Do you know what happened to my husband?" Mom asked, acidic.

He tugged at his tie. "I'm aware."

"Then you'll understand why I'm pulling Nikki out of this school. Today."

"Mom!" I was arguing about getting to leave school? The world had gone mad.

"Get your things," she demanded. "We're going."

Principal Flagstaff stood as Mom did. "Mrs. Tate, that's your decision. Certainly. But isn't this a bit of an overreaction?"

"If there's paperwork, email me. Nikki!"

I was on my feet, gathering the cards off the desk. Mom left the office.

"Sorry," I said to my principal, though I wasn't sure what I'd apologized for.

News radio squawked on our way back to the casino, occasionally interrupted by Mom's mumbling. She wasn't talking to me. It could be a while before we engaged in anything resembling civil discourse. I'd seen her like this before, most memorably during the early days of Dad's incarceration, when Andromeda's had been on the brink. *More* on the brink. I'd stirred up something she didn't want me near. It was breaking her.

"Mom." I didn't know how to continue.

The radio announcer's voice boomed, "*BREAKING NEWS*," followed by the station's synthesizer theme. "*Body discovered in Northeast Las Vegas this morning. Police are reporting that Daniel Bartholomew Harris, a local attorney, was found dead in the predawn hours, the apparent victim of a brutal robbery . . .*"

"Oh god."

Back off or else.

Not a prank, as my mom said. Not a prank at all.

CHAPTER  40

Freaked wasn't the proper term after hearing the news about Harris.

I sat in Andromeda's back office, pressing my palms flat on my desk because it was the only way to make them not shake. Mom, more freaked than me, insisted I stay within earshot. From her office, hunched over the phone, she'd break her conversation every few minutes confirming we were okay. Though we weren't.

"Nikki?"

"Still here." With four of the local news websites open on my monitors, all of them with similar reports. Pictures of Dan Harris from younger, better days.

Sitting there was torture, but when I broached the possibility of retreating to my room, Mom insisted I stay. She had lunch brought in and put me to work on a few spreadsheets. Anything to keep me near.

It went on like that for hours.

Davis: molly told me.

I held the phone beneath my desk, constantly flicking glances toward Mom's office.

Me: molly told everyone. ☹
Davis: how could someone get to your locker?
Me: idk. that's not the worst thing. dan harris is dead.

A text bubble with animated ellipses appeared while he typed something back. It stayed there a minute. Disappeared. A few seconds and it returned. Vanished again.

Me: still there?

Davis: not from natural causes, i take it.

Me: the news says a "robbery."

Davis: i'm worried about you. this is getting way out of control.

Me: i must be close to something. all this wouldn't happen if i wasn't.

Davis: thus the back off message. this is scary. you SHOULD stop.

Me: did you get in a lot of trouble?

Davis: you're changing the subject. someone else is DEAD, nikki. DEAD.

Me: mom's calling me. gotta go.

She wasn't, and I didn't. Needed to think.

Davis: text me later please. i'm trying to help.

I stared at the phone a while. Why didn't it feel that way?

Mom rounded my cubicle's corner. I slid the phone into my bag. "We're done in here," she said. "Come with me."

On the gaming floor I examined every patron with new suspicion. Back off or else.

"I've got a meeting with some prospective buyers in a few minutes," Mom said. "I want you to wait for me upstairs."

"Buyers." She was really going through with this. Andromeda's wasn't going to be ours anymore.

"They haven't made an offer, but this is a first step. We'll see."

"Buyers," I said again.

"Nikki, we haven't been communicating on good terms in a while. I want to fix that tonight. There's too much happening to be keeping each other in the dark. I have to do this first, so please, go upstairs."

More handling, more treating me like I didn't halfway run this place. If there was a meeting with buyers, I should've been included. "Sure, Mom. Whatever you say."

She continued farther onto the floor without me, angling toward a group of four well-heeled Japanese men huddled together near one of the *Star Wars*–themed digital slot machines, where you dropped tokens through one of the vents in Darth Vader's face-plate. They weren't playing. Only observing.

Mom bowed when they noticed her, and they returned the gesture. They moved in a pack to the Constellation Grill.

I passed the elevators for the staff entrance into the kitchen. Took a corridor I hadn't used in far too long, descended stairs into my card room.

Navigating the dark, I found the breaker box and lit the room, breathed stale air. The card table was as I'd left it, all the folding chairs collapsed and leaning against it. The door leading out to the alley was barred. At the old blackjack table, a change. A folded sweatshirt rested there.

The hoodie I recognized. Gavin's. Forgotten the last time we'd all been here.

The folding was new. I'd been to Gavin's house. They didn't fold anything.

Housekeeping? No. They never came down here. Circling the table for a closer look, I found more strangeness in the floor, out of sight. A cardboard box of files with the lid askew, a half-empty bottle of bourbon, and an iPhone charger dangling from an outlet.

Dad had been here.

I forgot about Gavin's shirt, examining this left-behind nest. Not only was Dad here. He was here often, judging from the bottle.

My back against the wall, I slid down, sitting as I imagined he did. The bourbon was top-shelf, probably straight from our bar. This space—this nook—felt cramped. Claustrophobic. He'd chosen this over a seat at the poker table that used to belong to him.

Did we drive you here? Mom and her obvious crush? Me and my anger? Did you get used to being alone, the same way we got used to being without you?

Taking the lid off the box revealed a yellow folder resting atop the other files. I flipped through. A lot of forms. City records, supply invoices, receipts. Financial relics of fiscal years gone by.

There was no way to know what Dad ultimately sought in these files where the smudged debits and credits bled into each other. The only significance I saw in any of it was the dates. These were records from the year Andromeda's Palace opened.

I rifled through more folders, gawking at the astronomical amounts it took to get the casino up and running. Each subsequent file like time travel, tracking backward from opening day to when the first patch of starry carpet was laid.

The last batch of folder tabs were marked "mortgage" and "loan docs" and "business plan—final." I almost ignored them, anticipating more nonsense numbers. The business plan struck my curiosity. How did Dad convince a Las Vegas bank to back his cardplayer paradise?

It was in a regal red file folder made of fine card stock, more like fabric than paper. Definitely meant to impress whoever got their hands on it.

Spreading the folder in my lap unveiled an introductory letter I'd never ever read in its entirety. I got stuck on the names above the salutation, written in fancy script:

Bertram Carlino, Nathaniel Tate & Jonathan Reedy
Doing Business As the Poseidon Group

"They were partners!" I slammed the business plan on the table, generating a thunderclap and a jittery start from Mom and her guests. "Not just friends. Partners!"

Mom recovered fast, plastered on a congenial grin. "Excuse me, gentlemen."

She picked it up, touched my shoulder oh so gently, and guided me away.

Her smile remained fixed, her words oozed anger: "Have you lost your entire mind?"

"Dad started this place with Mr. Carlino and John Reedy? You didn't think that was important enough to tell me before?" I jabbed a finger at the folder. "The Poseidon Group? All that construction around town? We're a part of that?"

"No," Mom hissed, "we are not. Not anymore."

All the struggles that had blurred together over the years— short payrolls, cutting the hours of Mr. Héctor and workers like him, fears of shutting down. The Poseidon Group was everywhere. Rich and dominant and set to rival the biggest developers in Vegas for the next century. My dad, our family, had a hand in the origins of a rising god.

But no more.

Tendrils uncurled and stretched in my head, reaching for answers that felt as close as Mom, yet as distant as the highest peak of the Nysos. My parents' reaction to Davis, all those Poseidon Group Property pictures in Dad's phone, the folder and the bourbon and the charger in my card room. Was Dad looking through this stuff on the night he died?

The Japanese businessmen left their booth, trading anxious, telling looks. Mom spat at me, "Don't you say a word." Then, "Gentleman! Would you like more drinks? Please, let the waitress know. Anything you want is on the house."

"We are very sorry," the eldest businessman said, not sounding sorry at all. "We have pressing matters at another property. Your proposal will be taken under consideration. We will be in touch."

"But—" They were in motion before Mom finished.

"Wait here." Mom chased them.

Nope. "I'll see you upstairs."

"Nikki!"

I exited the Grill swiftly, grabbed the first elevator to our floor. Mom's head whipped between the buyers and me. She quick-stepped my way, heels clacking. "Hold it."

The elevator doors shut, and I did nothing to stop them. If she couldn't be open with me, then I wasn't obeying her. We were going to have this out.

I prepared for the fight to end all fights. The elevator opened on our floor. I hustled to our room, entering while registering an oddity too late.

My exterior door was open.

Inside shadows felt deeper than usual and the temperature was off, like wading into tepid water. Perfect for hiding.

So occupied with Mom, I let the door close behind me. The lock clacked at the same moment my internal alarms sounded. There was a presence. I wasn't alone.

My hand grazed the light switch. A glove clamped painfully over my wrist.

"Leave it," the intruder said. "Much more cozy like this."

CHAPTER 42

In the dim room, he felt a dozen feet tall with gorilla strength, the power to rip me apart. He exerted grinding pressure on the delicate bones in my hand. The involuntary scream shooting up my throat hit a roadblock when his other gloved hand formed a seal over my mouth.

"Come on." He increased the pressure on my arm, using it like a ferryman's oar to steer me deeper into the room. My mattress caught the back of my knees, forcing them to buckle. He released me and I rocked backward onto my bed.

Horrors presented themselves. What he might do—what he *could* do—in this intimate space of mine. I became a pill bug, curling into myself, knees to chest. Prepared to piston my legs at him if he came closer.

There were no weapons here beyond what might be improvised from disposable nail files or scattered hairpins. I'd fight, though. I told myself that, screamed it inside my head, though the terror kept me from producing actual sound.

"You need to stop your digging," he said.

My muscles unclenched. His words sank in.

He smacked my foot lightly. "Say you understand."

I understood. This was Back Off Or Else, live.

He pressed, the roughness of his voice ringing false. Exaggerated. "Say 'I will stop digging into things that aren't my business.' I need to know we're on the same page. Do it before I break your nose."

"I will stop digging into things that aren't my business."

"Good. That was easy. Things will stay easy if you mean it. Do you?"

"I—I do."

"You better. For your sake, and your mother's. Are we clear?"

"Yes. There's something you should see first." I reached for the lamp next to the bed.

"Careful." His fingers grazed my shoe.

"It's all right." A switch flip and the room lit. "Behind the drapes, there are photos you should take with you."

His black mask swiveled that way, and I quickly took in all that I could despite the sudden brightness stinging my eyes. He wasn't nearly as big as he'd seemed in shadow, and his excessive dark clothing had a slimming effect. The black denim pants, the leather jacket over his navy-blue turtleneck. A split in the drapes gave a partial view of the photos affixed to the glass, proof that I wasn't lying. When he turned and crossed to the window, a slash of color broke his ninja motif. The yellow lining inside his jacket was sunshine bright.

He plucked at the edge of my drapes and dragged one hanging swath aside. Air puffed the mouth of his mask when he cursed in his real voice, the exaggerated gruffness forgotten.

I'd heard that voice before. Yesterday. At the Carlino's home, when he returned my bag.

Delano.

Photos of the Nysos, each shot with painstaking detail, were taped to the glass in neat chronological rows. My intimidator was drawn by the meticulous nature of it all. His focus on me broken, giving me the only chance I had.

I ran.

CHAPTER 43

The door leading into the hallway was not an option. It opened *into* my room and would cost me precious seconds if I stopped to pull it. I'd learned that playing hide-and-seek with Molly as a kid. The game I was in now would come with a much harsher lesson if I lost.

Thanks to Mom, I had another play.

When she removed the locks from my interior door, I never bothered closing it. Now the only barrier between mine and Mom's side of the suite was *her* interior door. I threw all my weight at it.

Please don't be locked. Please don't be locked.

I hit the door without bracing myself, consigned to break my arm and/or dislocate my shoulder if she'd engaged her dead bolt.

The door gave, swinging away as I flung myself into Mom's room, my unused key card still in hand.

"Hey!" the intruder yelled.

Spinning, I slammed the door behind me, turning the lock in one smooth motion.

The door rattled in its frame as the man collided with it. I didn't wait to see how long it held. I ran again, out of the room, praying that lock bought me the time I needed.

I wouldn't make the elevator and wasn't going to try. But I had options. Seven, to be exact.

The room across from Mom's had no Do Not Disturb placard dangling from the knob; it would do. I keyed in and closed it softly, bracing it with my back.

The guest space I'd infiltrated was "housekeeping neat." The bed was unmade. Soggy towels fragrant with soap and shampoo made a damp mound on the bathroom floor. I faced the door on tiptoes so I could peer through the peephole.

He emerged from my room, his neck twisting back and forth as he stalked the corridor. Seeing no motion, he went for the exterior door on Mom's side of the suite, thinking I was still inside. He hammered the door with his fist twice before abandoning the tactic and lifting his knee to piston a kick at the lock plate.

A clear ding, louder than my slamming pulse, signaled the opening elevator. How long since I'd come up here? A minute? Two? Long enough for Mom to catch a car?

The masked man turned that way.

"Hey!" A man's voice shouting. "Get away from that door."

My intruder did a quick about-face, ran. Seconds later another sprinter whirred by. Behind him, my mom, yelling, "Nikki!"

In a frantic attempt to gain entrance to the room, to me, she fumbled her key card. I popped from my hiding place across the hall. "Mom."

She spun and threw her arms around me protectively. Tomás continued chasing the intruder. I was glad to see him for the first time in *ever*. He popped into the stairwell for a second, then returned to the corridor, grim-faced.

"He's gone," Tomás said, lifting his windbreaker sleeve to his mouth like he used to, before remembering he was no longer wired to the rest of the security team. He motioned with his chin. "Open the door so I can call it in."

Mom obliged, and we entered the suite together, all three of us—also a first. Tomás got on the phone. "Barry, it's me. Look, we got a trespasser in the stairwell, likely trying to get out of the hotel. Get someone by the doors and elevators. He's approximately six two, in all black, masked, but I'd bet he's lost that by now."

Something occurred to me, the bright liner fabric. "He might have on yellow. His jacket might be"—I struggled for the word—"reversible."

Tomás side-eyed me but didn't question it. "Could be wearing a black or yellow top. Call me in the Tate residence when you get him. Do not let him slip through . . ."

Rattling off more instructions to his former teammates, Tomás quarterbacked the situation deftly, as he'd always done. Mom sat me down on her bed, examining me for knife wounds, bullet holes, and claw marks. "Baby, are you okay? Tell me what happened." Her patting and rubbing was a comfort I'd forgotten, triggering the shakes as she massaged away my adrenaline rush.

I told. All of it. When I recited the *stop digging into things that aren't your business* part and said I was certain Big Bert's man Delano was the one relaying the message, Tomás shot Mom a look.

"We gotta call this in, Gwen," he said. "It's gone too far now."

"What's gone too far?" I asked.

Mom ignored me. "I know, I know. But how much do we say?"

"As much as we have to. As little as we can."

Stiff nods from Mom. "Make the call."

On his cell that time, he drifted to the window, and by the way he talked, the phrases he used, I knew he was on the phone with police.

"Nikki," Mom said.

"Yeah?"

"When they get here, do not mention the Carlinos."

"I . . . wasn't planning on it." If we agreed on that, we had to agree on something else. I couldn't be boxed out anymore. "What's really happening, Mom? Do you know who killed Dad?"

She shrank some, withered, but gave me a straight answer for once. "The Poseidon Group. If not directly, then the ambition, and the betrayals, and everything else behind that godforsaken venture."

"So you're saying Big Bert . . ."

"No. I'm not saying that. You're not either."

"You can't keep doing this to me."

"I know. We talk to the police. When they leave, I'll tell you the rest. Promise."

She stood with supreme effort. A loser's stance. Time to pay up.

CHAPTER 44

We gave our statements in the offices downstairs, while the cops did their CSI thing up in our rooms. Not before Tomás helped me peel the taped photos from my windows, and Mom removed a thick envelope from the safe in her closet, smuggled it downstairs with us, then tucked it deep in her desk drawer.

Detective Burrows was back, completing an eerie reenactment of our last time together.

He asked his questions in his same disinterested tone. Mostly what I told was true. The description: a guy in black. He broke into my room and lay in wait. He pushed me onto the bed, but I distracted him and escaped. I didn't mention our conversation.

Burrows read messages off his phone, frowning. "The officers upstairs say the lock wasn't jimmied. Any clue how he got in?"

Sure. My key. A copy, anyway. I checked the hotel's key management software and it said I opened my room door a half hour before I actually walked in. Yesterday at the Carlino residence, Delano had plenty of time to lift my key and duplicate it before returning my bag.

But I told Burrows, "No idea." Because Delano wouldn't have done it on his own accord.

More questions. Was anything missing? Could it be someone I knew? An angry boyfriend?

Mom sneered. "I don't think so," I said.

Burrows flipped his notebook shut. "Well, hotel room break-ins are one of the more common crimes we see. Thankfully, no one was seriously hurt."

"This time," Mom said.

"Yes. This time. Mr. Garcia, did your team catch any footage on the guy?"

Tomás said, "We're still reviewing, but he might've slipped through."

Burrows shrugged. Hey, a grown man stalker accosts a young girl in her bedroom, whatcha gonna do? "I'll call if we get any leads."

"We'll be waiting by the phone with bated breath," Mom said.

Tomás escorted the cop onto the gaming floor. I watched through the office doorway as the investigators joined them, along with an extra person. Again, an agent from the Nevada Gaming Control Board made an appearance, chatting with Tomás and the police.

"Why's the NGCB here, Mom?"

"Be patient. We'll talk when they're gone."

I stretched my thin patience waiting on the magical moment when all would be revealed. Tomás returned, finally, holding a fresh business card in his fingers. He took a seat and slid the card across the desk to Mom.

It was the NGCB agent's contact info, positioned beneath the organization's seven-point star logo. It was a cheap print job, so the logo was blurred. Seeing it smudged like that reminded me of something I couldn't get my head around.

Mom said, "Nikki, close the door."

Time to talk. I did as told, the smudged logo sliding to the back of my mind.

Mom opened a desk drawer, removed the fat envelope from it, and dropped it on the desktop. Prying open the brass fastener, she shook the contents out before us. Papers. A DVD in a scuffed and cloudy plastic case. She rotated her computer monitor so we could both see and slipped the DVD into the disk drive. Tomás sat at an angle that would prevent him from viewing whatever we were about to watch. He didn't seem concerned, so he'd seen this already. That pissed me off a little.

A few mouse clicks and overlit gray scale images filled the screen. I leaned forward, made sure I saw what I saw. It was our once-popular poker room, my table—the one in the basement—was center frame, packed with fuzzy pixelated players. The time stamp indicated a summer night. Six years ago.

The night John Reedy died.

CHAPTER  45

"This doesn't exist," I said, tapping the space bar, freezing the footage in a silver still. I'd done my homework over the last week, knew the sticking points that sealed Dad's courtroom doom. "All the articles and records say there's no recording. *You* said there's no recording on the witness stand, Mom."

"I know. That was a mistake. Keep watching."

Hesitant, the ominous directive injecting icy fear into my system, I tapped the space bar again. The video continued, silent, no sound recording on this particular system. Dad was center frame, his back to the camera. John Reedy was visible in profile a couple of seats over. Leaning on the wall, in an animated conversation on his cell phone, a bloated Bertram Carlino.

The founding members of the Poseidon Group. Together for the last time.

I didn't recognize anyone else at the table. There were a couple of guys in sunglasses and hoodies, an older man in a suit with his necktie tugged loose, a younger dude in a T-shirt and baseball cap with the brim low, casting his pale face in a shadow smudge. A typical poker table motley crew.

The game progressed dully. Watching security footage of a poker game was like watching security footage of a cornfield. I couldn't see anyone's hole cards, there was no ESPN-style commentary like you got during World Series of Poker broadcasts. Totally uneventful. That fateful time stamp the only clue something bad was coming.

Players pushed their cards away, folding. One after the other until it was only Dad, John, and the guy in the ball cap. He showed first; whatever he had got Dad nodding respectfully. Then Reedy and . . .

Suddenly, the brim on the one guy's hat jerked that way. Players who'd folded earlier were on their feet. Something was wrong.

Before Dad showed his cards, the old guy in the suit grabbed one of the hoodies by his collar and signaled for someone to flip his cards. The other hoodie guy bolted, never to be seen again.

I knew this act too well. Thought of Chuck Pearl and broken glass.

Hoodie redirected the angry energy toward John Reedy. Dad got into it then, grabbing fists full of Reedy's shirt. Screaming in his face.

Big Bert stomped into the fray, pulling Dad off Reedy. Tried to. The Carlino touch incited Dad more. He flung Big Bert's meaty paw away and pummeled Reedy with quick punches. One, two, three.

More guys joined Big Bert, finally prying Dad away. Reedy crab-walked backward, yelling things and wiping blood from his lips. He rose smirking, mouthing off.

Dad broke free of those holding him back, pointed at John. Screamed at him. Though the video was mute, I knew what he said. It's in articles and courtroom transcripts.

"I'm so tired of cleaning up your mess, John. Don't ever come back. Next time I see you, I'm gonna kill you. Guarantee."

Reedy scoffed. He talked trash all the way out of the frame.

Spectators left, too. The remaining players followed. Dad's posture was different, his arms wide. Welcoming. Pleading. There's no way I could know exactly what he said. Probably anything to keep the game going, to assure them the trash was gone and Andromeda's was still a haven for real cardplayers.

Big Bert and the guy in the hat were last to go. Big Bert said something, but Dad shook his head and tossed back the rest of a drink that remained on the table. Big Bert stepped from view then. The player in the hat lingered, motioned at the cards scattered across the velvet. Dad waved him off. When the player turned, light caught his profile, and his jutting chin and clenched jaw tickled a memory. Then he was gone, and Dad kept drinking, finishing another glass that hadn't belonged to him. Finally, he stepped from the frame, too.

Mom stopped the footage, returned the disc to its case.

"Why hide this?" I asked.

"Bad advice," Mom said. "The lawyer working your dad's case at the time said it was best not to introduce the footage."

"What kind of lawyer tells you to lie like that?"

"The kind paid for with dirty money."

I nearly asked why but realized what I'd never seen in my research. Mention of Big Bert Carlino's presence that evening.

"You found the paperwork yourself," Mom said. "They were partners. John, Bert, and your dad. John had put together a cheating ring, and it threw shade on all their names. We know your father didn't kill John. That leaves who?"

Should have seen that one coming. "The lawyer told you to lie because Mr. Carlino wanted it that way."

"By the time we understood that it was too late, I'd already lied on the stand. Perjury."

My head jerked.

"Don't look at me like that. I would've still told the truth. I didn't care if I got in trouble. It would've been better than a murder rap. But your dad, he wouldn't give in. Never thought he'd be one of those stories."

Those stories. We all knew them. Black man railroaded by the justice system. Circumstance trumping reasonable doubt when it was supposed to be the other way around. All those were words from Dad's letters, seared into my memory.

Mom said, "No one was looking for more evidence, or even really looking at the evidence they had. Stands to reason it was in their best interest not to."

For a second I was back at the airport with Davis. Talking about how Big Bert paid Cardinal Graham to keep his son out of the legal system he despised so much. Did his money do the opposite with Dad? Did he buy my father's murder conviction to cover his own tracks?

"The prosecutor offered your father a deal. He wouldn't take it. Believed right up until the end that a jury wouldn't convict him of murdering his friend over a card game. That's where his reputation worked against him. All those interviews, that competitive nature that made him famous, put him on death row. The jury didn't even deliberate an hour.

"Weeks after, I got a notice from a law firm I never heard of, terminating the partnership for Andromeda's and giving me sole ownership. You know that's not how business usually works, right? When a partner gives up his share, he needs to be bought out. Not this time. Big Bert Carlino *gave* our family a casino. He washed his hands of us. Do you know why?"

I did. "Keep you quiet."

"That's why I'm telling you. You gotta stop what you're doing, baby. Making noise over this will only get somebody hurt."

"Somebody else, you mean? Reedy's dead. Dad's dead. Dan Harris is dead. And we're supposed to take it."

"Bert owns police and judges and lawyers. Dan Harris worked for him."

That stopped me cold. "No. That's not right. He got Dad out! Why would Mr. Carlino pay for a lawyer to get Dad's case overturned if he's responsible for the murder that put him in jail?"

Tomás—I'd forgotten he was in the room—said, "We don't understand it either. When your dad fired him and wouldn't tell your mom why, she asked me to do some digging. I followed Harris to the Nysos, saw him get escorted upstairs by Carlino himself. After that, I had a friend who's good with unearthing digital secrets look into paper trails. Dan Harris's law practice has had the same primary client for the last three years. The Poseidon Group."

"You followed him, like you followed me? That was you at the Cosmo? El Potrillo?"

Mom shifted uncomfortably in her chair. "I asked him to do that. I wanted someone watching you while I worked on our arrangements."

"Selling the place."

"Protecting us."

Tomás reinserted himself, backed her up. "Nathan wasn't just running around town that last week. He started something."

"What?"

"We don't know for sure. All we know is they're involved." He tapped the Nevada Gaming Control Board business card.

Mom stared at the floor. "When we brought your father home, he couldn't let it rest, not after Bert took so much from us. He was drunk and angry, and maybe I was a little mad, too. I told him if it bothered him so much, he should walk it off. The next time I saw him, he was so different. A man possessed."

I'd been blaming myself for the way I treated him. Mom had, too. I just didn't see it until now. "It's not your fault."

"Do you really believe that?"

I wanted to. For her sake and mine. I nodded.

"Thank you. But I'm not worried about fault anymore. Not after tonight."

Her fear, it felt oppressive. It was leading us somewhere I didn't like.

Tomás said, "Something's changed with Carlino, what he was content to let lie now has a lot of blood spilling all over town. It's like he's erasing a trail. Your dad, Dan Harris. Anyone who's too close to this thing. *Anyone.*"

"He's sick," I said.

A static charge crackled in the room, magnetizing the adults, drawing them closer to me.

"You get that from Davis?" Tomás asked.

"No. Mr. Carlino coughed up some blood right in front of me. I don't think he noticed. He seemed used to it."

"His weight loss," Mom said. "I thought he'd just gotten vain."

Tomás grabbed a notepad from Mom's desk, scribbled rapidly. "That's something. If it's serious, maybe he's trying to protect his business. Maintain investor confidence by keeping it quiet?"

"The Gaming Control Board, though?" I said, refocusing us all. "What would they have to do with that? Those agents got here so fast tonight, and before." I picked up the card, again stuck on that logo with its obscured, yet familiar edging. Gears ground in my head. I kept thinking of that old lady yelling "El Potrillo" when she spotted Tomás. Why?

He exhaled, a loud defeated rasp. "I've spoken to the board. They don't have answers. Only questions. Have we had any unusual fraudulent activity? Odd customers? Strange stuff for someone to come ask in person when a phone call would do."

My chest seized. Separate threads of thought slammed into each other, fused.

El Potrillo. At the Cosmo. Right before I met, and chased, Freddy Spliff.

"Baby?" Mom said.

"I'm fine. I'm fine."

Tomás wasn't wrong. Those questions from the NGCB were suspiciously plain, hiding the agency's true intentions. What those were, I didn't know. Freddy Spliff might.

The logo on this card was the same one on the van that snatched him.

CHAPTER 46

The adults kept talking. Half of me heard them. The other half kept stitching information together. The Gaming Control Board— not the halfway house helpers he claimed—grabbed drunk Freddy. I'd bet it wasn't because they liked his company. That flash drive he tried to give me, they wanted it as much as I did. More.

"What if Dad *did* find a way to take Mr. Carlino down? What if we got our hands on the information he had? We could finish what he started."

"No, we can't. It's killing me inside, but the warning was clear," Mom said. "We make too much noise, maybe we don't see the next guy coming. Maybe we disappear to a part of the town that's still desert. Do you understand?"

I understood. "He wins."

"It's not a simple thing," Tomás said. "What happened to your dad and Dan Harris wouldn't be something Carlino did himself. He doesn't do the dirty work."

"But—"

"Listen. There still haven't been any hits on the DNA they pulled off Nathan. With nothing in the system and no witnesses, unless they find another murder weapon in some lowlife's house, we don't even have an assailant who ties to Carlino."

"It's gotta be Delano. He's the one who threatened me. He does the dirty work."

Tomás's face tightened. "Not necessarily."

"If we got some of his DNA, could they test it against what was under Dad's fingernails?"

"Maybe. But how would you—"

"Doesn't matter," Mom interrupted. "We're not talking about this anymore. Go upstairs and pack a bag."

"Where are we going?"

"Tomás has extra rooms. We're going to stay with him." The way she said it, no nonsense, and the way he braced, I knew they expected a fight. I didn't have time for that anymore, not with what I'd just learned.

"Okay." When I stood, I slipped that disc off Mom's desk with fingers made nimble by years of trick shuffles and slipped it into the waistband of my pants while they made plans for our retreat. "I'll go get that bag now."

"I'll have someone escort you." Tomás fished his phone from his pocket to make arrangements for my safety, making it less and less possible to dislike him. I couldn't have eyes on me now, though.

"Can you send someone in like twenty minutes? I need a quick shower, and I don't want any guys hanging around my room while I do. I just . . ." I let it hang, didn't need to say more. I'd seen the work schedules for the week and knew the two female security personnel we employed were off tonight. He only had guys to send.

Tomás didn't take me at my word. He waited for Mom, who tried looking through me. I hugged myself for effect.

Mom nodded. "Twenty minutes. Thank you for cooperating. I know it's hard."

She shouldn't thank me yet.

I returned to my room, where only the light stirring of items indicated anyone had been there at all. As Mom asked, I packed a bag quick, and my mind worked quicker. I had to get this right the first time. Then I took the service elevator back down and avoided the Constellation Grill entirely. I sent texts on my way to my card room.

> **Me:** can you sneak out?
> **Molly:** i can, but SHOULD is the real question.
> **Me:** please. more important than anything. get gavin if you can. meet at the IHOP on the strip.
> **Molly:** yay, IHOP. can i tell gavin you're treating? i guarantee he'll come.
> **Me:** fine. whatever. be there in 20.

I rushed through my card room like I was being chased. It was good to get into that mode, because I knew, very soon, I would be.

Gavin's tent-sized sweatshirt still rested on the blackjack table. I snatched it on my way because, really, I didn't know when I'd have the chance to return after tonight. Whatever happened in the next twenty-four hours, it might mean I couldn't come back here ever again.

Exiting through the alley, I circled the building and caught the valet on duty messing around on his phone. He was a newer guy, only a little older than me. This could work.

Tense, but needing to play this exactly right, I waited just beyond his line of sight. He was goofing off on company time, chuckling at whatever text, game, or funny animal video had captured his attention.

"Excuse me." My mock authority voice was on point.

He jumped six inches and attempted to slip his phone into his pocket. He dropped it; the pavement-to-screen crack was wince-worthy.

"You know the policy about phones during working hours."

"I'm sorry, Nikki, I—"

"Unbelievable. I'm not in the mood for this tonight. Just give me the keys to one of the town cars."

"I can pull it up for you."

"Is that what I asked for? Keys. Now."

He crouched into the cabinet at the base of the valet stand, unlocked it, and selected the fob for a motor pool vehicle.

"Thank you. I think I can overlook you breaking the rules. I didn't see you on your phone, and you didn't see me. Understood?"

Squinty and suspicious now, he still agreed. "Sure. Have a good night, Ms. Tate."

At a swift walk, I found the car and got the heck out of Dodge. To finish this.

CHAPTER 47

Molly and Gavin were still en route by the time I reached the International House of Pancakes. Gavin kept me updated and also provided, what else, their orders. Blackberry and vanilla double-dipped French toast for him. Breakfast Sampler, with extra bacon, for her. I asked the waitress to bring a pot of coffee, too. That was mine. Because I needed to be *more* wired and neurotic.

> **Mom:** Don't do this to me. Please come home.

That was her ninth text since I hit the road; the first one came a mere five minutes after I left the Loop.

> **Mom:** Do you understand how bad you're SCARING me
> right now?

I thrummed my fingers on the table before responding.

> **Me:** i'm safe. i won't be back tonight.
> **Mom:** TELL ME WHERE YOU ARE RIGHT NOW!!!
> **Me:** i'll check in tomorrow morning. try to rest. i'm fine.

Then I blocked her.

The waitress returned with my pot. Bypassing the cup and pouring the scalding hot brew straight down my throat crossed my mind.

The doors chimed. Gavin muscled them open against a chill breeze and held it for Molly. Her hair whipped around her face in wild tendrils, her cheeks stung red. They came to me and squeezed in on the other side of the booth, cozy.

The waitress returned with their food.

"Perfect timing." Gavin unwrapped the silverware from a paper napkin cocoon.

"Your food bribes give you away. You're buttering us up for something," Molly said.

"I like bribes." Gavin's mouth was crammed with gooey whatever.

"Guys, I don't have time to joke around tonight. Someone attacked me in my room a few hours ago."

Gavin stopped eating. Molly grabbed my hand across the table. "You okay?"

"I'm fine, just need your help." I told them as much as I could. I went through everything from recognizing Big Bert's man Delano, to Dan Harris, to the NGCB snatching Freddy Spliff. I was about to start in on my plan when my phone buzzed.

Davis: you there?

I'd forgotten about him. Or blocked him from my thoughts like I blocked Mom's texts. There hadn't been much mental real estate available for the good Carlino right now. Given what I'd just told my friends—my suspicions about Big Bert and his lackey—it felt weird responding to Davis in front of them.

Phone in hand, I slid from the booth. "I've got something for you in the car."

Gavin perked up. "Yeah?"

"Your hoodie. You left it in the card room."

"Awesome. I thought my brothers got to it."

"No petty theft this time. Be right back."
My thumb was in motion before I hit the door.

Me: i'm here.
Davis: are you still n trouble? think you can sneak out? i want to
see you.

How crazy was it that, with all this going on, with his shady-
gangster-murderer dad trying to scare me off, part of me wanted to
see him, too?

Me: not a good idea right now. wish i could explain.

I unlocked my car. Gavin's sweatshirt had fallen onto the floor
of the passenger side. I leaned in to get it.

Davis: you can explain. in person. i'll come to you.

From the driver's side of the car, I had to cat-stretch and plug
the hoodie up by the inscribed tag. The silver inked *Gavin* glowed
under the sodium arc lot lighting. I flopped into the driver's seat
then, and attempted dissuading Davis to come. Really, dissuading
myself to let him.

Me: probably better you don't know.
Davis: let me decide. if it's bad news, pancakes will soften the blow.

I almost responded, almost gave in to his comforting charm.
One question stopped me.
How'd he know we could talk over pancakes?

One sneaker had been resting on the pavement. I reeled it in, slammed and locked my door. Twisting in my seat hard enough to bang my elbow on the wheel, I scanned every angle, every shadowed corner, looking for the light from another phone. A bluish ghost haze exposing some sinister watcher's grinning face.

Only cars in the lot. All of them empty. My eyes dropped to my hands. Phone in one, Gavin's shirt in the other. The fabric clutched tight, absorbing the dampness from my insta-slick palms.

Davis knows I'm at IHOP. How? He knew about that GPS Location History stuff. Could he be tracing my phone?

I scrolled back through his messages from earlier, before the incident in my room.

Davis: i'm worried about you. this is getting way out of control.
Davis: thus the back off message. this is scary. you SHOULD stop.
Davis: you're changing the subject. someone else is DEAD, nikki.
     DEAD.
Davis: text me later please. i'm trying to help.

How helpful are you, Davis?

My world tipped oh so slightly, skewing into paranoia. Those cards from my locker—the dead man's hand—were still in my back pocket. Never had the chance to remove them. I laid the phone on my thigh, snaked my hand into that pocket to retrieve them.

Fanning them on the passenger seat—BACK OFF OR ELSE—I glanced back to the texts.

Davis: thus the back off message. this is scary. you SHOULD stop.

Back off. Why'd he say that in his text? Sure, Molly could've told him exactly what she saw on the cards, and he could've been reciting it. Still . . .

I leaned over the cards, studying the silver ink scrawl on each. Gavin's hoodie with its exposed tag was still in my other hand. A fresh text came through.

Davis: you there?

No. No, I wasn't.

My vision blurred, my throat constricted to a pinhole. Then it all reversed itself, allowing me to vomit a ragged sob.

Davis hadn't tracked my phone. He'd sent a spy.

◆

The door chimes were faint beneath the pulsing in my ears when I stomped back into the restaurant, aimed at our booth. Molly's concerned expression morphed to straight-up alarm when she saw me. Maybe fear. Someone should be afraid.

Gavin plucked syrupy blackberry chunks off his plate. I flung those playing cards in his traitor face. "How could you?"

He flinched away. The nearly weightless cards spun in varying directions.

"Nikki!" Molly said, on her feet, pressing her body into me like we were on the soccer field.

I sidestepped her as gently as I could, which wasn't gently at all in my current state. She stumbled beyond the range of my tunnel vision, and I extended the arm holding Gavin's hoodie as if the garment was a weapon. "The handwriting's the same, Gavin. On this tag and on those cards."

He wouldn't look me in the eye, wouldn't deny it.

A man in grease-stained cook's whites suddenly flanked me. "Whatever this is, you need to pay for your meal and go before I call the cops."

My eyes were on fire. Tears poured down my cheeks and dripped onto the sticky tiles. I turned away and bit into the meaty part of my hand. Stop crying. STOP CRYING!

"Here," Molly said, pushing her own money into the man's hands. "That should be enough."

Gavin ejected from the booth and cleared the building with all the athletic speed and grace that might make him famous one day. Molly's arm looped into mine and she guided me back into the night where that Judas was.

He hovered by her SUV, his catcher's-mitt hands plunged deep into this pockets, and his eyes bouncing to everything but me.

"What's this about?" Molly demanded, dragging me into a loose huddle with *him*.

"Tell her what you did!" I said.

Molly's not stupid, never had been. She handled her own follow-up. "You didn't put those creepy cards in her locker, did you?"

"I didn't *want* to," he said.

She sagged beside me. "Why? What could've made you—"

"Davis paid you"—I willed myself composed—"right?"

"Yes, but it's not like you think."

"I think you like bribes. Food. Money. God, if he offered you food and money, would you toss me into traffic?"

"Nikki, he said it would keep you safe. He said it would help."

My composure cracked. "Do you feel helpful?"

"Stop it!" Molly said. "We should go."

The threatening cook stood at the restaurant entrance, his own phone pressed to his ear.

"I'm not going anywhere with *him*."

"Nikki, I'm sorry." He reached for me. I slapped his hand away.

"Did you tell Davis I was here?"

He shrank back.

"Really?" The intensity of Molly's disgust was something I'd never thought possible, not toward Gavin. Never.

Gavin looked smaller and weaker than anytime since I'd known him. Good. I pulled free of Molly, tossed him the incriminating shirt. "I can't do this right now."

"Wait," Molly called, "I'm coming with."

"I told you, not with him."

"I know. That's why I'm asking you to wait. I need to give him cab fare."

"Molly?" Gavin sounded half as wounded as I felt.

She said, "Don't. I'm with Nikki one hundred percent on this one. You messed up big."

I watched the rest from my car, leaning into the steering wheel, gripping it until my hands hurt so I wouldn't tip sideways and ball up from the pain in my chest. My friend could be bought? That was almost worse than knowing it was Davis who bought him. I couldn't even go there yet. The implications were darker than the night surrounding me.

Molly pulled away from Gavin while he waved his hands in pleading gestures. She came to my window and didn't look back.

The pane descended, Molly leaned in, her own tears cresting. "Lead the way."

CHAPTER 49

The way led to a convenience store first. Second, a safe secluded place. The airport observation lot. Molly parked, then joined me in my car as I opened the plastic clamshell housing my new prepaid phone. On Dad's phone, Davis continued texting. I ignored them.

Molly asked over jet noise, "What are you doing?"

"Trying to activate this thing." I flipped the ceiling lamp on, washing us in yellow light, still squinting over the tiny print in the instruction booklet. "You ever turned one of these on before?"

"No. I never turned on an untraceable burner phone before. And I'm talking about that crap show with Gavin."

"He sold me out. Don't tell me you're defending him."

"Am I sitting in the car with you, or with him? I'm backing your play here, but you need to hear everything."

I glanced up from the advanced calculus that was my phone's activation procedure, afraid. Was she in on it, too?

She said, "Gavin's dad lost his job."

The construction job that barely paid the rent and fed Gavin's family. The job he used to supplement with money from my, now nonexistent, card games.

"When did that happen?"

"The week you weren't in school. Before the funeral. He— we—didn't want to tell you because you deserved your time to grieve. He was scared his family wouldn't have a place to live next month and he kept it to himself because he didn't want to add to your burdens."

The fury I'd been hanging on to since we left the IHOP was sapped. I fought to stay indignant. "That's still not an excuse for what he did."

"It's not a *good* excuse. But who put him in that position?"

I bared my teeth. "You're blaming me?"

"No! Your rich boo-bear living up on Mount Olympus or whatever. You think Gavin would've ever considered doing something behind your back if Mr. Moneybags didn't throw cash his way when he was most desperate? Think about how close he got to you. To all of us. How he exploited it. That's some Lex Luthor stuff."

I'd exiled Gavin, but his presence remained in the form of sci-fi references. He would've complimented Molly on her judicious use of Superman lore. I would've laughed at his unabashed nerdiness. My anger swirled with waxing shame. "I have been thinking about Davis. He will be dealt with."

"Should he, though? What he did was gross, and what he talked Gavin into was grosser, but was he wrong? We're dealing with *murder.* I'm scared for you. That you're not scared, too, is really, really wrong."

"Would it be wrong if it was your dads? Or Bethany?" I barked.

She flinched. "All I'm saying is—"

"Cut Gavin some slack. I get it. I don't know if that's going to happen. That might make the UVA plan super awkward if me and him don't smooth things over, but—hey, what's wrong now?"

Her demeanor shifted. From the fierce intensity of giving me the business to a constipated discomfort. This wasn't about her wolfing that bacon.

"It's not important right now," she said.

"Would be helpful if I knew what 'it' was."

She sighed. "The UVA thing. It happened during that same week."

"You got in?" I didn't think she could accept offers or anything this soon.

"No. Me deciding *not* to go to UVA."

A half mile away the glaring wing lights on an approaching plane shone like low-hanging stars, getting bigger and brighter before shooting over our heads.

"What brought that on?" I focused on that empty runway, waiting.

"I don't know. Bethany started city league soccer, and she's wanting to run drills in the backyard. Dad Jerome started taking an improv comedy class, and Dad Dan is practicing his heckling. It's feeling like I'd have a hard time leaving them, is all."

"So you're not going to college?"

"Of course I'm going to college. I'm going to be a Runnin' Rebel."

That strange conversation in the Loop, when Gavin slipped and I thought he'd blown her cover about some guy. *You've been way preoccupied ever since you and—*

The conversation I'd misheard. Not *"you and—"* but "U-N."

As in UNLV. University of Nevada, Las Vegas.

"Oh my god."

"Their coach came by the house. The stuff she was saying was really cool, and—"

"I can't do this right now."

"Nikki."

"We'll deal with it, all right. All of it. I gotta get this phone set up, and you gotta help me. I know you're scared for me, but I need to see this through. Can you have my back for one more day?"

"I'll always have your back."

It's the same thing I would've said.

♠

It took twenty minutes of concentrated effort, groaning, and teeth sucking to get the cheap phone operational, confirmed with a test call to Molly's cell.

"Now what?" Molly asked.

"Now I program all the numbers I need into the new phone, and you're going to take my dad's phone home with you."

I started the task, scrolled through Dad's contacts list.

"Why would I do that?" Molly asked.

The phone lit with another Davis text. "Because I can't take him texting me all night. And I'm paranoid. I turned off the tracking features, and I blocked my mom's calls, but I don't know if her and Tomás can figure another way to find it. I'm almost certain they're going to try before long. So I'm giving it to you."

"What am I supposed to say if they come to me?"

"The truth. You don't know where I went."

"Where are you going?"

"Molly, you seem to be missing the point."

"You're not going to do anything stupid?"

"No." Not tonight, anyway. "I'll be in touch with you in the morning before school. But don't tell my mom that and do not respond to any of Davis's texts. I need to get through tonight, then tomorrow we execute my plan. Besides taking the phone, there's something else I need from you."

"Should I be scared?"

"Not yet." I told her what I wanted. No fear on her part. Not even when I mentioned abduction.

"Oh yes." Her killer smile radiated pure joy. "I like that idea a whole lot."

"Awesome." I punched the last number into my burner and gave her my dad's phone. "Now go. I'll see you tomorrow."

She hugged me awkwardly over the gearshift. "Be safe tonight."

When her SUV was taillights in my rearview, I called one of those transferred numbers. It wasn't one of Dad's originals, but one I'd added only a day ago.

"Chuck, it's Nikki Tate. Favor's due."

CHAPTER 50

GPS helped me find the Danvers Motor Inn on North Eighth Street, a dingy pay-by-the-hour/day/week spot that boasted Free HBO and New Coke Machines on its marquee. A couple of unsavory types lurked by one of those new vending machines, eye-molesting me. "Smile a little, girl!"

I snarled like I was rabid, and the mouthy one quieted down. I had no time for these motel trolls tonight. Chuck's Lexus was parked by the exterior stairs.

On the second-floor landing, I double-checked the messages I'd received, then scoped for room 217. A discarded pizza box and an empty gin bottle rested on the walkway next to the door. I knocked hard. "Open up."

"Put your battering ram down. I'm coming!"

The door swung inward, revealing a significantly scruffier Chuck Pearl, sweaty orbs staining the underarms of a dingy T-shirt. He backed from the doorway and made a grand sweeping gesture with his arm. He slurred, "*Entrez*, mademoiselle."

With my hand tucked into my bag, and my thumb caressing the trigger on my pepper spray, I stepped inside.

Chuck Pearl's room smelled the way the motel looked, like bad decisions and last resorts. Considering what brought me here, the poetry of it was not lost.

"Living the high life, huh, Chuck," I said, glancing around the dirt hole.

He glowered. "Seems there's some validity to that whole 'cheaters never prosper' thing. Especially when you're around."

"How quickly we forget the glory of unbroken bones."

"I know, I know. That's why I told you where I stayed. Let's get square and never see each other again."

"Fair enough. I need a place to crash."

"You're a minor, right? I'm fairly new to Nevada, but I'm sure you and me in here overnight would be frowned upon."

"Relax." I freed the hundred-dollar bill I'd folded into my hip pocket. "The sign outside said there were vacancies. I'm not old enough to get myself a room, but they'll rent another one to you."

"Can I keep the change?"

"Sure, Chuck. Also, classy."

He plucked the money from my hand. "Be right back."

Alone in his space, I snooped. It wasn't part of my plan, but I couldn't resist the jumble of enticing paperwork and gadgetry on the scarred TV stand. Two dozen brochures for attractions around town. Touristy maps and a photos of the larger Strip resorts. Loose playing cards. Several dice that rolled a little too fast when I tipped them slightly. Some kind of electronic box with Velcro straps and a length of stiff wire looping from it. Underneath it all was a detailed layout of the gaming floor at the Monte Carlo, adorned with hand-drawn X marks and red ink circles.

Chuck returned and found me seated on the edge of his bed, the blueprint spread beside me. Without looking up, I asked, "What is this?"

"Mine." He grabbed the blueprint and rolled it into a tube, then handed me a room key. "You're two doors down. We're even."

"What's that about?"

"Are you my stalker now? You know what I do. It takes knowledge and planning. It takes finesse. Just tell me, right now, if you're going to mess that up for me, too?"

I rolled my eyes. "I'm not going to step on your action at the Monte Carlo. Question, though. You got any info like that on the Nysos?"

♣

Chuck's short answer: no. The Nysos was too new. Too sophisticated. It might take years to get truly detailed plans from the underground contacts he dealt with.

He had some official Nysos cards, though. Sealed from the factory. He tossed me a deck from a trunk he'd wedged between the bed and far wall. "Consider them a going-away present."

I flipped the shrink-wrapped box over in my hands. "You don't hate me as much as you want me to believe, Chuck. You really don't."

"Why do you want security information on the Nysos? I thought you were Captain Vegas, the gambling den protector."

"When a place deserves protecting."

"Oh, I see. A grudge." He rubbed his face. "Will you let me do you a solid here?"

"You said we were square. If I let you do me a solid, then I owe you one day."

In a Don Corleone voice, he said, "That day may never come."

I couldn't help smiling. "Go on."

"Steer clear of that place. The streets say Carlino's bad news. Worse than most. Whatever you've got against his establishment, it ain't worth it. Live to play another day. Let it go."

"Thank you. But I can't."

"Why not?"

"I'm serious when I say I can't get into it. But I'll tell you a story my dad once told me. You ever hear of the fifty-million-dollar coin toss?"

He shook his head, closed the trunk and used it as a seat.

"Okay, it happened in a high-roller room. Sometimes when he told the story, it was the MGM. Another time, it was the Tropicana. Or the Palms. That the location changed so much shines some doubt on its accuracy. Still, there's a high-roller room. It's a fight weekend, so it's packed with a bunch of millionaires, maybe a couple of billionaires, having a good time. In walks this drunk dude with two models on his arm—"

Chuck's grin widened. "My kind of guy."

"Exactly. He was a tool."

His grin vanished.

"Dude's bragging about how he's worth fifty million dollars. He wants to see who in the room really has balls. He'll strip naked before he backs down from a bet. Annoying stuff. What he doesn't know is there's this Texas oilman in the room, and the Texas oilman was raised so humble, the bragging dude disgusts him. So Texas steps to the bragging dude and says, 'Okay, let's do a coin toss.' The bragging dude's laughing like, yeah, whatever. 'How much?' Texas oilman says . . ."

I let it hang, same way Dad did when he told it. Chuck filled in the blank. "Fifty million."

"Yep. Texas oilman's all like, 'Heads I get fifty from you, tails you get fifty from me. Being that you got a fifty-fifty shot at the win, it almost seems like destiny.' Bragging dude's not bragging anymore. He's looking around, waiting for people to laugh at the joke. Dead. Silence. Of course, he doesn't agree. It's a ridiculous idea to think someone's going to risk everything they have in the world on a coin toss. The bragging dude backs down, and the Texas oilman says he understands. But then adds, 'I'ma need those clothes, son.'"

"No way." Chuck's as wide-eyed as a kid listening to a bedtime story.

"Yes, way. The bragging dude had to strip, but the Texas oilman let him keep his shoes and boxers. He left the high-roller room like that. Alone. His dates seemed to like the Texas oilman better.

"When he was gone, the ladies ask the oilman, 'How would you even settle a fifty-million-dollar bet?' The oilman's all like, he would've made the bragging dude get a business manager on the line to confirm he actually had the money liquid, which would've proved what the oilman suspected: He didn't really have fifty million dollars. Then the girls are like, 'What if he did have it?' Oilman says, 'We would've flipped, and if I lost, I would've had my manager cut him a check. I'm worth way more than that.'"

We sat there a moment, the air-conditioning unit humming, the only sound in the room. Chuck said, "What's that story got to do with you and the Nysos?"

"Sometimes a bet isn't about winning. It's about everyone seeing you take on the douchebag in the room."

Chuck blinked once. Twice. "All righty, then. Your bard skills are right up there with your charm. Maybe we should call it a night."

"One more thing . . ."

He groaned. Waited.

"You got any more decks from Andromeda's?"

His eyes flicked up and to the left as he prepped a lie.

"Chuck!"

"Fine." He hopped off the trunk and yanked it open, all previous caution gone. He popped up, threw me a deck featuring Andromeda's silhouette. I pocketed those, too. Though if Mom's plans went through, they might be collectors' items more than a means to cheat us. Can't cheat what isn't there.

"Good night," I said.

"I think your assessment's overrated. Sleep well, anyway."

CHAPTER 51

My room was just as crappy as Chuck's, and I made an on-the-spot decision to sleep on top of the comforter, fully dressed, but my initial attempts at slumber failed. I rewatched the security video of that last card game between Dad and John Reedy a few times on a laptop I'd taken from Andromeda's. I paused the video to rest my burning eyes. When I opened them again, sunlight streamed through the blinds. Total shock, I slept and I was not devoured by bedbugs. Win-win.

The nightstand clock read 6:15 a.m. I dialed Molly from my burner; she picked up on the first ring.

"I'm so glad to hear from you," she said. "I barely slept at all last night."

"I'm fine. Did my mom come to you?"

"No. She called the dads. They gave me the third degree, but I told them we got pancakes, then played it like I was in the dark on everything else."

"Good. I don't want any blowback coming your way."

"How's that even possible? I'm an accessory already."

"So you did what I asked?"

"I talked to Gavin. It's all set."

"Awesome. I'll meet you in about an hour. Depending on what happens, I'll tell you what's next."

"Nikki, are you really going to be able to go through with this?"

By "this" she meant a minor kidnapping, and possibly some mild torture. "Brand-new day, brand-new me. See you in about an hour."

Fifteen minutes later, I was out the door, ready to infiltrate the school. The door to Chuck's room was wedged open by a house-keeping cart. The Lexus was missing from the parking lot.

Good luck, Chuck. Don't go getting your face smashed in.

♥

Navigating my car around my milling classmates, I grabbed a spot on the far side of the student lot, closest to the football field since I wasn't planning on entering the actual school. I was a few minutes early for my meeting with Molly, so I did the thing I dreaded. Called Mom.

She answered hoarsely; I knew she'd been crying. A lot. "Who is this?"

"Me. I know you're mad—"

"Where are you?"

"I'll tell you later today. I promise." There was more to say. I stopped myself. Waited for the inevitable pushback. Her silence was unnerving. "Mom?"

"I'm here."

That she wasn't screaming and making threats panicked me. A nightmarish thought blossomed. Big Bert's man Delano lurking over her, a gloved hand resting gently on her shoulder. "Are you okay?"

"I'm not. I don't know how soon I'll be able to forgive you for putting me through what you have."

"I'm sorry about all this."

"I just lost your dad. How selfish are you, Nikalosa?"

That stung more than being told I'm grounded for the next year. Selfish? I wasn't doing this for me.

She'd see.

"I'm sorry, Mom," I repeated. "I'll be in touch." I ended that round of torture and proceeded to the football team's building, feeling mean enough to start the next.

Molly was waiting with the door open. "Hurry up."

With me inside, she let the door swing shut, and the electronic lock caught. That she was able to get in here at all let me know the first part of the plan worked.

"Is he going to do the rest?" I asked.

"That's what he told me."

Our voices echoed in the Lion's Den, reverbing in the emptiness. Awesome.

Been too long since me and Davis had some quality time.

◆

The electronic lock buzzed and clacked open, allowing their voices entrance before their bodies followed.

"—talk in here?" Davis said. "Why can't you just tell me what's going on with Nikki?"

"Inside," Gavin said. "We don't want anyone seeing us."

The door settled back into its frame, sealing them in.

"We had a deal." Davis stepped deeper into the building. "You're supposed to—"

"Go on," I said, revealing myself with Molly behind me. "I'm real curious about this part."

His mouth shut, an audible snap.

Gavin sidled by me. I resisted the urge to shy away. My deep and angry feels toward him hadn't gone away in a night, but I'd factored him into my ultimate plans before I knew of his betrayal. I needed him. Thanks to Molly, I had him.

Davis recovered quickly. Frighteningly so. His charm cranked to one hundred. "Nikki, I'm so glad to see you." He raised his arms as if he might attempt to hug me, but dropped them just as fast. "Can we—can we talk?"

"We're going to. Have you been playing me this whole time?

"I think there's a bit of confusion here—"

"Gavin, grab him."

This wasn't his nature anywhere other than the football field. If things between us hadn't taken a turn, I wouldn't dream of asking this from him. But they had. I trusted Molly relayed all that would be required when she got him on board.

That size and speed that had college scouts salivating was something to behold in a room full of people who were essentially munchkins to him. Gavin lunged forward with force, shoving his hands into the grooves of Davis's armpits, hoisting, and spinning him up against the wall.

"What were you trying to keep me away from when you had Gavin put the dead man's hand in my locker?"

"I was trying to protect you." He pushed against Gavin with the same effect as pushing against a brick wall.

"The easy way to do that, 'Hey, Nikki, my dad's sending our crazy butler to your house; don't be there.'"

He stopped struggling, genuine puzzlement creasing his face. "What?"

"Don't act like you don't know."

"I don't." Any anger he'd fought to hide was now apparent, aimed at Gavin. "You didn't tell me that."

"I'm done spying for you," Gavin said.

Davis's eyes bounced back to me. "What happened when he came to you? Did he hurt you?"

"Like you care."

Davis's body went slack with what I thought was resignation. Then he tensed, jabbed his fingers into the meat of Gavin's right shoulder.

"Ow!" Gavin's arm went lip, and Davis was free.

Molly, silent until then, put herself between me and Davis.

"Come on," Davis whined, "I'm not going to do anything."

Gavin lurched to the side, massaging his bicep. "Tell that to my arm. The whole thing's numb."

"I jabbed your axillary nerve. The pins and needles will wear off in a second."

I stepped around Molly. "What *are* you?"

"If you let me explain, I'll tell you every—"

He was airborne, lifted and slammed into a big rolling cart of towels.

"My arm's better now," said Gavin. "Try that again and you lose teeth."

"Not likely." Davis did some weird twist move that straightened Gavin's arm. Gavin rocked sideways, then somehow, Davis's legs were wrapped around Gavin's shoulders and neck in an attempted choke hold.

"Enough!" I shouted.

They stopped their Tasmanian Devil twirl and detached from each other.

Gavin lurked over my shoulder as I stepped to Davis. "Tell me what's happening. If I get any feeling that you're lying to me, I promise you can't take all three of us."

"I haven't been playing you the whole time, Nikki. Just since yesterday. That's when I gave Gavin cash to put those cards in your locker. Nothing before that. I wanted you to leave it all alone."

"Why, Davis?"

"Because we went to see that lawyer. I didn't know how to tell you, so I didn't."

"Tell. Me. What?"

"That I recognized him. I knew he worked for my dad, and that meant whatever you were looking for was worse than you could imagine."

CHAPTER 52

I waited. How could anything be worse than what I've imagined? Worse than what I've lived?

"Harris," Davis continued, "recognized me, too. I'd seen him at my place a few times in the last year. Never knew why and didn't care. Until you found him."

"You should've said something!"

"I didn't know how. When he started hinting about needing money to remember, that was for me. Or, rather, my dad. I was scared you'd picked up on it, but then your mom and that biker's card game distracted you, so I sat on it."

"Before you decided scaring me off with poker lore was a good move?"

"I was going to tell you at my place. But Ced interrupted; then my dad showed up."

"You still could've told me. Call. Text. You had options."

Carefully, he stepped closer. I stepped back.

"I couldn't tell you. Not without my phone. This is the part you really need to hear."

Molly and Gavin were church mice quiet. First bell sounded. Nobody here was worried about tardiness now.

Davis continued, "Dad grilled me after you left. Where I was, what I'd been doing. I told him about Harris because, I don't know, that extorting my family for money—in front of you—didn't sit right."

"And?"

"He calmed down. Was just like, 'Is that so?' If you know him, you'd know how weird it was. Later that night, I get out of the shower, and my phone's gone. I'm thinking he took it, or had Delano do it. I go looking and no one's in the house or picking up their cells. I tear the place apart looking for it. Nothing. Next morning, I wake up, my phone's right on my nightstand. I go to the Location History to see where it's been, and some of it had been deleted. Where my phone was while it was missing overnight, and everywhere I'd been with you."

Davis stopped talking.

"So you're saying someone took your phone, covered their tracks and yours?"

A vigorous nod. "That scared the crap out of me. I called Gavin and offered him a grand to put those cards in your locker."

Anything beyond "a grand" was lost on me. To Gavin, I said, "A thousand dollars?"

He misunderstood my outburst, turned away shamefaced. I yelled because that amount was mind boggling. I might've done the deed myself for that much.

"He told me no. Then I offered him five," Davis said.

Gavin got in his face. "I'll give it back. I don't have all of it. But I'll work that off. Wasn't worth it."

Davis wilted, despite having shown that Gavin's intimidation tactics were useless on him. "You're right. It wasn't."

"Why now?" Molly asked. "You had to have known this might be related to your dad when you saw the pictures in Nikki's room. You didn't try to scare her then."

"I wasn't convinced anything led to my dad. Not until the lawyer."

"You played along to get close to me?" I said, chewing my lip after. The physical pain was better than the other kind that seeped in with every one of his shady confessions.

"Yes, but I wasn't being deceitful. I wanted to be there for you. I like you so much, Nikki."

A confusing warmth spread through my chest. *Traitor,* I told myself. Out loud, "Do you still?"

"Of course."

"Enough to help me bring my dad's killer to justice?"

He froze. Finally, "My dad wouldn't have killed yours."

It didn't sound like murder was beyond Big Bert. It sounded like murder was *beneath* him. The same way he might say "My dad doesn't do laundry," even though he always had clean clothes.

"Delano?"

He looked to the ceiling, beyond the ceiling, for some divine intervention. It didn't come. "It wouldn't matter. Whatever happened, it would've been done in a way where no one can find proof."

"What if someone could? Would you help? Could you prove you liked me enough to let me take down the man who came into my home and threatened me?"

"You want to go after Delano? How?"

"Will you help?"

He glanced from me to Molly to Gavin and back to me. "For him. Yes. Tell me what you want me to do."

"Leave."

"Huh?"

"Walk into the school, go to your first class, and continue with the rest of your day."

Confusion tugged his lip up like on a fishhook. "I thought you wanted my help."

"I do. And I'll get it when you take me to the football dinner tonight."

I felt the postures of my friends change, their own confusion setting in. I'd explain soon enough.

Davis said, "That's all you're telling me? Something's going down at the dinner?"

"There are two more things. One, make sure Delano is on the property. Two, be pretty. Now go."

He hesitated and I stomped my foot, firing a cracking echo around the room. "Go!"

Quickly, he went, stopping at the door to say, "I really am sorry, Nikki."

"Make it up tonight if you mean it."

When he was gone, Gavin and Molly closed on me with obvious questions.

"What are you going to do at that dinner tonight?" Molly asked.

I pointed to Gavin. "Not as much as him. Davis showed you how to break into to the safety alert systems for Vista and Cardinal, right?"

"Yeah, why?"

"Phase Two."

CHAPTER 53

I explained my version of the Phase 2 plan. It did not go over well.

"No," Molly said. "I won't let you."

"You can't stop me."

"Make a bet. I win, and you—"

"No."

"Then I'll—"

"No. I won't force you in on this. But it's my last shot to do something for my dad. It's happening. Right?"

That question was for Gavin, who hadn't resisted at all. His guilt was useful that way. "I got you."

A flustered Molly said, "I still get a question."

"A question?"

"Our previous bet. You owed me three questions. I have one left."

I'd totally forgotten about that.

"Do you honestly, swear on a Bible, think what you just described will work?" she asked.

Gavin said, "It doesn't matter. We have to try."

Molly threw her hands high. "All the crazy is in here."

"We have a better shot if you're in on it," I said. "That's my honest, swear-on-a-Bible answer."

"No pressure at all."

"Give me Dad's iPhone back." I extended my hand. "I'll need it."

She rooted in her bag, gave it over. "Where are you going?"

"That's a secret. You love me just enough to tell my mom."

Her pinched face was not a convincing rebuttal. "I could fill her in on this Phase Two insanity."

"Maybe. But you shouldn't have reminded me of our bet. I never got my demand."

"That doesn't apply here."

"No-strings freebie. You. Must. Comply."

She was vibrating mad, unused to being outmaneuvered. "I'm putting you in a terrible position, right? Making you choose between my well-being and our friendship. I'm not heartless. Tell my mom whatever you want. My demand is you wait"—I checked the time on the phone—"eight hours."

"Oh, like that's helpful."

"More than you know. See you tonight. Dress to impress. I've got errands to run."

I left them to it and went about my next task. Not errands plural. Only one. It was overdue.

♠

Freddy Spliff's temporary residence was faded sandblasted brick and gnawed siding with iron bars set in the window frames. In the yard, a sign mounted on two wooden posts identified the place as Help House. A close grouping of punctures in the *H* and *O* of *house* might've been bullet holes. All together, it made the sign seem more like a plea than a title.

I climbed the rickety front steps onto a wraparound porch crowded with mismatched chairs. Mailboxes were mounted on a rack next to the door, each with a removable label. *F. Spliff* was third from the left.

Pressing the doorbell triggered a buzzer inside. The man who answered had long, streaky gray hair tied into a ponytail and looked like an old rock star except with thick glasses. His magnified eyes stared, blinked slow, like he was taking snapshots of my internal organs. "What do you want?"

"Is Freddy Spliff home?"

"He expecting you?"

"Not exactly."

The man fidgeted, and I got it. What good could possibly come from a teen girl popping up for an afternoon visit with an ex-con? "I think he's job-hunting. I'll check, but you might have to come back later."

It was far from convincing the way his eyes flicked to the left, like Freddy was in the next room. I took a deep breath, prepared to shout Freddy's name. Freddy saved me the trouble by coming out from hiding voluntarily. "It's okay, Malcolm. She's the daughter of a friend."

The old man—Malcolm—said, "Well, y'all talk on the porch. We don't want anyone getting the wrong idea."

Freddy nodded and joined me outside. Malcolm closed the door behind him, slammed the lock in place. If Freddy didn't have a key, he'd have to ring the bell when he wanted back in. It didn't seem to bother him.

"You shouldn't have come here." He wore the same pants and shirt he'd had on at the Cosmo, took a seat in a wobbly, varnished chair. "I already told you I was messed up when we talked before."

So why sit? I opted for a dusty lawn chair. "I don't know if you'll tell me anything I want or need to hear. But there is a matter of you having what belongs to me."

"You want the flash drive."

"You said it was my dad's. Which means it's mine now.

However messed up you were, that drive was real enough for those guys from the Gaming Control Board to snatch you that day."

Freddy twitched as if I'd tased him. "Nathan said you're a smart girl. Everybody I know who got kids says the same thing. Me included. Nathan might be the only one who ain't exaggerating."

My purpose in coming here grayed. Dad thought that, even when I was being a jerk to him. "Were they—" I blinked my eyes dry and swiped nonexistent dust from my face. "Were there agents in the room when I called you? Did they tell you to get rid of me?"

He nodded. "It didn't take much convincing, though. Girl your age shouldn't be mixed up in this."

This. Something so extreme they snatched him up like we live in a police-state. "Why'd they come for you like that?"

"Nathan was already stirring up trouble with Metro and attorney's office. Imagine if Gaming Control got dragged into it. They didn't want anything proving he'd been helping them when he died. He must've mentioned my name in one of his meetings. They tracked me down."

All this CIA-style kidnapping and cover-up stuff upgraded them from annoying to frightening. "Do you know what Dad was helping them with?"

"Catching cheaters."

If he'd said "catching gremlins," it would've made as much sense. "Why would they recruit him for that?"

"They didn't." Shadows crested his brow. "Nathan went to them. There was loads of details on the drive."

"The one they took." I cursed.

"Sure." Freddy pulled a different flash drive from his shirt pocket. "Good thing I made copies."

I pulled my laptop from my bag and booted up right there and plugged in the drive. There were a few text files. All the photos I already had. A couple of numbered folders. The data on the drive took up a fraction of the device's space. Good news. Easier to comb through with midday temps rising and my warming computer balanced on my knees.

"What's relevant here, Freddy?"

"His notes talk about the crew he spotted working tables at the Nysos his first night back. Poker, blackjack."

I'd skimmed that first text file and saw similar notes. The cheaters were a motley crew dressed in a manner that would prevent a casual onlooker from recognizing they knew each other. Corporate types paired with dreadlocked stoners. Vacationing grandpas and ditzy sorority girls. Communicating through discreet hand signals. Stuff that dealers, or gaming floor supervisors, or pit bosses should've easily caught . . . unless some of them were involved, too. Dad noticed because one of the crew had rigged a Hold'em game he'd sat in on. It was an eerie déjà vu for him.

Each new set of notes was in a different, dated file. I moved onto the next, where Dad returned to the Nysos and followed one of the dealers to an East Side apartment complex, then to a bar where that dealer met someone from the crew. It was then that he first contacted Gaming Control.

"Why do this? What was in it for him?"

"I asked him the same thing when he came to me for help organizing it all. He was skittish at first, didn't want me in too deep. He broke after a while, though. Told me a story about Al Capone."

That tore me from my laptop. "The gangster?"

I'd seen his picture in the Mob Museum, one of the city's most popular attractions, down the street from Andromeda's. What'd he have to do with Dad?

Freddy grunted a confirmation, then said, "He was a big-time Chicago mob boss. Never went to jail for all the people he killed or the lives he ruined. But he also didn't pay his taxes and that's how the government eventually got him. Nathan was obsessed with that story."

"He wanted to get the person who killed John Reedy, by any means necessary."

"Right you are."

"He thought Big Bert Carlino was running a cheating ring?"

"Never said who. You'll notice there are no names in those notes. Everything he wrote was cryptic." Freddy tapped his temple. "Said it was safer for me."

Not for me, though. Maybe before I started poking around, but I needed that information for leverage now. Cryptic could get me hurt. Or worse.

The notes were obscure and the pictures I'd seen before. None of this was helping. "I don't get it. If Big Bert's Al Capone, why would Dad think *this* was the way to get him? He wouldn't cheat his own casino."

"I don't know what to say. I wish I'd asked more questions." His voice took on the quality of an old dog's growl; he turned away from me, hiding his face. His shame. "That last night, I should have."

"You saw him?"

"One last time, I did. He wasn't making sense. He'd just met with his Gaming Control contact. Whatever they talked about had him upset. He kept saying, 'I never asked what it was. I never asked.'"

Freddy was right. Nonsense. "That's all? He didn't say or do anything else?"

He pointed a crooked finger at my computer. "Created that last text file. I've looked at it a bunch of times but don't know what it means."

"Cryptic." I felt deflated clicking on a file I expected to be as comprehensible to me as ancient Sanskrit.

The opposite was true. I understood it too well.

Dad's note read: *bludgeon = bat*.

I knew it all.

CHAPTER 54

That headline from so long ago—"Local Man Bludgeoned to Death; Casino Owner Charged"—slammed into my conscious thoughts with enough force to make me dizzy.

Bludgeon, a vague descriptor the media ran with in the absence of a murder weapon. John Reedy could've been beaten with a crowbar or a frozen leg of lamb for all anyone knew. When the "real killer" was found with the *bludgeon* in his possession, we only cared about big-picture stuff, Dad coming home. The details escaped us.

All the research I'd done in my grief-stricken haze. All the hot rage and confusion and uncertainty and anxiety. All the nights staring at the ceiling, obsessing over who would, and how did, and what now? All of that, and I'd missed the same, obvious question Dad had.

What, exactly, was a bludgeon?

The recorded security footage from Andromeda's was still in my computer. A couple of touchpad swipes set the disc drive spinning, and opened a window into a frozen past. I didn't play it, didn't need to see ghosts fighting again. Neither of them was the cardplayer that required my attention.

The young man in the baseball cap, the bent brim obscuring most of his face. I knew what I was looking for now, and that familiar jawline jumped at me like 3-D. He was more muscular these days. The facial hair was new. There was a reason I felt I'd known Davis Carlino on his first day at Vista and had such an intense reaction. Call it a trace memory of the night things went so wrong for my family. But it wasn't really Davis I remembered.

It was Cedric.

First in line for the Carlino empire. A slick, always-on hustler. Former baseball star.

bludgeon = bat

Cedric's bat.

He'd killed my dad. And John Reedy. Probably Dan Harris, too.

"Dad was after the wrong Al Capone." We both were. I closed my laptop without shutting it down, and I pocketed the flash drive. "Freddy, I gotta go."

Phase 2, my grand plan, based on the same wrong assumptions that drove my father until the night he discovered the truth and died because of it, wasn't going to work.

♣

The world rang. A sharp trilling triggered my reflexes, so I stomped the brake, inspiring angry honks from the car behind me. It shot by on my right, the driver giving me the traffic finger in passing.

Back in motion, I recognized the sputtering tone as an incoming call on the car's hands-free system. Molly's number flashed on the dashboard display. I thumbed a button on the steering wheel to open the line. "Yeah?"

"Got your text," she said.

I'd sent the message an hour ago, keyed it while idling at the first red light I hit after leaving Freddy's. I knew classes were in session and didn't expect a quick call. Which was fine. I needed the time to process all I knew. To let the fixer in me work on the problems with Phase 2.

"I'm in bathroom stall, and it's gross," she said. "Can you tell me what it meant?"

"Exactly what it said. Change of plans."

"I never agreed to the first plan," she reminded me.

"If you're not going to help, you could always hang up." I waited. "Hello?"

"I'm here."

And I kept going.

♥

The Doolittle Community Center was one of my favorite places in the city, always my intended safe house until it was time to execute "all the crazy" I'd plotted. This place was where I'd met Molly and Gavin on a Friday Funday during citywide summer camp. Where I'd learned to swim and got in trouble for betting M&M'S in unsanctioned card games with other kids. I entered like I always had, checking in at the front desk with a bag containing none of the athletic wear or equipment most patrons carried.

I entered the women's locker room frumpy, in denim and sneakers. When I emerged an hour and a half later, the clothes I'd come in now stuffed in my duffel, I knew everyone in the place would remember I'd been there. That was okay. All the hiding was done now.

A half hour later, I entered the cavernous Nysos parking deck, veering away from the valet line and descending deeper underground for self-park options. I chose a space in a sparsely populated corner, and sat. My A/C on and my radio off. I could do this. For him.

I sent the first text.

Me: are you good to go? any problems?
Gavin: it's working. i can send on your signal.
Me: do it!

Minutes passed and nothing happened. I started to worry.

Then the phone buzzed in my hand, the screen lighting with the image and message I'd requested. Gavin came through for me. Now the rest.

Me: decision time. in or out?
Molly: already in the lobby.

Thank. God.

Me: you know what to do. feel free to tell my mom anything you
    want. and make sure your phone's charged.
Molly: i'm sitting on 98% battery. worry about your end.

Oh, I was plenty worried.

More exchanges with more people. Me playing puppet master, yanking on strings that might not be attached to anything at all. It was 4:45 p.m., and there was one more text to send.

Me: are you ready?
Davis: i am.
Me: see you soon.

CHAPTER 55

A parking deck elevator delivered me to lobby level. I stepped from the elevator car and strolled past the same valet I'd seen every time I'd been here. And he saw me, twice. The result of his neck-cracking double take.

That funeral dress Mom bought me was a stunner when you took it out of its intended context. Those bell sleeves were an unplanned bonus, making me think maybe I had some luck on my side. Add in heels that accentuated every hard curve in my field-trained calves and quads, and my hair forming a bouncing black halo around my face, I knew everyone would be looking at all the things meant to distract.

Loose groups approached the revolving-door entrance, and familiar faces were among them. Vista players and their plus-ones arriving for the dinner Davis arranged. They greeted me by name, and we stepped between spinning glass panes that created a fast draft, the mild wind nudging, then ejecting us into the atrium.

Windows taller than my school allowed cascading waves of light inside without the accompanying heat. Dark marble at our feet was polished to a mirror's finish. Chrome—or possibly silver—sparkled in so many places it was hard to process, like camera phone flashes in a dark concert hall. There were waterfalls. Jewelry stores. A tattoo parlor. A seafood restaurant that transcended vowels, its sign simply reading FSH. Ahead, like the entrance to a forbidden cave, was the shadowed start of a gaming floor that stretched a city block. The lights and lines—the shine—felt like standing inside a diamond.

Dinner was somewhere on the second floor. A pair of long

escalators ascended and descended ahead of us, but we did not go. Our host was on his way to greet us.

Davis, dressed in a tailored blue suit that looked simple but probably cost a few thousand dollars, a white open-collared shirt, and a purposely loose tie, rode the scrolling stairway with his hands clasped behind his back. Per my instructions, he was pretty.

The football players emitted warm vibes. Shouts of "Daaave!" and "Carlino's that dude" had replaced their disdain. Davis shook hands, patted backs, accepted their gratitude, remained fixated on me.

When he got to me, he was no longer the shining host. "Nikki, I can't have you mad at me. I know what I did was so messed up, but I want to fix it. I mean it. I've been keeping tabs on Delano all day. I know exactly where he is right now. Me and you can get whatever you need. Just tell me—"

"That's not important anymore, Davis."

"I don't understand."

"You remember that day at Caesar's, when you told me you were in the dark about the things your family was capable of?"

"Yeah?" His inflection cautious.

"Do you really want to help me? Because it may mean learning some things best left in the dark."

"I do want to help, but you going after my dad scares me."

"That's not important anymore either."

"I'm totally lost."

I detected movement to my left, by the gaming floor. "Play along and you'll see."

Before he could question further, the host I'd actually come to see joined us.

"Nikki Tate," Cedric said. "So glad we're finally going to do this."

CHAPTER 56

Davis remained at my side, silently observing, while Cedric led us across the gaming floor. We came to a corridor blocked by a velvet rope. A stocky black-clad security guard with a nametag that said Kurt unclipped one end of the velvet rope and greeted us. "Mr. Carlino."

Cedric gave a nod. "Make sure we're not disturbed."

He pushed through a set of leathery upholstered doors at the end of the low-lit hall, and we followed. Davis's fingers grazed my arm, signaling me to slow. "What is this?"

"We're both going to get answers. If you want them."

"But—"

Cedric poked his head into the hall. "You two can make out later. Come on."

We obeyed and entered the Nysos High Roller Room.

High ceilings. A subdued luxury unlike the exaggerated hotel atrium. There were no windows. The outside world could never peer in at the one percenters who visited, and the only view concerning the players here would be stacked directly in front of them. All of it in a space big enough for a half-court basketball game and empty enough to trigger a hotshot of adrenaline. Me. And them. Alone.

"I appreciate you agreeing to poker lessons," Cedric said. "I believe in paying professionals for their time. We should talk about your rate."

"I'm not a pro, though."

"From what I hear, you will be. So how's this? I front you some chips. Whatever you still have by the time we wrap up, you keep."

The hustle continues. He needs a coach, even though he was holding his own with the best players in town at, what, fifteen? Sixteen years old? He had no intention of me leaving here with *any* chips. We were playing the game before the game.

"I don't know," I said. "That's generous of you, but there's something I'm really more interested in than money. Your brother."

"Excuse me," Davis said.

"Oh, yeah?" Cedric's wide wolf grin and "attaboy" vibes he projected at his little brother were far from subtle.

"He's always so secretive," I said, throwing a hand on my hip. "He's probably got girlfriends back in New York."

Cedric's grin shrank, likely considering his Bro Code Liability. "What do you have in mind?"

"It's this thing Molly and me do. We bet questions. I win a hand, I get to ask a question that must be answered honestly. You win a hand, same deal."

The gleam in Cedric's eyes was back. "So the chips would just be symbolic. For bragging rights."

"I'm a minor; it wouldn't be legal for me to play for money in a licensed establishment. I'm a stickler for the rules." See, we could both BS through this.

Davis stepped off the sidelines. "This isn't a good idea."

Cedric did my work for me. "Chill, bro. We're going to have fun."

"Yes," I agreed. To Davis, I said, "If you're up for it, you could even deal."

"Great idea," said Cedric. "I'll get the cards and chips. We'll use that table."

He motioned to the room's center, where a pill-shaped chrome-and-leather table resided.

"Are you going to sit down?" I asked.

Davis seemed deflated. Or defeated. He took the dealer's seat.

I sat on the opposite side of the table at a slight angle. Cedric returned with an empty card shoe, a bundle of Nysos-branded card desks sealed in plastic, and a rack of chips. He sat on my side of the table, but with two seats between, turning the three of us into the points of a loose triangle.

"I think we're ready," he said.

"Me, too."

"How do you want to start, Nikki? I want to follow the expert's lead."

"You familiar with five-card draw?"

He pressed back into his seat. "I am. Not many people play it these days."

"Since it's just the two of us, let's forget about the card shoe. We can use one deck. You'll learn faster when there are no community cards working for you. That's how my dad first taught me."

"Excellent. A lesson in the style of Nathan 'The Broker' Tate." Cedric slid the shoe to the far end of the table and popped the plastic on his card bundle. He removed a single deck and tossed it underhand to his brother, a perfect throw from the former Mr. Baseball.

Davis shook the cards free and shuffled the deck several times while Cedric divided our symbolic chips, all real denominations no smaller than twenty dollars.

"I was hoping the master would take it easy on the student tonight, but given the stakes, you're about to run me, huh?" Cedric said.

"You're probably better than you think."

"I hope so. Let's get it started. Ante up?"

I tossed a twenty-dollar chip into the pot. Cedric did the same, told Davis, "Whenever you're ready."

The youngest Carlino slung the cards and got us going. And Cedric—the student—won the first four hands.

Heads-up poker was different from playing a full table. When there are multiple people—three, four, five—you have the option of backing off. You can fold more, save your chips when you get garbage cards. When there's just two of you, it's the opposite. Every hand you bet. Every hand someone's losing. That someone was me.

Cedric took another pot with a measly pair of tens. It made his life. "Nikki, I gotta say, you're bringing out the best in me. I never play this well."

I was nearly out of chips. Them being symbolic and all, Cedric just shoved some from his pile my way. He was having too much fun for me to go bust. Our real currency was information, and deferring his prize questions to Davis seemed to give him some special brotherly joy.

On Cedric's first two wins, when he prodded his little brother to ask the won question, Davis softballed it and asked for the name of my favorite restaurant. It's The Egg & I. Awesome crepes. Cedric threw a chip at his head for that.

"Come on, man. I'm doing all this work for you. Ask something good!"

Davis's reluctance got the best of him, and he flubbed the second one, too. Where do I want to live after college?

Cedric groaned, took the third question himself. "Not to be rude, Nikki, but maybe your dad would've given me a better challenge. Not trying to dis you, I'm just saying, you think I could've held my own with him?"

"It's hard to say. My dad was a pro. And you're way better than you let on. Ultimately, no. I don't think you would've done well against him. Not without hustling him like you did me."

His good-natured sheen dulled. He made a show of pushing his winning hand toward Davis for the next deal. "Maybe he wasn't as good as you thought."

"World Series of Poker finals twice, that's as good as anyone thinks. He would've crushed you."

His jaw clenched like a fist. "Bro, deal."

Davis hesitated, so I nudged. "Cards, please."

He dealt the hand. Cedric and I bet, and discarded, and drew new cards. When we showed our hands, he was the winner again with three of a kind. "Crush that."

Davis said, "I'll take the question this time."

"I don't know, bro. You gonna man up and ask something real?"

"I got this," Davis said. "Nikki, where are we going from here? You and me, I mean? How's this all supposed to turn out?"

That was three questions, and no good answers for any of them. I settled on the most honest thing I'd done that night, and said, "I don't know."

"You think you're too good for my brother or something?" Cedric was clearly agitated now. Just like I wanted.

I said, "You have to win another hand if you want me to answer that. Play again."

And we did. All of Cedric's moves were aggressive and smug. He tossed his chips like a sadistic child tossed rocks at stray cats.

We showed cards. I had two pair with an ace kicker. It was not the hand Davis dealt me—that would've been another loser—but while Cedric was distracted by anger, and Davis was distracted by his concerns for me, I used some sleight of hand to improve my situation, easily beating Cedric's pair of sevens. "Wow, look at that. Must be the start of a comeback."

Cedric swept up his cards and flicked them at his brother. "Can't win them all. What are you going to ask him?"

"My question's for you. It's a juicy one."

He laughed, an exaggerated sound. "You girls flatter me. Look, I'll tell you flat out, Molly's hot, but I'm aware of our age difference. It was all fun flirting. Nothing else."

"Actually, I was really curious about why you killed my dad. I'll let Molly know, though."

CHAPTER  57

I'll give it to the sociopath. He didn't crack. With remarkable dexterity, he danced one of his chips across his knuckles, spun it from his pinky into his palm, repeated the move. Not even a mild tremor in his hand.

"You're not serious," Davis said.

I didn't speak to him. I spoke to the murderer who'd taken so much from my family. "When I realized a baseball bat was used to kill John Reedy, and it was you at the table with them that night, a bunch of things made sense. Not all of it. I don't know if a sick mind like yours can ever make total sense to anyone sane. Enough, though."

My blood pulsed so hard through every part of my body, the edges of my vision bounced with each heartbeat. Only sheer will kept me in that seat. I wanted to run, or scream, or fight.

"Say something," Davis demanded.

Cedric didn't say a thing. He left his seat with a nimbleness that likely served him well before his forced retirement from baseball. He rooted in my bag before I could do anything but yelp.

"Leave her alone," Davis said, pushing up from his chair.

Cedric froze him with a finger. "Sit down."

"Do it," I said to Davis. Cedric hadn't hurt me. Didn't even touch me. He'd taken Dad's iPhone.

He dropped it on the carpet. Drove the heel of one sneaker into it. His shoe rose and fell a few times, forcing me to flinch away as shards bounced from the impact.

He collected himself. His calm voice was chilling in the

aftermath of that tantrum. "Let me guess. You had the voice recorder running. Thought you were going to get me saying something wild."

Not exactly. "Are you going to answer my question now?"

He crouched by the broken glass, metal, and circuitry. Mocked me by speaking loudly at the demolished device. "Whoever this was intended for, I did not kill Nathan Tate."

Returning to his seat, he said, "Play another."

"Sure. Deal, Davis."

"Really?" he said.

"Really."

While Davis shuffled, I kept talking, kept pushing buttons. "I watched the security footage a lot. You were going to win that hand, right? Teenage wannabe about to take a pot from a celebrated pro. Exciting stuff, I can dig it."

Cedric checked his cards, threw three away. I tossed two. Davis replenished our hands.

"Another player caught one of Reedy's cheaters at the table. Messed up your moment, and you couldn't let it slide. You caught up with him later and"—I made a swinging gesture with my arms and clucked my tongue against the roof of my mouth—"home run."

He tossed chips in the pot, as did I. We drew more cards. Cedric said, "Show them."

I won with a straight. "My next question. Did you mean to kill Reedy, or was it an accident?"

He refused to answer. But he didn't leave. Despite the deep disgust it gave me, I understood him now. Leaving on a losing hand was not an option. He needed to win, needed to be on top. I wasn't going to let it happen.

Despite his non-answer, we went again. I kept talking. "Here's the part I don't get, the cheating ring. That's what that was when Molly and I caught you getting off that party bus? You were mad at Reedy for doing it, then you start running the same scam. That's how my dad got your scent, you know, because he saw your flawed little plan, like, immediately. Seems pretty stupid, particularly when you're ripping off your own casino."

He showed his cards. He was flush with diamonds and feeling cocky again. Couldn't keep quiet. "This isn't my casino yet. I make my own way. Dirty and clean. Show 'em."

I fanned four jacks and an ace, and his fist crashed into the table, making his chips jump.

"Next question. Did you kill my dad because he was onto your scam or because he knew about Reedy?"

"Deal."

Davis was a statue in his dealer seat. What was this like for him? I'd shone a light on all that darkness his family gathered. Shown him what no one wanted to see and it was taking its toll. By my watch, it was 6:01, the football dinner would've started, and fear was getting the best of me.

My grand plans and machinations. There should've been results by now. But there was nothing.

"Deal!" Cedric shouted.

My father's killer, seated mere feet from me, was reaching a boiling point.

Davis complied, got another hand going. I played distracted, flicking glances at the only way in or out of this room. When Cedric got his coveted win, would he let me leave?

The hand progressed. At the end of betting, he showed his cards. Two pair, kings and sevens. "What do you have?"

Suddenly the double doors swung open, and Kurt the security guard entered, clearly stressed. "Mr. Carlino, we—"

"Wait!" Cedric popped from his seat, stood over me. "Show yours."

I did. My highest card was a jack of clubs. A losing hand. Cedric's whole face lit with sadistic joy.

"You win." I fought to sound firm, unafraid. "Ask away."

He leaned close, whispered in my ear, "No question. Just this. Your d-bag dad wouldn't play me. Not even a single hand for the ultimate bet, my freedom. I always wanted to take down a Tate. Now I've done it twice. You got lucky, Nikki. This beating is way better than the one your daddy got."

He pulled away, wearing a mask of innocence. A salt slime filled my mouth. I'd bitten into my tongue so as not to snap and rip his face off. I'd come too far for it to go down like that.

"You might want to check with your man over there. I think there's trouble on your floor," I said.

He faltered, spoke to Kurt. "What is it?"

"The football team event upstairs, it's down here now. There are a lot of large, angry boys getting rowdy on the gaming floor."

Davis rounded the table. "What's going on?"

Coldly, I said, "Wait for it."

Cedric was flustered with Kurt now, barking at him. "So throw them out."

"It's not just them. There are also bikers, and a really aggressive lady threatening to call the FBI. They're looking for her."

Kurt motioned in my direction, and Cedric stomped to me. "What—"

"There's something you should know before you ask that question. You didn't actually win it."

Raising both forearms, I snaked two fingers into the cuff of my left sleeve and pulled free a couple of playing cards sporting the Nysos logo, courtesy of Chuck Pearl. I repeated the gesture on the other side before laying those cards on the table. "I have more. This dress is really great for hiding them. So you see, the hands you won, you didn't win. The hands you lost, you didn't lose. We were never playing a true game, Cedric Carlino. Didn't my father make it clear? You aren't worth the effort."

I couldn't tell how much he heard. He stared at the cards I'd used to cheat and stall while my backup arrived.

Kurt held the door open. Shouts of "GRIF-FIN BLOOD! GRIF-FIN BLOOD!" flitted through, the commotion growing, a rumbling like a large boulder rolling closer to crush Cedric. Just as I planned.

Davis's brother snarled, leapt at me, and coiled his fingers in my hair, yanking me from my seat in an explosion of scalp-scorching pain that consumed me so I couldn't manufacture a scream.

If he was to be crushed, he intended to take me with him.

CHAPTER 58

"Sir!" Kurt the guard screamed, finally leaving the entryway. Maybe he meant to intervene, to stop his boss from assaulting a woman in front of him, even if it meant his job. He was too slow, though.

Davis clocked Cedric across the chin, jarring him enough that he released me. The sudden freedom sent me backpedaling and I landed on my butt.

Cedric steadied himself, brushing at his clothes as if Davis had sullied them. "You choosing her over me? Over family?"

"I don't want anyone to get hurt." His fists were clenched, but furtive. He only used them when had to. Because of who he was facing, Davis couldn't see what was so clear to me. This was a time when he had to.

"Like that ever happens." Cedric rushed forward, sank a fist into Davis's stomach all the way to the wrist.

Davis collapsed in a ball with a groan, and Cedric lorded over him. "See what I mean?"

Wheezing, Davis got his knees under him. Cedric hit him again, flattened him again, the collision a wet crunch.

"Stop them!" I shouted.

Kurt the guard might've been chivalrous enough to help me but didn't budge when it was the princes of his kingdom brawling. If he wouldn't step in . . .

I ran past him, through the corridor and onto the gaming floor. The sight of the chaos I'd created was an invisible wall, killing my forward momentum.

The Nysos security team was a minority among the groups of tussling high school athletes and riled-up spectators. Half of the combatants were Vista players, easily spotted in their dinner-appropriate khakis and dress shirts. The others were CG, jeans and tees. They pushed, shoved, threw wild punches. The Cardinal Graham mascot head went airborne like a popcorn kernel, then flipped end over end back into the scrum.

I scanned the ruckus for the biggest, tallest person who wasn't Gavin. Found him. "Goose! Help!"

The biker, a wistful observer on the edge of the melee, heard me, as did several others. With meaty arms and a bulldozer gut, he cut a path through the lightweight teens and overwhelmed hotel security. Him and his Pack mates. A torpedo of leather and tats aimed directly at me. With stragglers in their wake.

"Nikalosa!"

Oh crap. My mom.

I dipped back into the High Roller Room, knowing they'd all follow. We were getting to the end of it now.

Cedric left his groaning brother on the floor, set his sights on me. He took three big, angry steps before aborting his approach.

The Pack spilled in. Flanked me. Even their bulky machismo couldn't deter my mother from muscling her way through, with Tomás and Detective Burrows and Molly tailing.

I exchanged a knowing look with Molly, the old telepathy at work. She broadcast a message back to me. *Ready.*

Mom wrenched me to her, and though I knew a full-on reaming was in the near future, she gave me a constricting hug. "Oh my god, what are you doing?"

"Leaving," Cedric announced. He told Kurt, "I want these

people escorted off the property immediately, or I want Metro here to arrest them."

Burrows said, "Metro is already here."

"Perfect. I demand—"

"Just one minute," a voice boomed from the congested corridor. Another person joining the fray. The people jam parted for Big Bert.

"This is my establishment," he said, "and I'm the only one who makes demands here. Somebody tell me what's happening."

"Mr. Carlino." I stepped to him, or tried. Mom attempted tugging me back. I spun to her. "Let me finish. For Dad."

I felt Big Bert watching our exchange until he keyed on the moaning by the center poker table. He rushed to his downed son, triggering a coughing fit. Despite his respiratory struggles, he comforted Davis and shouted to no one in particular, "Get medics in here."

Orders from the King of the Nysos reanimated Kurt the guard. He forced his way from the room while radioing for help.

Big Bert levered Davis to his feet, wheezing the whole time like he was the one with the broken nose. "You did this?"

The question was for Cedric. No one else was under suspicion.

Cedric said, "Dad, Davis's lunatic girlfriend—"

"Stop. Talking." Big Bert craned his neck, sweeping his gaze across everyone present. "Clear the room. This is a family matter."

"Nope," I said. "Nobody leaves. I've got something to say."

Big Bert zeroed in on my mom. "Gwen, I thought we had an understanding."

Mom stepped closer, slipped an arm over my shoulder. Joining me. "What understanding is that exactly, Bert?"

Tomás gravitated to my other side, refusing to let us stand alone. "Say what you need to, Nikki."

Here we go.

"He's killed at least three people. Including my dad," I said, pointing to Cedric. "And I can't prove it."

CHAPTER 59

"Can't?" Detective Burrows said. "As in can*not*?"

"Correct," I said.

"No proof?"

"Uh-uh." I added, "He's also running this shady cheating ring, but I can't prove that, either."

Detective Burrows directed his ire at Molly, who didn't seem to notice. She was recording the proceedings on her phone. Burrows said, "You called me."

"I made her tell you we had additional info, but I've got the same vague, circumstantial stuff you've got," I said.

Cedric, for his part, laughed so we saw all his teeth. "She forced her way onto the gaming floor, knowing she's underage. I'm certain that riot outside is her doing." He actually pled his case to the cop. "What else do you need to drag her and her gang off our property?"

"Did she hurt that boy?" Burrows motioned to Davis, who was alert and rapt like everyone else.

Cedric gave a dismissive wave. "Dad, back me up here. Tell him to do his job and maybe we won't have our lawyers eat their young."

Big Bert shook his head oh so slightly.

"As much as I hate to admit it, he's got a point," Burrows said. "I don't know what we're all doing here, other than you wanted it this way. You better explain yourself."

"It's the Al Capone thing," I said. "Dad wanted to tie Cedric to the cheating ring because there's no way to link him to the murders. That's not going to work either because the Carlinos are too good at running this town. I'm sick of it."

With everyone fixated on my little speech, my sudden movement was as surprising as I needed it to be. I closed the gap between me and Cedric, raked my clawed hand fast and hard across his cheek, ripping skin and drawing blood. He stumbled, roared, cocked a fist I'm sure he would've swung if not for so many witnesses.

"Did you see that?" he shouted. "She attacked me! I want her arrested and punished to the full extent of the law!"

I went directly to Burrows, arms extended, the fingertips on one hand pink with Cedric's blood. "Cuff me. Take me now."

Mom was there in an instant. "Nikki, why?"

"It's okay, Mom."

Burrows brought out the bracelets, snapping them over one of my wrists, and then the other. Cedric kept ranting, his words obscenity-laced now. Big Bert and Davis, though, they got it.

What was the family motto? Never get arrested. Never end up in the system. Really smart way to keep incriminating DNA away from the system.

There were ways around it.

"Cedric," I said. He kept ranting, so into his feelings and threatening lawsuits, I had to yell. "Cedric!"

He snapped to. "What?"

"My dad got some of his killer's skin under his nails. For my last bet of the evening, I'm going to say the skin under my nails is a match. You want in on that action?"

Every bit of malice and color drained from his face. Murmurs all around the room.

"Please take me to jail now. And, Cedric, don't feel bad. You wouldn't be the first player to get done in by a dead man's hand."

CHAPTER 60

There's this thing in Nevada called committing a breach of peace. Other parts of the country might call it inciting a riot. In the months following that day at the Nysos, I became well versed in the jargon since I was being charged with a bunch of crimes relating to it.

The timeline that a city prosecutor would eventually share with me and Mom and my criminal defense attorney looked something like this:

4:27 p.m.—At the prompting of Nikalosa Tate, Gavin Lafaie executed the first leg of a plan N. Tate dubbed "Phase 2" and sent an inciting message to the entire Cardinal Graham High School football team. G. Lafaie copied N. Tate on the message to confirm her instructions were followed. The contents of the message were a photo of the Cardinal Graham mascot's head next to signage clearly indicating the gaming room of the Nysos Casino Resort, and the message read: "Come and get it you [expletive]."

4:36 p.m.—At the prompting of Nikalosa Tate, Margaret Martel notified the following individuals of N. Tate's whereabouts inside the Nysos Casino Resort: Gwendolyn Tate (mother), Tomás Garcia (family friend), Det. Raymond Burrows (lead investigator on the Nathaniel Tate murder case), and the Nevada Gaming Control Board public line.

4:40 p.m.—Nikalosa Tate sent several misleading text messages to a number of individuals to lure them to the gaming room of the Nysos Casino Resort. Among the individuals contacted were members of the Wolfpack Motorcycle Club, and several people who identify as professional cardplayers, though many have varying criminal records. N. Tate's message read: "Whale Alert! Phil Ivey's playing at The Nysos. Get. Here. Now."

5:00 p.m.—Nikalosa Tate, a minor, illegally traversed the gaming floor of the Nysos Casino Resort, and engaged in several hands of poker while all the parties she'd manipulated gathered in force.

6:00 p.m.—Nikalosa Tate . . .

The timeline continued, entirely accurate. All the premeditated stuff I engineered. Legally speaking, I was kind of up a creek.

These weren't inadvertent repercussions. My plan did not backfire. My arrest, and what happened immediately after, was still the plan. This was the game *after* the game.

Going into this, I knew I'd be throwing a big rock into a pond, and there would be an epic splash. I was looking at potential jail time, and that was terrifying. The toilets alone. There were other dangers, though. Accusing the son of a powerful man with connections to the legal system, a powerful man who may not be above permanently burying problems. Without the proper precautions, evidence could disappear. *I* could disappear. I needed insurance that whatever happened, Cedric's role in my father's, John Reedy's, and Dan Harris's deaths didn't get lost in the shuffle, so to speak.

While Metro collected samples of Cedric Carlino's DNA from my nails, Molly performed one more task. The final leg of Phase 2, which wouldn't make my incriminating timeline. From a fake account, she uploaded a video to YouTube of me confronting Cedric, spliced with the chaotic footage of Vista and CG fighting over a mascot head.

That crap went viral in like a day.

Sure, most of that was probably the allure of a Worldstar-like brawl, but me announcing that Cedric Carlino was a killer couldn't be ignored. A few days in, YouTube pulled the video (likely at the request of some persuasive Nevada law firm). Within hours, two more versions appeared with different titles, posted from different user accounts. They took those down; four more appeared. A virtual hydra.

A rabid media went all in on the racial optics of a young black girl in a life-threatening battle with a white Casino magnate.

That breaking news stoked the fires more. TV, radio, web. Even got my own hashtag. #NikkiVsNysos

Dan Harris would've been proud.

Mom, not so much.

Other than the first round of processing and interrogation, I never spent a night in jail. I *was* placed under house arrest. Not by the city—they were still gathering evidence against me—but by my mother. Total lockdown. Part of it was punishment, Mom made sure I knew that. Part of it was protection. Because Cedric remained free. Evidence was not an arrest, not charges filed. Those things took time. Anything could happen while we waited.

So, no school—not that I would've been welcome there anyway after I got half the football team locked up and the Cardinal Graham game forfeited. No phones. No friends. For the first month, I only saw my mom, Tomás, assorted Andromeda's staff, my new home-school tutor, and a bunch of meh streaming movies.

Month two had Mom releasing the iron grip a little. Mostly due to necessity. She needed my help finding us a new place to live.

Andromeda's Palace had been sold.

◆

Those Japanese guys dropped out of the running, but another group of investors was waiting in the wings, willing to take the casino off Mom's hands for a slightly reduced price.

Who knew Mr. Héctor had such well-off friends?

Years of saving and dreaming had gotten him what he always wanted. A place to explore his passions. He worked our valet stand until the day the sale closed. I sat and talked with him while movers loaded our personal belongings into a truck destined for the Rancho Grande home Mom had bought. A real house. No more room service.

"I'm glad it's you." I sat on the smokers' bench in Andromeda's Loop, perhaps for the last time. "She should go to someone who loves her."

"I don't love her," he said, "at all."

"Huh?"

"Andromeda's Palace will undergo a major renovation, Nika. What do you think about"— he held his hands high and wide, framing the invisible name—"Ximena's?"

"What's it mean?"

"The one who hears. It was my beloved's name. It fit her well, she was a good listener. She'd like the sound of tourists spending their money here." He clutched his stomach as if stifling his belly laughs.

I never met Mr. Héctor's wife. She passed away before I was born. But I didn't have to know her. "It's beautiful."

"Exactly. Out with the old, in with a sexy Mexican vibe."

"Absolutely." I didn't know how convincing I sounded.

"I'm going to change the name of the Goddess Room, too," he said.

"Oh." I suppressed a flinch. Or tried.

"I'm thinking of calling it Nathan's Room, and putting a plaque in your father's honor right by the door. It's not sexy, or Mexican, but it fits. Yes?"

The Andromeda of legend was a chained prisoner, a sacrifice. She was freed, lived a long, long life, and was said to have been placed among the stars after her death so we'd always remember her. A poker room in Downtown Vegas wasn't the same as a constellation, but I had a feeling Dad would've been cool with it.

"Yes," I said, "it fits perfectly."

♠

Month three, no ninjas had come for me in the night, and I hadn't discovered a single horse head in my bed.

We were still settling in to the new house. Tomás came over a lot, playing Mr. Fix-It. Installing ceiling fans and voting on accent wall colors—almost always agreeing with my picks, inciting mild Mom wrath. Occasionally, my lawyer called, reiterating how slow the gears of justice clanked and that the city was still putting together a case against me. But there was hope. I was a minor, so I should be looking at only a short stay in juvie. Yay?

Those days were hard. Stuck at home, a cell looming, while Dad's killer held no such concerns.

Seemingly secure in his assertion that his baby-eating lawyers would quash all the murder nonsense despite compelling DNA evidence, as well as the GPS on his favorite car putting him close to Andromeda's on the night of Dad's death, and a witness describing someone who looked like him near Dan Harris's office before *he* died, Cedric never broke stride. He partied hard, set the town on fire. Literally, in one case, when he lit a bottle of vodka aflame at his birthday party. He was determined to show his face at any and every available opportunity. Nothing to hide here.

And where was Davis in all this? In an email—a connection to the outside world Mom hadn't severed—Molly informed me he left Vista, too. Had vanished completely. In the absence of facts, the rumor mill turned him into a gangster Carmen Sandiego, placing him at all manner of seedy, exotic locales around the globe. When I had trouble sleeping in the new place, I wondered where he really was, and what my scheme had done to him. I wondered if I had the right to care.

Christmas came and went. We watched the New Year's ball drop on TV. Mom ran out of reasons to keep me confined and allowed little freedoms back into my life. She returned my original iPhone. I received it with the same sense of wonder and apprehension as my dad when we gifted one to him. *Oh. I remember those.*

Netflix at Molly's (with regular half-hour check-in calls to the freshly returned iPhone). A Saturday afternoon at the mall, where Molly attempted pointing me toward cute boys, and I tried not to act like a vampire staring at a crucifix. I wasn't ready, and it didn't make me a bad wingwoman either, because she wasn't in the market.

In my absence, she and Gavin got closer. She overexplained the whole thing during our first outing, wanting to tell me face-to-face, worried I'd be mad at her for forgiving his betrayal. It'd been too long. I'd been too alone. I missed my friends. My response to her confession: "I look forward to being your officially licensed third wheel."

As Mom's comfort grew, I was allowed more excursions. Safe things. I didn't dare tell her what happened to me at the Vista vs. Clark's Magnet School basketball game.

It was an evening contest. I'd been granted an 11:00 p.m. curfew. I rode with Molly and sat in the stands with the Vista faithful, nervous at first. There was some side-eye, whispers, but ultimately, my former classmates let me be. I used to go to school with them, and used to be worth their time and ridicule. Now I was only visiting.

Gavin was a three-sport athlete, and he dominated this competitive season like he did the first. Molly cheered every sunk layup, jump shot, and free throw. She was only slightly louder than me. When the coach called Gavin to the bench for a much-needed break, he waved at the stands. To her. Us. I mouthed, *I want a dunk.*

He mouthed back, *You got it.*

I don't know if he fulfilled the promise.

Two minutes until the half, my phone lit with a text.

Davis: Are you here at the clark game?
Me: yes. are you?
Davis: Can you meet me outside?

I craned my neck toward the exit. Should've recognized how weird it was. If Davis was back in town, why reach out like this? But I wanted to see him. Despite the dead man's hand and whatever part he played in all that happened, I didn't want him beaten and bleeding on the High Roller Room floor as our last joint memory. I told Molly I was going to the bathroom.

Outside, it was chilly, barren. A sea of parked silent cars. All wrong.

A Lincoln limo pulled up to the curb, stopping with the opaque back window directly before me. The glass whined down, Big Bert spoke.

"I'd like a word."

CHAPTER 61

Run.

Recognition of his voice dropped me into a sprinter's lunge. Him leaning into the light, showing me his face, rooted me in place. He was not the Big Bert I recalled.

Sunken cheeks, dark circles under crackling red eyes, skin a shade of yellow that couldn't be blamed on hazy lamppost light.

"Please," he managed. Followed by the wet rattle of things tearing loose in his chest. That cough hurt *me*.

I didn't move, couldn't look away.

"You don't have to be scared. Call whoever you want. Tell them where you are. I'll leave the door open while you sit. I'd come stand with you, but that's hard for me now."

Standing was hard?

"I'm sending a group text to everyone I know." I held my phone so he saw my thumbs twitching. "Outside with Bertram Carlino. If I'm not back in ten minutes, send the Navy SEALs."

He chuckled; it didn't sound much better than his awful cough. "Funny girl."

It'd be funnier if he knew I didn't send that text. If I had, Molly would come running with reinforcements ASAP. Despite our history, I was intrigued.

The limo door swung open.

I sat, keeping the toe of one sneaker on the asphalt for a hasty retreat, if needed. The weight he'd lost since I last saw him . . . unsettling. His suit draped his frame like a blanket, as if there were room for someone to join him in it and snuggle. Anyone calling him Big from now on would do so out of tradition. Or obligation.

"Are you all right?" There was no way he could say yes.

"I hope to be."

"Are you following me?"

"No. I'm here for the game. My business has a sports management arm, and I'm told Clark's point guard is one to watch. I"—he coughed, lighter this time—"loved basketball as a young man. I wanted a good night."

"Then you saw me."

"Then I saw you."

"Nice move faking like you're Davis. That's not creepy."

"I'm sorry for that. I was hoping to move past deception this evening. It was careless of me to start that way."

I squirmed. An alarming thought popped in my mind. "Is Davis okay?"

"His mother tells me he's adjusting well to the change."

"He's in New York?"

A nod.

"Without his phone, I suppose." Now that the fear dulled, disappointment set in. I wanted to see him. There wasn't much I wanted lately. "What is this?"

"I'm sick, Nikki. I was diagnosed with lung cancer three years ago. I won't have the chance to say I'm a four-year survivor."

Not shocking. Did a dying man have anything to lose? I shifted closer to my open door.

"I've done a lot of wrong in my life," he said, "and I've been making amends ever since I was diagnosed. You may not know this, but I hired Daniel Harris to take on your father's case."

"I knew. Nice after you let him go to jail in the first place."

"I didn't mean—" He reconsidered his words. "I should've done something sooner."

"You mean you should've set up some other fall guy sooner."

"I went about it wrong trying to convince Nathan to take a deal. I thought things could be okay for everyone."

"Except John Reedy."

He leaned forward quicker than a fleshy skeleton should. I suppressed a flinch. Bert said, "John was my friend, too."

"I hope I never have a friend like you."

His turn to flinch. He grew smaller before my eyes. "John, me, your dad. We were supposed to be *the* guys in this town. Kings. We met as young men, each of us with different resources, a different angle. Andromeda's Palace was our start, and our finish."

"The Poseidon Group."

"You know about it, then?"

This was my first time hearing any of this. If this was a trap, I was caught. "Not much."

"My background led to prime real estate opportunities. Your father's card skills were lucrative, and gave him access to heavyweights in town. John's potential, it never shifted from underworld dealings. He didn't evolve. Grew bitter at your father and me because we did. But I don't think that's why he turned on us, cheating our own establishment right in front our faces. He was just the first of us to admit what we all"—coughs erupted, machine-gun fast—"knew. Three heads can't wear one crown."

That hacking continued, alarming the driver, who lowered the black partition. "Sir, are you—"

I cursed. "Oh no. No way."

Delano, the goon who'd manhandled me, in my home, was driving.

"Close the partition," Bert wheezed. The divider rose between us again.

"You sent him to my room! That's your way of making anything right?"

A few heavy, labored breaths passed before he answered. "He had instructions not to harm. He didn't, did he?"

"You're insane." I couldn't leave his rolling tomb fast enough. "I'm gone."

"Wait."

"If you don't tell me what you want right now, I'm calling the cops." Phone in hand, touchscreen lit, I dialed a 9 and a 1, let my thumb hover.

"Your charges will be dropped, as will any pending against your friends and classmates. I've called in favors. You'll be able to go on with your life. And . . . and you'll see I'm not pulling strings for my own benefit anymore. Evidence against Cedric is stacking up by the day. My lawyers will do their jobs, but his case will play to a just conclusion. As Nathan intended."

"My dad didn't intend to die."

"None of us do. Not like this." He waved a pathetic hand over his gaunt frame.

Then something mean inside me got it. What all this was about. Why he was here.

"You're confessing." Not like criminal, but church. This car was his confessional. I was the priest.

"Your indulgence is a comfort. But there's something else I'm seeking. I was wondering—hoping—that you'd see this talk as a good-faith gesture and consider a request. I was hoping you'd persuade my son to call me."

Oh, you sad, sad man. "I haven't spoken to Davis in months. I don't even have his number in—"

A business card protruded from the car, pinched between his index and middle fingers, trembling as if the thick paper was a flake of heavy steel. An odd sense of politeness made me take it, and I made out the ten digits scrawled on the back clearly, despite the low light.

"If you have his number," I said, "call him yourself."

"He doesn't answer for me."

"Use somebody else's phone. You know that trick."

"As soon as he hears my voice, he hangs up."

"Then I can't change his mind."

"You can! He cared—cares—about you a great deal. You both hate me the same. If I can sway you . . ."

I spun the card back at him, unconcerned if it hit him in the chest or wedged in his eye. "And you think you're not pulling strings for your own benefit anymore."

He called after me, desperate and worn, coughs punctuating his speech in strange places. "Nikki. I am. Sorry. Please. Will. You forgive me?"

I kept walking, and when I spoke, it wasn't loud enough for him to hear. "I might. But you'll never know."

♣

I didn't make it back into the gym, settling for a bench by the concession stand. Too shaken to make it further. A worried text requesting my whereabouts led to Molly joining me. I told her the crowd was overwhelming after being confined for so long, not a total lie.

"You wanna go home?" she asked.

"If that's okay."

"Always."

We left, and there was no limo in the lot. At home I found Mom curled in bed, watching renovation shows on HGTV. She said, "You're early."

I kicked off my shoes, crawled into the bed, nuzzled my face into her shoulder, and looped my arms around her.

"Hey," she said, alarmed. "Is something wrong?"

"Nothing at all. I just love you."

"I love you, too. Can't help thinking there's a follow-up."

There was. A condition that we'd never, ever be so at odds we couldn't tell each other what we felt. I didn't need to explain, though. She and I were better than that.

♥

All of the things Bertram Carlino promised came to pass.

The following Monday, my mystified and ecstatic lawyer called. The city dropped all charges against me. I'd practiced my surprise face in the mirror and pulled it off pretty well while Mom shouted, and danced, and thanked the lord above.

A week later the top news story: Bert Carlino watching his oldest son taken from the Nysos in handcuffs on charges of murder and racketeering.

Three days after that, Bert made the news again when the cancer won.

The Poseidon Group was no more.

CHAPTER 62

Molly lay in the hammock, fingers laced behind her head and elbows splayed. She stared up, sunshades protecting her eyes, and sunscreen keeping her from roasting on this unusually hot February day. "What do you think that cloud looks like?"

Gavin splashed in the pool like a toddler. Not swimming exactly. Actively not drowning. "Which cloud? There are a bunch."

"That one." She still didn't indicate which.

From a comfy deck chair, I had selected on a me/Mom/Tomás Home Depot trip, I sipped ginger ale through a twisty straw, guessed wildly. "A rabbit."

"Wrong. It's obviously Spider-Man."

"Yep." I pushed my drink aside and began shuffling a card deck I'd brought poolside. "Obviously."

Gavin said, "Peter Parker or Miles Morales?"

"I don't know, the one who does this." She thrust her wrists about in exaggerated gestures that were either web-shooting or interpretive dance.

Gavin attempted a backstroke, sank, resurfaced sputtering.

"Be careful." I sped up my shuffle, worked in more intricate tricks. False cuts, shooting a card airborne and letting it drop back into the deck like a pop fly into a catcher's mitt. "I'm not getting my hair wet saving you."

"This is different," Gavin said.

"How?" Molly asked. "You've always been a terrible swimmer. She's always been no-nonsense about getting water on her hair. Why *did* your mom buy a house with a pool?"

Gavin said, "No. I mean not hanging in the Loop."

I stopped shuffling. "Better?"

"Mostly. It's way better than the three of us crammed on a bench in a forever-nicotine cloud. Also"—he seemed at a loss—"just different."

I couldn't say I knew exactly what he meant. How can you ever know *exactly* what someone else means? Even your best friends. I *felt* a change, though. Molly's sudden quiet convinced me she did, too.

Molly wasn't going to UVA, but Gavin was. Given their new status, the logistics of that arrangement were fuzzy. I wasn't going to ask for clarity. Not my circus, not my monkeys.

My Vista Rojo days were over, over. I'd keep getting tutored through the spring. Next fall, it was new-kid status. The Meadows, maybe. Or Coronado. Or I'd let the tutor see me through graduation. With all the individual attention, I could finish early, then travel some. Mom's recommendation.

Selling Andromeda's was huge for us. Even after all the debt (and my legal fees), there was money left over unlike anything we'd ever seen. I could go anywhere, do anything. No more chains, and no more rock to attach them to.

My new backyard, with the deck, and the pool, and the stainless steel grill Tomás might fire up later was crazy spacious. Certainly an upgrade from the shoulder-to-shoulder smokers' bench. Me here, Molly there, Gavin in the pool . . . there weren't great distances between us, but that change I felt might mean the gaps were larger than we knew. And growing.

That was okay. Friends shouldn't stay together forever. Bertram Carlino taught me that.

"Different." I shrugged. "Good thing we adapt well."

Molly kept finding obscure figures in the clouds. Gavin managed floating for a solid four seconds before near-death, and I returned to my first friends, the cards. Tranquility that couldn't last. That's not what my life was.

My phone rattled in the chair's cupholder, reminding me.

I picked it up, went numb. "Guys."

They perked, listened. I pushed my phone at them. "It's Davis."

◆

Gavin reacted poorly, with colorful language. Then he washed his hands of the whole thing—literally, with pool water—and continued his kiddie splashing.

Molly's response was much more nuanced. "How do you feel about it?"

"I don't know." I reread the message for the ninth or tenth time.

you might not recognize the number. this is davis. i won't text
     again if you tell me to go away.

I knew he'd come back, for a short time if nothing else. Bert's funeral was two weeks ago. He and his mother had been in all the news footage and in the papers. Davis kept his head down and hand up to block the good shots. He couldn't hide from me. I clicked off the article without reading it. Couldn't click away from him. I'd thought of him ever since.

The number Bert tried giving me, I didn't remember it. If I knew it, at some point I would've reached out first. When my emotional pendulum swung away from that desire, cutting an arc toward Davis using Gavin against me, I was relieved for my lack of a photographic memory.

He hadn't forgotten mine.

Molly said, "You could tell him to go away. Like it says."

"I know."

"But you haven't."

"Do you think I should?"

She raised her palms defensively. "Does what I think *really* matter here?"

"I guess it wouldn't hurt to see what he wants."

Molly cupped a hand to her ear. "Speak up. You're mumbling."

Me: hey.

Davis: you didn't say go away.

Me: no. what's up?

A new text bubble started, stopped. Started again. A tickle in my stomach turned to a twist, then full-on anxiety. What was he going to say to me? Molly crammed herself into my chair somehow so she could see, too.

Davis: i'm going to the scene of our first crime tonight. if you bring burgers, i'll bring the picnic blanket—aka the car.

We turned to each other so fast, Molly and me bumped foreheads.

"Ow," I said, rubbing the point of impact. "He wants to meet."

She had a stink-face, prodded her own potential bruise. "Jeez, Tate. We already know you're going. Get your burgers, and I'll get my nunchucks. 'Kay?"

♠

I got In-N-Out burgers. You can't go wrong with In-N-Out burgers. Molly insisted on hanging at the Walmart a couple of miles away. With her nunchucks.

He waited in the same spot we'd had that night. No fancy sports car, but a simple Chevy sedan. I wouldn't have recognized him if he'd been in it . . . but he was on the hood, knees pulled to his chest, eyes on the sky.

My approach was slow in my sweet new Mazda. He didn't know this car. I could keep driving, and he'd be none the wiser.

Plus, the flutter in my belly would make it tough eating burgers. What if he was mad at me? He had to be. I was mad at him sometimes. We might fight. This was so stupid. Go home, Nikki. Go home.

Those thoughts and more were mudslide thick. I pushed through them, angling my car into the space next to his. I grabbed the food bags in the passenger seat extra tight, willing the shakes away.

If it was bad, I'd leave. That was all.

He slid off the hood, greeting me as I exited my vehicle. We met between the cars, a tight space that forced us against our respective vehicles so as not to touch.

"You came," he said.

"You sound surprised." Like I didn't consider passing him by. "Your hair's different."

Sweeping a hand across his new buzz cut, he shuffled a bit, shyer than I remember. He deflected. "I'm glad you showed. I'm starving."

He looked it. He'd lost weight, too. Nothing as drastic as his dad toward the end. I didn't think he was sick. Tired, though? I could believe that. He was heir to the Carlino kingdom. That crown, the one that couldn't be worn by three heads, was all his now. Probably heavy, too.

I offered him the burgers. "Dig in."

He went elbow deep in the bag, grabbed a bundle of fries, consumed them nearly whole. He crawled back onto the hood. "Come on up?"

"Will it dent this time?" My words, followed by instant regret. A reference to what happened to the last car bearing our weight, the last night things were okay.

He rolled with it, though. "Dents come out."

I climbed on, slid a bit. He gripped my forearm, steadying me. My emotional pendulum swung toward mad. Why did he try to fool me instead of trust me?

"You're still angry." He retracted his helping hand and I steadied myself.

"Sometimes I am." The pendulum swung away. I claimed my burger. "Are you back for good?"

"Don't know yet. Dad left everything to Mom. But she's letting the advisory board run all the businesses so she can focus on Cedric."

Millimeters away from my next bite, I lost the urge. Bert promised no string pulling to get Cedric off. Did Cedric's mom have different plans? "Focus how?"

"Getting him ready to go in. She even hired this jail coach to prepare him."

"That's a thing?"

"You'd be surprised what sort of services are available at the right price."

"No, I wouldn't. Not anymore."

We ate. Not in silence, no such thing with the planes coming and going. We ate in tolerance. Between bites I tested his presence and proximity. Could I stay here? I wasn't conceited enough to think he wasn't doing the same. I thought long and hard about what I'd say when the food was gone. I settled on "I'm sorry about your dad."

"Really?"

"Of course. I know what it's like. You *know* I know what it's like."

"No. You don't."

The pendulum swung. "Seriously?"

"Calm down." There was a snap in it. He was angry, too.

"This was a bad idea."

"Nikki." He inhaled hard. "I meant you don't know what it's like because you were proud of your dad. Your dad was innocent. Your dad tried to do right and tell the truth. That's the legacy he left you."

What do I say to that? I stopped short of asking if he'd spoken to Bert before the end and knew that his dad wanted his love, if not his respect. No. That was between them. I watched another flight take off. I didn't leave.

"You come back here much?" he asked.

"When he's on my mind. I like it better here than the grave-yard. I'm not a flowers-on-the-tombstone kind of person. If I play cards again, I think every game will be for him. That'll be my flowers."

"If. You haven't played since the Nysos? At all?"

"Been occupied." My time in isolation was a hurdle. That was over, now. I'd even gotten some texts from Goose. I was nervous. I didn't need to play for an escape or tuition. Both were available to me if and when I needed them. Would sitting down at a table even feel the same?

He didn't press but pointed at a jet tracing a luminescent line across the sky. "You still think about it?"

"Flying away. Sure. I just don't feel so hard-core about not coming back."

"How did you deal?" Davis asked, a complete left turn. "I mean, when your dad went through his trial, and people shoved cameras in your face, and treated you like you did something wrong when you didn't."

The answer he was looking for, I didn't have. Not when the monsters in his family were real. "It's the murderer the press really cares about," I said, trying to help him without lies, without letting Cedric off the hook. "Not his family. Ignore the other stuff."

He nodded. Cordial. I knew it was easier said than done and had a feeling he knew it now, too.

I remembered. Even shielded, I got lost. Buried. Dad was the world.

Cedric had a jail coach to take care of him. No one took care of the good son.

My hand found its way to Davis's. Our fingers naturally twining together, I squeezed, and I still felt our old connection.

"If I stay, can we start over?" he asked, looking at our hands. "After everything that happened, can we be okay?"

"Do I have to answer tonight?" I asked. "That's not me saying no," I was quick to add.

"You don't have to. I have another question: Are you at least happy to see me? Even a little?"

A tighter squeeze. "More than a little."

"That's good enough."

Another plane took off. "I bet that one's going to Miami," he said.

"How can you possibly know that?

"I don't. That's why it's a bet. We are in Las Vegas."

"That's sound logic."

"Well, tell me, what you think?"

What I thought . . . all bets were off.

ACKNOWLEDGMENTS

Here we are again! It's a special kind of reader who sticks around for the acknowledgments. I'm one, and you're one. We like to know who's knocking around backstage.

This book had a lot of assistance getting from my head to your hands. I'm going to TRY to mention everyone here, but with the usual disclaimers. 1.) If it's right, it's thanks to them; if it's wrong, blame me. 2.) If I somehow forget you, blame the head, not the . . . you know.

First, the Usual Suspects: Adrienne, Mom, the siblings, and the rest of the family. I have a weird job that you're all okay with. That's cool and I love you.

Jamie: We did it again. Now we gotta figure out the particulars of a gym assassin story. I'm thinking franchise potential here.

Jody "The Editor" Corbett: You have awesome boots and fishing-line jewelry. More importantly, you dragged this book out of me with superhuman patience. I'd like to change a single word on Page 19, Line 12 . . . but it's probably too late for that now, huh? So, I'll just thank you and hope you want to do this again sometime.

Special shout-outs to: Phil Falco, the designer responsible for the beauty of the book you're holding; Elizabeth Tiffany, the production editor who handles all the little details that would overwhelm mere mortals; Jana Haussmann, of the legendary Scholastic Book Fairs, for supporting this labor of love; and the collective Publicity and Sales team for all of their hard work in getting Nikki Tate's story to all you readers who, I hope, dig her as much as we do.

Daria Peoples (a writer/illustrator superstar in the making) and Jermone Riley: Thank you for helping me get Vegas as close to right as I'm capable of. I want to come back and have exotic tacos with you at China Poblano soon!

Eric Liu: Thank you for the insight into the world of pro poker. What you do is amazing, and if I ever see you at the table, I'm walking away.

For telling some awesome Vegas stories and other miscellany help, thanks to Robert Riley, Becky Binion Behnen, Amy Hisler, Crystal Lone, Ken Chilton, and Jen Rofé.

A special shout-out to the We Need Diverse Books crew: Ellen, Dhonielle, Karen, Sona, Gbemi, Thien-Kim, Kristy, Bryce, Steph, Nicole, Elsie, Jenn, Amitha, Hannah, and all the rest.

And thanks to you, Dear Reader.

Now, deal!

ABOUT THE AUTHOR

Lamar Giles is the author of *Fake ID*, which was an Edgar Award finalist and a YALSA Quick Pick for Reluctant Young Adult Readers, and *Endangered*, which was also an Edgar Award finalist. Lamar is a founding member of We Need Diverse Books. He resides in Virginia with his wife.